WINTER'S END

WINTER BLACK SERIES: BOOK NINE

MARY STONE

To my husband.
Thank you for taking care of our home and its many inhabitants
while I follow this silly dream of mine.

DESCRIPTION

Sometimes, the beginning is the end.

For thirteen years, FBI Special Agent Winter Black has been haunted by a man who performed heinous acts. Murdering her parents. Abducting her baby brother.

For thirteen years, she's suffered mentally and physically. Often doubted her sanity and ability to move forward to achieve her goal of bringing that brutal man down.

Thirteen years of regret. Of hope. Of fear. Of hate.

But now, the boy she longs for has transformed into a man she fears.

She has to face him. Catch him.

Maybe even kill him. Even if it means the end of her.

Winter's End, the ninth and final book of Mary Stone's gripping Winter Black Series, examines the intricate battle between love and hate. Right from wrong. Leaving you breathless and asking...what would you do?

1

It was dark.

I didn't like the dark. The aloneness that went along with its presence felt like a living thing. At least the moon was trying to look in on me, so I didn't feel so by myself. That was okay because I sometimes laid in my bed and watched the moon right back, so that was fair.

What time was it? Blinking hard, I leaned toward my nightstand, turning my clock so I could see—

Thud.

A sound ruptured the silence, making me jump. It was like something had fallen, creating a hollow echoing sound that didn't belong in my house. Was that what had woken me to begin with? I was usually a very good sleeper. Mommy said so. But I was awake now. Very awake. I didn't like it. Maybe I was such a good sleeper because being asleep made me not think about the dark.

I wish I wasn't thinking of it now. It was watching me.

Heart making my ears feel full, I sat up, pulling my blanket to my chin, peering into the dark shadows of my room.

The closet was closed, which was exactly the way I liked it. It scared me when the door was cracked open, giving evil enough room to peek through. I could feel it sometimes watching me when my closet was like that. Feel it waiting. Hoping. Wanting me to get too close. Ready to attack. Gobble me up.

Was it the monster who'd made that noise? Was it placing its hand on the knob right now, ready to open the door and leap?

Scraaape.

Holding my blanket tighter, I almost screamed, but managed to keep the sound behind my teeth. If I'd screamed, the monster would know I was awake. And it would make my big sister laugh at me in the morning. I didn't like to be laughed at, which was why I'd stopped using a nightlight in my bedroom. I wished I had my nightlight now.

Stupid sister.

The scraping sound came again, making it hard to breathe for a while. It came one more time, and this time, instead of freaking out, I tried my best to recognize the sound. Was the monster carrying an ax, dragging it on the floor? Heading my way? Or was it already under my bed, waiting for my feet to hit the floor so it could chop off my toes and catch me before I could run?

"Stop being a baby," I whispered to myself as I scanned the entire room, too afraid to turn the light on. I hated being called a baby, especially by my sister. I was six years old, practically a grown-up, for cripes' sake.

Maybe whatever I'd heard had slammed my closet door shut, and whatever it was could be in there now. Or worse, maybe it was now in my room. Trying to look everywhere at once, I peered into the shadows, but nothing moved. Nothing was crawling over the floor or across my ceiling.

Being super careful, I peeked over the side of my bed, expecting something to jump up at any second.

Which was worse? Confronting the monster or waiting for it to confront you?

I didn't know.

Frozen with indecision, I thought through my options. If the monster wasn't in my closet or on the floor or ceiling, it could only mean one thing. It was under my bed.

I needed Daddy. Monsters were afraid of Daddies. I pulled the covers up to my chin and locked them in my fist. Monsters weren't allowed to dig under blankets, Daddy said so. If I stayed under the blankets, they couldn't get to me. I couldn't cover my face, though, because that made it hard to breathe. Besides, I was too scared. I had to see if one of them rose from the floor and reached for me.

None did.

Just when I thought it was safe again, I heard another thud, and my heart started galloping in my chest again. But this time, I knew something I hadn't known before. The noise wasn't inside my room. It had come from down the hall. From Mommy and Daddy's room.

As I listened with all my ears, I realized that the sound was familiar. It was the same sound I made when I tried to use the bed as a trampoline. Mommy didn't like that. Daddy said I had to work on my...dismount, whatever that meant. Instead of landing on my feet, I always landed on my butt on the wood floor in my room, and this new middle of the night sound was kinda like that.

Which was funny because I didn't hear Mommy or Daddy jumping on their bed. The bed squeaked when I did that, and the headboard hit the wall. I wondered if I'd slept through that part and only woke up when they fell. I grinned, thinking how funny it would be if one of them needed to work on their dismount too. I wanted to go and see and laugh with them. I wanted to see them on their butts, just like me.

But getting up meant turning on the light. That was scary. Monsters didn't like Daddies and blankets and light especially. That meant they'd keep you from turning on a light if they thought you were going to.

I thought about this a long time and finally pulled my arm free of the covers because I was brave—Mommy said so—and that was what brave boys did. I reached up as hard and as long as I could, and I still nearly missed the dangling chain, making it make a clinking sound against the metal pole thingy that held the light.

When it was finally in my hand, I pulled it really hard, hard enough to send the lamp dancing across my nightstand. The race car at the bottom of the light glowed, and the light shone off its little windshield in a hundred different places that were dazzling.

At least the light was on. The monsters had to leave me alone now. I saw Captain America watching from a poster I put up a couple of days ago. I knew that he was only paper, but I kept thinking that if monsters ever did show up, Cap would sound an alarm. 'Sides, now that I was up, I was thirsty, and a glass of water would be just about right.

I grabbed my giraffe. Mommy and Daddy got him for me when I was little, and his neck didn't stay upright too much anymore, but that just meant he leaned into me harder. He's Raff. He reached things for me when I couldn't because I didn't tall well. I liked Raff even if Winter thought it was a stupid name.

My sister called a lot of things stupid. She was thirteen and nearly a grown-up. She called me "Stupid" too. I thought maybe she didn't do well with names and forgot mine was Justin because she called me Stupid a lot.

My footie pajamas made little whisper sounds as I headed

to the door. It was kind of hard for me to turn the knob because my hands were all sweaty. I wished that Raff was real and that he could do the doorknob for me. He was good at knocking things off shelves and stuff, but he couldn't quite do twisty round parts, and doorknobs were all twisty round parts that should be banned by every house in America.

Peeking into the hallway, I could tell that my parents' door was open. When their door was closed, that meant I had to knock, and even when I did, Daddy got grumpy. But if the door was open, then it was okay to walk in and wake them up. They were probably already awake if they were making *thud* noises.

Still, I was a little worried they wouldn't like me seeing them "have fun" because Daddy told me that—in exactly those words—when I walked in one night when they forgot to close the door and were doing something not sleeping.

I told him that I liked to "have fun" too, and he told me that I needed to talk to Mommy about the "birds and the bees," which was confusing because, while birds were fun to watch, bees only wanted to sting with their butts. I didn't want to sting anyone with my butt, and I absolutely didn't want them stinging me.

Grown-ups were so confusing.

"Should we go in?" I asked Raff in my very quietest whisper.

Raff nodded. He nodded at a lot of things. I liked that about Raff because, sometimes, I needed someone around to tell me "yes" because everyone else was so good at saying "no."

"Okay," I whispered. I held Raff tight, my fist gripping his long neck as I walked into the room. After all, his plastic eyes were watching me like the moon was watching me, so it wasn't like I was alone. Mommy and Daddy couldn't say no to *all* of us, could they?

Only they didn't say anything at all.

I stopped and stared because Daddy was right there, kind of hanging off the bed, his head back, and looking at me upside down. One arm was kinda up over his head, the other was somewhere in the blankets. It was a funny way to lay. I didn't like the way Daddy was looking at me. He was looking at me the way Raff looked at me. Daddy's eyes didn't blink, and they looked kind of shiny and plastic and not real at all.

There was a kind of third eye on his forehead now, which I knew hadn't been there before. I wondered where he got it, and why he'd put it there. If I had a third eye, I'd put it on the back of my head so I could see things that came up from behind me. Because monsters liked to come up from behind little kids, so they could gobble them up before they could scream.

Scream...

Scream...

I must've made a noise because the moon came out to look and see what was going on. Mommy and Daddy's bedroom window got brighter, and I started to see the red.

It was everywhere. I thought that it must be ketchup. If it was, Daddy must have broken a whole bottle 'cause the ketchup was covering his face and rolling in and out of his open mouth. I wanted to ask why Mommy and Daddy had ketchup in bed because I wasn't allowed to eat in my room. But Daddy wasn't swallowing, and I didn't think he'd answer if I asked.

I hoped it was ketchup. I prayed it was ketchup because it was starting to look like it did when I fell on the rocks and cut my arm. When that happened last summer, the blood ran and streaked down the skin from wrist to elbow.

Mommy bandaged my arm, and Daddy fixed the bicycle, but there wasn't nearly so much blood then as Daddy had now. He was covered in it. I thought it must hurt, but

Daddy's eyes still didn't blink, and he was staring at me like he didn't want me to be there.

Mommy bandaged owies. That's what she did. She wrapped them and put that stuff on the cuts and scrapes that stung like crazy, but you had to have it. I liked it better when she put the bandage on and kissed my forehead and smiled, and the world was all right again. Mommy could bandage this; she could put some of the stinging stuff on Daddy and make him better and get me and Raff a glass of water.

I trotted to the other side of the bed. I saw Mommy's feet first, only they didn't stand up. Her feet looked funny all slack like that, and I thought she must be very tired to sleep in such a twisty way. I thought if I touched them, she'd wake up and giggle because Mommy was ticklish. But I was scared to, and I didn't know what to do.

Raff said that he'd touch them, he just needed a boost. I lifted him, and Raff touched his face against her feet, but nothing happened. I tapped Raff's nose against her, but she didn't move her feet. I didn't want to look at her face for some reason. I couldn't.

Suddenly, I didn't want to see, I didn't want to know. I wanted to go back to my room and hide and crawl under the blankets and stay there until the moon and Daddy stopped looking at me with unblinking eyes. I wanted the sun to come up and Mommy to make pancakes and for Daddy to be late for work and rushing around complaining like he always did.

I wanted to go away until life was normal again.

But even as my heart was telling me to run, my feet wanted to know. They moved closer, around the corner of the bed. I didn't ask them to, they just did. The moon came too, and I could see that Mommy was covered in red. The sheets, the pillows, the blankets. Everything was red.

I guessed the blankets didn't save her. Daddy didn't save

her. Maybe some monsters weren't afraid of Daddies or blankets, after all. I wondered if they were afraid of the light.

I decided I didn't want to know those kinds of monsters.

Mommy was looking at the ceiling. She was staring at it, but it looked wrong when she did, the way it looked wrong when Daddy stared at me. I was still close to her feet. If I tickled her, maybe I could make her wake up. I reached for her foot like I'd reached for the lamp, but when I touched her foot, it was cold, and it didn't move under my fingers.

It wasn't real. It wasn't alive. It wasn't her.

It couldn't be.

I wanted Daddy, but he was still upside down. For a minute, I wondered if he was laying like that so he could slide off and check for monsters under the bed. Or maybe he already checked…and one of them got him.

My whole body shivered, and my heart began punching at my ribs.

I shook Mommy harder until her whole body moved. Her head turned, and there was something wrong with her neck because it twisted funny, and suddenly, there was more blood. It was on my hands and on my pajamas.

This wasn't my Mommy and Daddy. I was really scared now, and I wanted them to wake up now.

I turned and screamed for my sister. She could set this right because Winter always fixed things, like when she fixed the lampshade I hit it with my ball. She could wake Mommy and Daddy, and if she wanted to call me Stupid, I didn't care. She could call me names and beat me up and make fun of me all she wanted if she'd just wake them. Then I could get a glass of water and a kiss on the head, and they could tuck me in.

Only, I couldn't scream. My mouth was open, but nothing came out, even though a part of my chest was breaking, and the pounding of my heart crashed through my ears, and I was deaf with the throb-throb-throb of it. I couldn't even yell for help.

I made my feet move. I forced them to turn me around, to carry me out of there, to get away from plastic eyes and funny Mommy and Daddy shaped things. I was stuck, though, my feet sticking to the floor. I realize that it was because the red stuff was on them, the rug was full of it. My feet of my pajamas were red, and they left red footprints everywhere I stepped until I was in the hallway. I didn't remember getting there.

I left footprints from my Mommy's room to the hallway, and she was going to be so mad when she woke up, woke up, woke up, wake up. Suddenly, my voice came back in a shriek as loud as any firetruck.

"WAKE UP! WAKE UP! WAKE UP!"

I couldn't think of my sister's name. I couldn't think at all. I just needed everyone to wake up, everyone needed to wake up, everyone needed to wake up, and I screamed as loud and as long as I could.

But no one came.

Backing down the hallway, I didn't stop until my back hit my sister's door. I needed to go inside and wake her up. But…what if she had a third eye too?

Whimpering, I just stood outside her door, my hand on the knob. Raff told me to turn it, but then I heard a soft click coming from downstairs. It sounded like the front door.

Was the monster leaving, or was it opening the door for his friends?

I shuddered so hard my hand fell from the doorknob, and I huddled against my sister's door as footsteps sounded on the stairs. I waited for the squeak from the fifth step from the top, but it didn't come. The monster knew about that squeak.

My pajama bottoms grew warm and wet when a dark

figure appeared at the top of the steps. It had long black hair and it was walking up on its toes, very sneaky. Very quiet.

The dark figure stopped at Mommy and Daddy's bedroom door, and from the light coming from the door, I realized it wasn't a monster. It was Winter. My sister.

Nearly hysterical with relief, I tried to say her name, but the words were caught in my throat because it was tight and hard to breathe.

As she stared into our parents' room, she made a sound that kind of sounded like a scream, and her hand came up to cover her mouth as she stumbled backward.

She'd seen the ketchup too, I could tell. And she would clean it up and we'd all laugh in the morning as we ate our pancakes.

For a moment, I thought everything might be all right, but that was before more weird things happened. A shadow behind my big sister kind of pulled away from the rest of the darkness. The shadow shifted and changed, then grew bigger and bigger. After my heart pounded at least three more times, the shadow became a man. A full-grown man.

Yay, it's a grown-up. That was my first thought, at least. Maybe he could wake my parents. After all, he was an adult, and that was what adults did. They helped.

But instead of helping, he raised something he held in his hand. It was a long piece of wood, like a bat, but thinner. I knew that I should scream or say something, anything at all, but before I could even open my mouth, my sister turned and looked at the man. She didn't have time to scream either before the shadow man slammed the thing down on her head, and she fell. And just like that, she was staring at the wall like Daddy had been staring.

There was blood on her head now too.

My fingers were numb, and my brain was numb. Raff slipped from my fingers onto the floor, and he got blood on him too. He stared at me from the floor as if to say "get out get out get out," but the man stared at me too as he stepped over my sister, and threw the stick away into my parents' bedroom. His other hand held something that shone in the dim moonlight. It was a knife, but the knife was bleeding too.

He went down to one knee and smiled at me.

"Your Mommy and Daddy kept you from meeting me," he said. His voice was like a deep rumble, like Mr. Washington at the store. Mommy said that Mr. Washington talked like that because he smoked too much. I wondered if this man smoked too much. I could kinda smell the smoke on him, but everything around me smelled stronger, sweet, and funny— like metal I could taste with my nose.

"We're family," he said to me. "You shouldn't oughta be kept from your family." He looked toward my parents' room for a moment before turning all his focus back on me. He scooped me up into his arms. I wanted to reach for Raff, but my whole body was frozen as he stepped over my sister and walked calmly down the stairs and out of the door, me in my wet SpongeBob pajamas, and headed for a pickup truck parked in the street.

He set me on the passenger side and told me to wait. I thought, *I should run, I should hide, I should get far, far away.* He was a stranger, and I was not supposed to ride with strangers, but I couldn't move, and the words got stuck again.

He got in and fired up the truck. "You're a good boy," he said, his voice still a low grumble. "You obeyed me just right, and all you gotta do is keep on obeyin' me. 'Children, obey your parents in the Lord, for this is right.' That's from the sixth chapter of Ephesians. Do you know your Bible, boy?"

Mutely, I shook my head. My thumb was inching closer to my mouth.

"Didn't think so. That'll be a changin', boy. Gonna teach

you right." The truck started moving, and he looked at me sideways. "I was at your house just to meet you, and I'm going to take care of you from now on. Not right keepin' you from your family. Not right at all."

The truck rattled and coughed and belched smoke. I could see it in the mirror on the side of the truck, just like I could see my house growing smaller and smaller. We went through the neighborhood, past where I was allowed to ride my bike. I looked in the mirror at my house behind me and missed Mommy and Daddy and Winter and Raff-Raff. He drove down roads I didn't recognize until my home wasn't there behind us anymore.

"How about we call you...Jaime?" the man said suddenly. "My name is Kilroy. Some folks just call me Preacher."

I put my thumb in my mouth and nodded.

What else could I do?

I SHOOK MY HEAD. *God, what a waste of time.* Memories usually were. I'd sat down to talk, and instead, I got lost, caught in a whole lot of nonsense from a long time ago. More than thirteen years ago. Sometimes, I forgot that all that mattered was the here and now.

Justin was dead. Why couldn't I leave him buried?

I realized that the camera was still recording and had captured me sitting and daydreaming, reliving little boy nightmares. I cursed under my breath and called myself twelve kinds of fool as I took the memory card out of the camera and inserted a fresh one, a new one, one that had never witnessed the image of me lost in some pathetically childish dream. The first one would have to be destroyed.

When I sat back, I took a deep calming breath as I

assessed my image on the little screen. It was perfect, just the way I'd planned it for so long.

With the simple tap of a button, REC appeared on the bottom left corner of the monitor. I gazed into the camera, imagining how she'd feel when she was gazing back.

I had something to say and someone very important to tell it to.

Time to begin.

2

Special Agent in Charge of the Richmond Violent Crimes office, Max Osbourne, drew a heavy breath and gave Winter Black one of his more impressive looks. She'd seen the new hires flinch under one of those looks. Given that their department worked on catching the country's most violent criminals, that was saying something.

Winter didn't so much as bat an eyelash, willing him to see this as a good a sign as any that she was ready to take on bigger cases. He'd recently started giving her grunt work, and she knew it was because of her brother's case. It was time for him to believe that she could handle anything, including taking down her sibling.

"I want to know everything. I won't involve myself in Justin's case." She mentally crossed her fingers as she said it. "I just want to help with the Timothy and Mariah Young murder case."

She swallowed, thinking of Mariah, the sweet little girl who'd witnessed the aftermath of her mother and sister's brutal murder. Winter still felt like a failure for not keeping the father and daughter safe. They should have tried harder, done more. Anything more.

It had been like a knife in her gut when she'd learned Tim and Mariah had also been slaughtered, Preacher style. They were just the last of a long list of innocents who had survived the Danville Mall murders...only to be savagely killed by someone intent on finishing what Tyler Haldane and Kent Strickland started that terrible night.

Kelsey and Adrian Esperson

Sandy and Oliver Ulbrich

Willa Brown

Dana Young and her twelve-year-old daughter Sadie

And now Timothy and ten-year-old Mariah. An entire family wiped out so cruelly.

By Winter's baby brother?

It appeared that way.

Max's stare was growing even harder as her mind wandered into the past. Did he growl a little under his breath? This was her boss, and by now, she was used to Max's bluster, and knew how to control the situation. At least she hoped she did.

"You can help as needed, but I'm not going to assign you directly to the case. Understood?" He pulled an open file closer across his desk. It was a newly assembled file, and the side tab held a very familiar name. *Justin Black AKA Jaime Peterson.*

She swallowed hard on seeing the names in print like that, side by side, as though they belonged together. She wasn't entirely sure how someone missing for so long, who'd gone through so much as Justin had to have survived, could all be encapsulated into a simple manilla folder. Her eyes longed to drink in the photo of her dark-haired brother that gazed out from its place on top of the paperwork.

Max cleared his throat, pulling her attention back to him.

"I shouldn't be talking to you about any of this, you understand me? This case...it's been going south for a while now. No sooner do we run down one name, one killer, than another crops up. The Preacher is dead. Now, we only need the third person from the manifesto."

The manifesto to which he was referring was an online letter that proclaimed the works that Kent Strickland and Tyler Haldane had written before shooting up a mall and killing a number of innocent victims. As it turned out, there was a third accomplice in the shooting, one who'd gone on a killing spree himself.

Was that Justin?

Winter still had a hard time believing it could be her baby brother. But then again, the last time she'd seen her brother, he'd been wearing SpongeBob pajamas and holding his favorite stuffed animal, Raff.

"When the connection to your missing brother came up," Max went on, "well, I hoped they would be wrong. But from what Kent Strickland's father, George, told Miguel and Noah, he gave a positive ID on Jaime Peterson. Apparently, he and Kent were good friends. They formed a..." Max checked his notes again before continuing. "They formed a club of sorts, using code names and secret handshakes, the lot."

Winter swallowed, lifting a hand halfway to her mouth, compensating for the gesture by brushing a single strand of glossy black hair back behind her ear as she nodded. She willed her blue eyes to stay carefully calm and serene. "Right. Do you know more on why they used the code names?" She already knew all this, and she didn't understand why Max was bringing it up again, so she played along.

"Yes, they'd apparently planned on being a military unit one day. They had code names for each other, the way special ops in the movies have. As you know, your brother was 'White Ghost.'"

Somehow, that was fitting. Jaime/Justin was a ghost of sorts, after all. One she'd been searching for over a dozen years.

"This is all according to Strickland, right?" Winter looked up, feeling a glimmer of hope that faded almost as soon as it started. Strickland might not be the most reliable witness, but there was no reason for him to lie, not now.

"He was most cooperative." Max gazed back at her from under heavy eyebrows. "Winter, you know that you're not on this case. You're too close."

Every fiber of her soul wanted to scream and yell and tear the office apart. Of course, she needed to be in on this, it was her *brother*, the child she couldn't protect, the last of her family.

A more rational part of her realized that was the exact reason she shouldn't be on the case. Her objectivity wasn't there. If an agent allowed her emotions to rule her case, she jeopardized not only herself, but also her partner and everyone who worked the case. Of course, knowing that didn't help the frantic energy that was building inside every cell of her body.

"I'm a professional." Her voice was calm, and the words came in measured tones. "I'm aware of the risks. I don't expect to be assigned to this. I just..." She stared at the desk and the folder that held all the information on her lost brother. "I just want to be kept informed. Please." She lifted her gaze, meeting his eyes squarely. Max returned her look with one of his own, a considering look.

I'm not being unreasonable. Under the circumstances, I think I'm being perfectly rational.

What Max had to consider was beyond her.

"I'll keep you in the loop."

Winter blinked. He'd acquiesced. Okay, there might have been a certain amount of reluctance, but he was willing to give her this much, at least. Winter could see it in his posture, in his expression that he was trying. Well, she would if a stoic iron-forged face like Max's could be considered to have expressions. He might have made a professional poker player with as much as he gave away.

Calm down. You know what he's not saying here. Don't run a victory lap just yet.

Winter understood what Max didn't say: he would give her little bits and pieces that he felt were safe for her to hear, and only when he felt it was safe to tell her.

Which, in the end, was still better than nothing. At least she hoped so.

The scream began again under her calm.

No. It wasn't better. Deep down, she knew it wasn't.

She wanted more. She wanted every scrap of information, of evidence. She wanted her brother back, dammit. She'd only been thirteen when he'd been lost to her. Now, after a lifetime of searching, she was so close. So close she could taste it. How in the hell was she supposed to stand back and let someone else bring him in?

She should be the one to see this through. Not some stranger who'd never met him, who didn't know him the way she did. They only saw the stone-cold killer, not the scared little boy who couldn't go anywhere without his stuffed giraffe.

"It's probably stupid to ask this, but I have to. How are you holding up under this? If you need some time off..." Max closed the file, the picture of Jaime Peterson—Justin Black, the protégé of Douglas Kilroy...Winter's long-lost brother and suspected killer—now covered up. Just like that, the meeting was over. This was all she was going to get.

Why was Max asking personal questions? She met his

gaze, suddenly unsure. This was *Max*. He'd always been approachable as far as bosses where concerned, but to Max, everything was all about the job, and to suddenly pry into the emotional state of one of his people felt wrong. Weird. Like he was looking for something.

Like he was expecting her to crack under the pressure.

Breathe. Just breathe. It'll be all right.

Winter smiled and looked away. *Remember, it's still all about the job.* Max wanted to know if his agent was able to work. He was a man checking a tool, making sure that it could work for him before using it. Making sure the tool didn't snap during a crucial phase of the job. This wasn't about her. This was about what she was able to do, about how she was able to work. Or not.

That bitter, visceral assessment might have been unfair, but so was this entire situation. She blew out a short breath in frustration.

He has a job to do, and for that matter, so do I.

"I'm all right." Winter looked him in the eye again. Maybe there was a little concern for her in there, more than just the job, but it was the boss she answered, not the man. "In fact, it would be easier on me if I concentrate on what I *am* able to do. Maybe I can't be involved directly in Justin's case, but I can still do other, more important duties. That's a lot better than sitting around obsessing on what I can't do, don't you think?"

"All right." Max leaned back in his chair, and Winter stood, realizing that the interview was over. Time to prove everything she'd just said and try not to think about how Justin had become Jaime. Or that Kilroy had taught him well. Most of all, she needed to remember there was nothing she could do about any of it.

Max was right, she was too close. The burn in her guts told her that.

Let the others handle it.

Which was all great, in theory. She was willing to be professional, but the emotions still churned in her guts, and the adrenaline that came from holding down the emotions surged through her blood. She stepped outside of Max's office and looked toward her desk and the mounds of papers waiting to be shuffled, the phone that never stopped ringing, and all the responsibilities of a job she loved. And that didn't even begin to address the multitudes of unread messages sitting in her inbox right now.

Instead, she turned in the other direction and headed for the exit, making a beeline to the gym. There was a lot of energy to burn off and building up a sweat always seemed to clear her head and help her think.

Today of all days, the aerobics and treadmills had no appeal. Today was a good day for the heavy bag. Thankfully, no one was using it, meaning she could dive in fairly fast while her adrenaline was still up.

She loved the feeling as the bag gave under her fists. She pounded on the canvas cover and pummeled Douglas Kilroy and Justin Black and a thirteen-year-old Winter who couldn't protect her little brother. She beat on her parents for getting killed. She beat on Max, on her boyfriend, Noah, on Strickland and Haldane. Then Kilroy again, the so-called "Preacher," the cause of all of this.

She hit him for what he did, for who he was, for dying with her brother's location on his lips and taking that to his grave. She hit him for what he did to Justin, for what he did to her, and most especially to her parents.

No matter how hard and how fast Winter hit the bag, it seemed there was no upper limit to the damage she wanted to inflict on Douglas Kilroy. She threw herself into every punch; the grunts and guttural sounds she made on every impact were a curse on his memory.

She punched for the ones murdered at the Danville Mall and those killed simply because they'd escaped. The Espersons and the Ulbrichs. Willa and the entire Young family.

Especially, Mariah.

By the time she ran out of people to pummel, her arms felt sodden, and her shoulders sang with the impacts to the bag. She straightened, stretching her back to find out that she'd been the focus of some scrutiny from those around her. She glanced around, suddenly uneasy.

This wasn't the usual ogling that men tried to hide when a woman exercised. These looks were more of surprise and concern. She looked around the room in surprise and no small amount of anger until she swore that, if she saw one more worried frown, she wouldn't use the bag anymore, but transfer the rage within to the next person who asked or even *looked* like they wanted to ask if she was all right. A person had a right to workout the way they chose.

Then it came back to her that the grunts and explosions of sounds coming from her mouth occasionally had had words buried in them, and she blushed, considering some of the more choice phrases she'd used.

She swiped at her face with the back of her hand, and that's when she nosed the blood. Her nose was bleeding, more than a little. Dammit. She reached for the tissue she kept on her person at all times to staunch the flow, but her hands were clumsy with the boxing gloves.

No wonder the other men and women were watching her carefully, as if she were an explosion waiting to happen.

Gritting her teeth, she ignored them, and they eventually went back to lifting round leaden weights and running on conveyor belts. Winter stood long enough to catch her breath, and a part of her marveled that the bag had withstood as much punishment as it had with no sign of damage.

That seemed unfair, considering how her fists and forearms still vibrated from her efforts. She remembered a scene in a movie where the hero punched holes in the heavy, thick canvas. Or maybe the one where the bag went flying off the chain. She decided the workout would definitely have been more satisfying if the bag had, at the very least, ruptured.

In between breaths, a new thought occurred to her, one at odds with the severe professionalism she'd worked so long and hard to achieve.

I don't need to be assigned to the case.

For a moment, she couldn't breathe at all. She walked calmly to where she'd stashed her water bottle as she turned this over in her mind. *I still have access to files under my own name. I can look into the evidence and work this on my own. Just so long as I keep my own little personal investigation hidden.*

She pulled the cord to the right glove with her teeth and shook her hand till the glove fell. She freed her left hand in a similar way and bundled the gloves together before taking a long drink. She could feel the water all the way down, crisp and cool.

I can do it. No one needs to know.

Excited now, Winter grabbed her towel, dabbed at her nose, and headed for the showers. A hot shower, a quick bite of toast, and the afternoon should go reasonably well. If nothing else, she could hold on to the cool and collected agent persona, and that would make it easier to prowl undetected in areas she wasn't supposed to be in.

She paused in the doorway and turned in silent farewell to the bag and the many victims of her rage it represented. For a wild giddy moment, she wondered if maybe it would be best to leave all that there, to allow the ghosts to wander the gym unmolested. Wasn't that what a professional would do?

No, it was what *they* would have her do.

I can't. I can't let this go any more than I can stop breathing.

I'm not ready to forget. I can't do that to you, Justin. You still need me.

By the time she got into the shower, the hot water only seemed to strengthen her resolve. The energy was burned off, and she felt more able to face the day, but she wasn't about to sit back and idly let the case go forward without her.

She needed to get in this. For that scared little boy she remembered outside of her parents' door. For her. Justin deserved better, and so did she.

And she couldn't do anything if she was bogged down in shit work for the Bureau.

Once she was toweled off, Winter braided her hair neatly and dressed in the fresh clothes she kept in her locker. Within ten minutes, she was heading back to her desk.

She stopped when Max called her name. "Come to my office." When she didn't move, he added, "Now."

Winter swallowed hard. "Yes, sir."

Dread crawled over her skin like a spider as he shut his door behind her.

"Winter, we have a problem."

It seemed her little outburst in the gym had already made its way to his ears. And just like that, Max put her on a leave of absence.

"For how long?"

His gaze was softer this time. "Until I tell you to come back."

iden Parrish picked up the file again. As the Supervisory Special Agent of the bureau's Behavioral Analysis Unit, he was expected to be right most of the time. If there was a time for him to be wrong, this was that time.

The problem was simple...he *knew* he wasn't wrong. He knew it in his bones and out in every direction. The problem was he didn't want to be right. Winter was a friend, even if their friendship took a strain now and again. That friendship meant something to him.

How would you feel if your long-lost brother was suddenly identified as a serial killer?

How was a person even supposed to imagine such a thing? The very idea was too foreign a concept, yet it was the very issue that Winter was now facing. That kind of thing had to mess with a person in ways one could hardly imagine.

The problem was that Aiden was only able to go so far with his concern. In his position, being too familiar with another agent was a bad idea with capital letters. Not to mention that it would be wise to take Noah Dalton, Winter's fellow agent and boyfriend, into consideration. Aiden didn't know if Noah was the jealous type, but since he was armed and trained to take people down…it was better to err on the side of caution.

He closed the file without looking at it, tapping the spine on his empty palm and grinding his teeth together. His analysis was spot-on, the profile would hold up, but interfering with another agent, that was new territory for him. He wasn't so sure about the steps involved there. Still, he couldn't do nothing. What kind of man, what kind of *friend* would he be if he just let it go and let the woman he'd met because of her parents' murder fend for herself?

He dropped the file on the desk in front of him and turned to see the solution open the door to his office. Dr. Autumn Trent knocked on his doorframe as she stuck her head in. "You wanted to see me?"

He motioned for her to come in, momentarily distracted by the tall, slender redhead. She could have easily been a model, but her mind was as sharp and insightful as any he'd ever known, as evidenced in the clear green eyes she turned on him. What's more, Autumn was a good analyst. Brainy enough to have a PhD, and canny enough to work in threat assessment, Autumn was truly a force to be reckoned with. More importantly, from what he'd observed, she was a good friend to Winter. Noah too. It only felt a little manipulative to exploit that fact.

"Have a seat, Dr. Trent." He gestured to the worn and patched chairs on the other side of the desk. Funding in the bureau was spotty, but replacement furniture for offices was never high on the list of priorities.

Still, when Autumn sat, she brought a touch of class to the place that was sorely missing.

"Thank you for taking the time to see me today," he added as he rose and closed the door behind her. He ignored the raised eyebrow and hitched one hip onto the corner of his desk.

"You said it was about Winter," Autumn prompted. She shot a look at the closed door. "A private matter, I take it?"

"I did, and it is." He reached out to pick up the folder again. "I've been going over the file on Justin, her brother."

"Are you going to tell me that you were wrong?" Autumn asked, a note of hope creeping into her voice. "Because I have to tell you, I would be relieved enough that I wouldn't even give you shit about it."

Even with her humor, he barely allowed himself to smile. "I wish I was. It would make things a hell of a lot easier if I were. Unfortunately..." he half shrugged, "it is what it is. Which leads to the problem. I'm worried about Winter."

Autumn crossed her legs and leaned back in the chair. For a moment, Aiden regretted the shabbiness of the furniture. "You called me down here to tell me you were worried about Winter? Of course, you're worried. *I'm* worried. We should be worried. You just told her that her long-lost brother is a murdering psychopath. What's not to be worried about?"

"I called you down here to ask you, as a friend of a friend, to keep an eye on her. She claims to be all right, and she refused to take time off. I thought with the upcoming holidays she might want to visit family. She has grandparents who she normally spends the holidays with, but in addition to her refusing to take time off, there are other...indications that she's not taking this well."

"Indications?" Autumn's lip curled up. She wasn't pleased with the assessment, though he could see in her posture, in the way her hands were folded carefully in her lap, that she was keeping her emotions under tight control. "I hardly think she's interested in Christmas right now."

Aiden took a deep breath. "Indications like trying to pound a heavy bag into powder. Like skipping meals and letting her work slide. Max...SAC Osbourne...is turning a blind eye, citing personal issues, and only assigning her to minutiae duties in case it could be potentially problematic for someone who..." he tried to think of a diplomatic way to continue, "someone whose head isn't in the game."

Autumn's shoulders relaxed. "Sounds like he's got a handle on this," she said, but there was still a note of question in her voice, not to mention a few slivers of ice.

Aiden rethought how to word his thoughts. "That's the official line, yes. It so happens that I agree with it too. But Winter is a friend. That might be tested from time to time, but a friend she remains. You and I at least have this much in common. We both want her safe, physically and emotionally, even considering her line of work."

That, at least, seemed to mollify her a little. "I happen to agree." She tilted her head to the side, looking at him curiously. "What do you want from me?"

Aiden shrugged. "Just...keep an eye on her. That's all."

Maybe he should have worded it differently. Autumn sat fully upright, her foot coming down to the floor with a bang as she uncrossed her legs and stood. "I am not going to spy on my friend for you."

"No. I'm not asking that. I don't want that. I'm not looking to be informed about her, I just..." He exhaled, striving to maintain his cool. "I just want you to do what I can't. Be there for her."

Autumn studied him closely as she sank back into the chair. At least she wasn't leaving. "Sometimes," she said quietly, "the best you can do is to let a friend feel her or his pain." She inhaled deeply, her normal sardonic smile and the flash in her eyes gone. "Seeing a friend hurting sucks, but it's better to see them hurt and get through it than to protect them from reality. Are you prepared to never see her *not* in pain?"

Aiden blinked. "Meaning?"

Autumn smiled, the light in her eyes returning, though slowly. "Meaning that the best thing I can do for her is to leave her alone and trust that she'll be all right."

"And if she calls you for help?"

Autumn's eyebrows shot up her forehead. "I'll drop whatever I'm doing and rush to her side. That's what friends do," she replied primly, her tone offended.

Aiden spread his arms. "That's all I'm asking. Just to be there for her until she gets her feet under her again."

"You didn't need to drag me down here for that," Autumn practically growled and shook her head. Her gaze was almost uncomfortable in its intensity.

She really was beautiful. It was odd how he tended to forget that until seeing her again. *That's a lie, you never forget how beautiful she is.*

"You asked me into your office for a reason. I suspect you're looking for more than a casual favor."

"I would like to know how she's doing. How she's holding up. You're in a better position to know those things right now than I am."

"I told you," Autumn's voice took on an edge, "I will not spy on a friend for you or for Max or even for the ghost of Karl Marx." She barked out a brittle laugh. "There you have it. I wondered when the altruism would run out. If you're looking for dirt to put in a report, you won't be getting it from me."

"I don't want you to spy!" he shot back, exasperated now. "I just want to know what's going on."

"What's the difference between that and spying?" She folded her toned arms over her chest and her head tilted to one side. Less in casual study than in absolute scrutiny, as though she thought him perilously trapped.

"Because," Aiden said through gritted teeth. "Precisely

because I'm *not* writing a report or handing the information over to my superiors. I just want to know for *me* how she's doing."

"I notice you're not concerned about Noah."

"Should I be? It's Winter's brother who's the killer, not his."

Autumn had the look of someone whose joke wasn't understood. He shook his head and shoved off the desk, tired of sitting still.

She pointed to the file. "There isn't a possibility that's wrong?"

"No." Aiden shook his head. "I mean...there's always the possibility. Noah and Bree are out there now interviewing Strickland again, maybe they can shed new light on all of this, but whatever he is, or whoever he is, we have to find him, one way or another. We *have* to. And when we do, that's when Winter will need you the most."

Autumn glanced down at her hands, idle now in her lap. "I can't imagine what it was like for a six-year-old to find his parents dead. Can you imagine being whisked away and raised as the son of that...?" She waved her hands around, words clearly failing her.

Aiden waited while she fought some hidden internal demon. Only her eyes moved for a long time.

Finally, she looked up, sighing as she answered. "All right, all right, but only for a short while." She waggled a finger at him. "But I am not spying on her."

"Still not asking you to."

"You know I would do anything for her. You know I will be there for her."

"I do," Aiden admitted, "but what I didn't know is if you would be there for me. To let me know how she's holding up." After a moment, he smiled and added, "And Noah too."

That made Autumn laugh, the sound appearing to be

genuine this time. "Yeah, I'll be sure to add him in my reports too."

Aiden retreated behind his desk and sat wearily in his chair, feeling oddly heavy despite this particular burden being lifted from him. "Thank you."

Autumn stood and straightened her skirt. "Tell me," she said as she headed to the door. "Why didn't you just call her in here like you did with me and give her the 'my door is always open if you need anything' line?"

"It's not a line," he said, watching her face as it changed from curiosity to chagrin to understanding.

"Oh my god, you did, didn't you? You already told her that." Autumn pressed her fingertips to her temple. "You and Winter? Really?" She took a step back and nodded as if seeing something she had been looking for. "Well, I can see that. I guess I really can."

"No." Aiden shook his head. "Not the way you mean, no. I'm worried about a friend."

She chuckled. "For your information, I haven't heard much from her for a few days now."

Aiden nodded.

She gave him a backward look as she opened the door. It was a thoughtful look with a hint of speculation that made him uncomfortable.

"What?"

She paused, her hand still on the doorknob. "Just wondering if you're the friend you're making out to be or if there's a hidden agenda behind this."

"No agenda." He held out both hands. "Just a worried friend."

"I think I'm choosing to believe you, Agent Parrish." She smiled at him, closing the door behind her as she left.

Aiden stared at the door for some minutes as the scent of

her perfume faded from the room. It looked even shabbier now than it had looked before she came.

"Don't go there," he cautioned himself and placed the file carefully on his desk again. There were other cases waiting for his attention. He'd done all he could do for now.

4

Concrete walls and floors took every click and creak and bang of steel and iron and concentrated the sounds, echoes chasing each other through the bare hallways. Manual and automatic gates opened and closed as Agents Dalton and Stafford checked in, relinquished their weapons, and stole deeper into the sterile tomb of a maximum-security prison.

They were led to the commons where prisoners would meet with visitors under the close supervision of the guards. They were led onward past that door, their footsteps a counterpoint to the closing and locking door behind them. The next door opened for them as they arrived, their escort falling away and leaving the rest to the guard inside the separate interrogation room.

There were four chairs set up in the room, each one bolted securely to the floor, metal monstrosities whose function was limited to causing lower back pain while being easy to keep clean.

Two chairs were behind a table, two were in front of it.

Only one was occupied. A middle-aged man with thick glasses and a nervous air stood quickly to greet them.

"Agents." He smiled as he said it, a meaty palm reaching out to the both of them, a tremulous smile creasing his face and little piggy eyes like small jewels sunk deep into the rolls of doughy looking skin.

Noah took his hand, though with some hesitation. "And you are?"

"Lionel Mathews," the heavy man answered, grabbing his hand for one of the most unpleasant handshakes Noah had ever felt. It was wet and not unlike having a dead fish laid in his palm. "US Attorney's Office."

Noah pulled his hand back. The offer was given to Bree, who somehow kept a poker face throughout the greeting, though he noticed she didn't linger over the handshake either, her dark skin a stark contrast to his paleness. Lionel looked very pleased to have held her hand, and a shadow of disappointment crossed his face as she pulled away.

"And what is the role of the US Attorney's office here today?" Bree asked him with a smile. "I understood that this case was over, and Strickland was found guilty and given life. Was I wrong about that?"

"No, Agent Stafford, you were not wrong at all. I'm just here to ensure that if there is a retrial or other types of legal maneuvering, nothing will be seen as possible...legal...shall we say, shenanigans?"

"Shenanigan?" Noah started to bristle, but Bree stepped in.

"We don't do 'shenanigans,'" she assured him.

"Oh, and I'm sure you do not." Lionel sounded more like a stereotypical southern preacher than a lawyer. The man had obviously missed his calling. "No, and I'm also sure that you all ask questions in accordance with the prisoner's rights and all. But when your boss requested this interview with a high-profile prisoner like this one, he was informed that the presence of a member of the US Attorney's Office would have to be in attendance. Did he not mention this fact to you?"

"Must have slipped his mind," Noah said, annoyance grinding into his bones. "Counselor, I don't think—"

The door on the other side of the conference room opened, and Kent Strickland entered. Chains bound his ankles and wrists to a strap he wore across his waist.

Strickland was led, not gently, to the table. They all waited as his hands were freed and relocked into the top of the table on the eyebolt set there for that very purpose. Noah noted with a certain satisfaction that the chains on his ankles were not removed.

Strickland looked from one to another of the three people in the room, a smarmy looking smirk playing on his lips. He sat back as much as he could under the restraint of the chains and waited. Wordless. Challenging.

"I'm Agent Dalton, and this is Agent Stafford." Noah indicated Bree, who stayed back a step from the table. The introduction felt unnecessary. Maybe it was. How much did Strickland remember or understand regarding his case? Prisoners tended to become experts in the details of whatever got them convicted in the first place. Why should he be any different?

"Secret agents." Strickland guffawed. "License to kill? Tell me, sweetheart," he turned to Bree, "what are you licensed for? Do they give licenses for that?" His tongue swept a loop around his lip in an obscene manner, but instead of holding her eyes, he matched Noah's stare. It was a move calculated to get under Noah's skin, to get his ire up.

Far from angry, Noah was mystified at the action. It was senseless and ultimately useless. Bree was Noah's partner, not his lover, and for her part, she was disgusted, not offended, and more than capable of taking care of herself.

Strickland's performance felt forced, a show of bravado for his own benefit. Maybe he was trying to bolster his courage, to convince himself he was in charge of the situation.

Making all of this irritating in the extreme. While Strickland was playing king of the exam room, people were in danger, or even dying. This whole interview was starting to feel like a waste of time.

"Lionel Mathews," the big man said, reaching out his hand before remembering that Kent couldn't reach. He pulled his hand back quickly, looking at the guard that stood behind Strickland. "Ah...US Attorney..."

Noah looked to Bree, who understood what he was thinking but was obviously not too happy about it. She took a deep breath and walked over to where the guard was standing and whispered in his ear. Bree was a very persuasive person when she had to be.

"Tell me about Jaime Peterson," Noah began, leaning forward in his chair as he got straight to the point. There was still a chance, however slim, that Strickland would act in everyone's best interest. As remote as that possibility was, he was determined to give the man every chance. On the other hand, he refused to leave empty-handed. This was too important. Too important to future victims, and most of all, too important to Winter.

"Jaime?" Kent seemed surprised by the line of questioning. "What about him?" Strickland's eyes took on a speculative cast, like he was trying to find an angle in the question that would benefit him.

"Start with where he came from."

Strickland blinked and considered this for a moment before he leaned back in his chair with an indifferent shrug. "Don't know. Don't care."

"You were childhood friends," Noah said, hoping a little

verbal prodding would make Strickland more forthcoming. "You're saying that you never asked him where he was born?"

"Why should I?" Strickland crossed his wrists and tilted his head to the side as if noticing Noah for the first time, and not quite sure how to classify him. "Don't matter to me."

"What about his grandfather?" Bree shot from behind Lionel's chair. She'd been moving around the room as though restless while Noah questioned the man. The man from the US Attorney's Office jumped. He apparently hadn't heard her move, which was precisely why she'd done it in all likelihood. Noah kept his eyes locked on Strickland's and stifled the smile that threatened to break the persona Noah was trying to project.

What Strickland thought of Bree's maneuvering Noah didn't know. His tone was neutral, even bored as he asked, "What about him?"

"Nice guy? Real friendly?"

Strickland shook his head. "No, he wasn't. I guess you would say he was a real bastard. But he kept it hidden. Everyone loved him." As if startled that he'd answered that question honestly, Strickland shot a lecherous look at Bree. "I bet you would have too, sweetheart." He blew a kiss at her and laughed when she didn't react. Noah looked up at the guard, but he stared straight ahead, making no move to silence the man.

Which meant he wouldn't put a stop to most anything; that could be good or bad.

"Tell me about Jaime!" Noah growled, sick of the whole thing. He imagined Winter's pale face, freaking out over the idea that Justin was not only alive, but actually *adopted* by a psychopathic serial killer. He couldn't begin to imagine how any person adapted to that kind of information. For that matter, it would be too much for anyone to take in, wouldn't it? And here Strickland was, holding the key, the information

Noah needed to put an end to this farce. But instead of helping, it seemed the mass murderer was intent on only playing games.

Noah bit back a growl, reminding himself he was a professional and that this wasn't personal, even though everything about this case had been feeling that way for a while now. He leaned across the table, until he was practically nose to nose with the man. The rules were you couldn't touch a prisoner, but getting into Strickland's personal space was a gray area.

Strickland's eyes widened for a moment, and incredibly, he laughed instead of rearing back. If anything, he leaned in, as though ready to share a secret. "Oh, wow. Jaime's being a problem, isn't he? Got you all flustered and bothered? What did he do? What did he do? You can tell me. It's hard to get news in here, you know?"

Noah stared at him, for all the world at a loss for words.

Thankfully, Bree wasn't. "Where was Peterson from?" she asked sharply as Noah pushed himself away from the table, giving himself some much needed space.

"Who cares?" Strickland yelled back.

Noah whirled and slammed his hand on the desk. Lionel jumped. "You do. If you let one more person die, I swear I will do everything in my power to get the judge to add their deaths to your sentence."

"I'm a lifer, jackass." The sneer was still in place, but there was just a hint of fear in those eyes.

"Yeah." Bree's usual affable smile was gone. She closed the distance to Noah's side, her calm unhurried speech a frozen counterpoint to his heat. "Life sentence. Maybe, with good behavior, you could be eligible for parole in twenty years. What about two or three life sentences? What age will you be when you see the light of day once more? You'll die in here."

"Agents..." Lionel fidgeted in his seat, clearly not happy with the tone of the interview.

Strickland laughed in her face. "Like I give a damn what happens to me now. Guard!" He lifted his hands as far as the chain allowed, indicating he was ready to go back to his cell. "This has been a lot of fun, but I think I'm done now. I'm going back to my comfy cell. There's a program on I want to watch. Besides, it's fried chicken tonight." He flashed them both an ingratiating grin.

Noah straightened and looked to Bree, who shook her head minutely. Noah turned his gaze to the guard. For a moment, the four of them were a frozen tableau, save Strickland, who looked between each of them with a sort of vicious delight.

The guard sighed and checked his watch. "Five minutes." He gave Noah a hard look and left the room.

"What...what's...five minutes?" Lionel asked, looking between the two agents wildly, his eyes widening in alarm.

Noah ignored him and slammed his hands down on Strickland's forearms, causing his wrists to leave the table, a move made impossible by the short links binding his arms there. Strickland screamed and cursed. "What the—"

"Agent Dalton!" Lionel half rose from his seat. The look on his face was complete outrage. Bree set a gentle hand on Lionel's shoulder, using an iron grip that Noah knew well. Bree forced him back into the chair.

"You're going to tell me about Jaime." Noah said each word distinctly, making every syllable a threat.

Strickland ground his teeth and swore again. "I *don't know*!"

"Agent Dalton!" Lionel's cheeks puffed red with the effort to get up. Bree gave him a steely look, and never so much as wavered.

Noah leaned forward, putting more weight on the arms,

not liking the tactic, but damned if he was going to let go now when he was so close...

"Fine!" Strickland gasped, and threw the word at him like it was a weapon. "Fine, you want to know about Jaime? I don't know, and that's the truth. But he told me once of a big house and a sister of some sort. I told him that there wasn't a use for sisters."

"Why not?" Bree added, her long fingers lost in the folds of the coat Lionel wore. For his part, the man was sputtering and turning red in the face.

"Because of his grandfather. Damn it, get off me!" Strickland tried to shake himself loose.

"Where was he from?" Noah growled, not letting up so much as an ounce of pressure.

"I don't know! His grandpa took him, that's all I know!"

It was very likely all he would get. The man really didn't seem to know. Noah stood back abruptly, disgusted with both himself and Strickland. The bastard. Strickland shot him a look of pure hate as the guard re-entered the room and began unhooking Strickland from the table and rejoining his bonds to the belt.

"You won't find him," Strickland muttered, rubbing his wrists. "Jaime's smarter than all of you." He followed that prophecy with a long list of curses that faded behind him as he was unceremoniously dragged from the room.

"Your superiors will hear of this...treatment!" Lionel sputtered, rising from his seat quickly enough that Bree had to step aside. Noah watched him go, knowing they'd both be called on the carpet for this, and honestly not caring a whole heck of a lot right now.

"That..." Bree exhaled noisily, "is not going to look good when our attorney friend there makes his report."

Noah turned to her, his eyes weary and hard. Being the bad guy felt new to him. What he'd just done left a bitter and strange taste in his mouth. He swallowed hard, trying to make it go away. "This is Winter's brother. I don't think there's any doubt now."

Bree shook her head. "No. No doubt."

"Winter is more important than the job. More important than anything."

He hadn't intended to say that out loud, but being in this place, after doing what he'd just done…? He shook his head. This wasn't him. He had no idea who he was anymore.

Bree slipped a hand around his elbow and gently led him to the other exit, behind Lionel. "I like her too, you know," she said, and he found himself smiling despite himself, grateful for her friendship.

"I know." He took a shaky breath. "But you're kind of in this with me too, now. I should have thought before taking things that far."

"Well…" Bree said as they headed down the hall to pick up their weapons, "the good news is that Max likes her too. Maybe what we did here will get buried. Paperwork has a way of getting lost on his desk all the time."

Noah snorted. "One can only hope."

5

Winter leaned against the cupboard door and stared down at the steam rising from the tea. Four minutes. The bag had to soak for four minutes before the tea was drinkable, and four minutes were a lifetime when she should be doing more important things.

Certainly more important than waiting for the tea to steep.

Noah was doing important things. He and Bree were doing important stuff like talking to Kent Strickland, getting more information, getting useful information, getting stuff *done*. Looking for her brother. This was her search...her failure all those years ago.

And here I am making tea...

She dunked the bag again, forcing it under the water with the flat of the teaspoon. It tried to rise, tried to escape and float to the surface, and she caught it, playing a game of drown-the-teabag.

Two minutes left. Traffic sounded outside the window, cars filled with people that hurried from one place to another, jostling each other and cursing each other for getting in the way of things they were doing. Important things. Actually *doing* things, not just standing in a kitchen that had been cleaned within an inch of its life, trying to kill a teabag in a watery grave.

Close enough. Maybe there was another minute left. Maybe not. Did it matter? The teabag was sufficiently water-logged, there was no point in holding its head under any longer. She scooped it out with the spoon and wrapped the string around it, binding the bag to the spoon and strangling the rest of the flavor from it before dropping it into the trash.

The spoon went to the sink, a solitary soiled spot in the basin that had been scrubbed mercilessly because it had felt important to do so.

So far there'd been no word, no indications, no further information. The question was, was it because there was nothing to say, or because there was nothing anyone was willing to talk about?

The case file from her parents' deaths over thirteen years ago had been officially reopened, the investigation was "pro-ceeding", but no one would tell her anything more than that. She'd been staring at the kettle all afternoon, watching water boil and quietly going mad.

Winter sipped her tea and made a face. That had been roughly four minutes. Now what? What does one do when waiting for her boyfriend to come home and give her details on her long-lost brother? There was no training, no amount of exercise that covered waiting with nothing to do.

She walked into the living room, cup in hand, and stared at the black screen of the TV. Turning it on, flipping chan-nels...it all seemed too much work to watch ridiculous dramas she had no interest in watching. She shifted her gaze to the CD player, but Noah's collection of 90s grunge music didn't hold much appeal, nor did a country music serenade. She thought about digging out a piece of jazz or even a favorite album from long ago, a thought that lasted all of a minute. In the end, she sat in a chair against the far wall and sipped her tea while the sounds of the city ebbed and flowed around her, an oasis in a constant storm.

Oasis? It's more of an isolation chamber.

Her mind had become one of those isolation/suspension devices where you'd go mad if you stay too long. A place without sight or sound or taste or touch, just alone with a panicked brain so desperately starved for input that it created its own. One that fed her a constant supply of waking nightmares that defied the conscious, rational mind.

Strickland. What would he say? What could he say? What terrible secrets could he reveal that Noah and Bree and Max and Aiden and everyone else will know and process and discuss LONG before any tidbits of it fell to one Winter Black.

Yes, that was professionalism. Yes, it was proof that she shouldn't be involved. But didn't she have a right? This was *her brother!* Justin. In her mind's eye, he wasn't an almost twenty-year-old man. He was still that charming endearing little snot-nosed spoiler of fun she remembered.

He stood before her in her mind's eye, his pajamas baggy and ill-fitting as though they stayed up only from divine intervention. He carried that stupid giraffe with him, the animal's neck clearly broken and lolling in the child's pudgy fist.

Winter set her tea down to concentrate on the spectral image in her mind. Sad-faced, one finger trying hard to not seek the mouth. It had been so hard to train him to not suck his thumb. Her parents had all but given up on that task. She hadn't, though. She'd hung in there.

Be real, Winter. You called him 'stupid' and tried to shame him out of it. When have you ever been a good sister?

Her phone beeped. The noise seemed apologetic, as if the phone was afraid of adding to her stress. Winter slapped the table, capturing the device in her hand. *If one more person or electronic device tiptoes around me, I will throw him/her/it against the wall.* She gripped the phone hard for a moment and forced her fingers to open, prying the phone from her palm and ignoring the marks it made in her flesh.

It was an automated notice. There was a new entry on the forum, the dark web creep show for people who got off on watching and discussing murder. This message was marked "WINTER." As the general public neither knew nor cared about her or her missing brother, it shouldn't be another cautiously worded sympathy message.

She moved to the couch and opened the laptop on the coffee table, logging in and picking the tea back up as the computer fired up and searched for the internet.

There was a new message, though the username was one she'd never heard of, one with a video attachment. It was cleared by the server, so there was no virus threat. That didn't necessarily save her from the content.

This better not be the equivalent of a dick pic...

After a moment's hesitation, she doubled-clicked on the file. And with that movement, the world ended.

No. *Her* world ended. As a video began to play, a young man in deep shadow faced the camera, a smirk playing on his lips.

The remains of the tea spread over the coffee table unnoticed and unstopped. The cup didn't break, but a small chip had appeared in the rim. Winter wondered why her brain wanted to focus on that tiny flaw. Protection. Her brain was trying to distract her, take her mind away from what was in front of her.

It was Justin. No longer a boy. Now a man.

Although his face was masked in shadow, the hurt and anger was clear. She superimposed the child's face over the man's. The mop of unruly hair was cut closer to the scalp now, the round face of childhood had narrowed into strong lines, but the man staring back at her was Justin.

My brother. Her hand slid to the monitor, and the back of her fingers stroked the side of his face. She stopped and whispered his name just to hear it out loud.

"Justin."

She moved the cursor over the PLAY button and hesitated. A cold fear began to creep up her spine.

"It's just flesh and bone," she murmured. This wasn't a ghost before her. Or maybe it was.

She just didn't know anymore.

Her finger barely touched the trackpad, and Justin exploded to life, even though he barely moved. He was staring at her directly.

"My name is Jaime Peterson. I think that things should be clarified, and to that, let me first address the deaths of William and Jeanette Black." He paused for a moment as if making connections in his head. *"They betrayed the true path, deviated from the commands Douglas Kilroy set down. They didn't understand the path, and they betrayed the way. They betrayed Kilroy. They deserved to die. All who betray and lie deserve to die. What Grandpa couldn't finish, I will."*

He glanced down at something in his hand and back to the camera. *"Which leads me to Winter."* His eyes seemed to bore into hers. *"You claim to be my sister. You're not. You're an impostor. I know this because I know the truth about you. You're not Bill's daughter."*

What? Winter stared at the screen, wondering if she'd just heard correctly.

He took a deep breath, and his voice took on a growl. *"Your life is a lie. Your very existence is an abomination. When you murdered Doug...that's Douglas Kilroy, in case you've murdered so many men that you can't remember them all...you took the brightest and best. You took my grandfather, my brother. He was more real to me than a sister that didn't even share my blood. He was my father, my sanctuary, and my best friend."*

"No," Winter whispered. None of this was true.

"You weren't there. You don't know. You don't know what he taught me. You don't know the way of the path. The way of truth. Thank God he was there for me, thank God he was willing to raise me. I was his. Only his."

Winter stared at her baby brother, the bile rising in her throat. She was going to be sick. Or pass out. Or something. She fought to breathe.

Justin shifted again and looked down once more. For the slightest instant, his face came a bit more fully into the light, but not by much. She still couldn't see him clearly.

"In his memory, in his name, I vow I will finish what he began. I will dictate the safety of the path to those who listen, but I will not tolerate fools. You have been very, very foolish."

Breathe in. Then out. Listen to what he has to say.

"I am finishing the task my grandfather set before me. He gave way to betrayal and false smiles, but don't expect that same failure from me."

Winter's eyes were fixed on the left side of the screen. Justin was shaking. It was subtle, nearly imperceptible, but once she saw it, she couldn't unsee the tremors that wracked him. The video ended, and his baleful eyes stared unblinking as the recording froze.

She was shaking too.

Winter reached out, stroking her fingers along his jaw.

It was every nightmare come true. It was every horrible thing that could have happened to him coming back on her in the daylight.

I need help. I can't do this alone.

Winter fumbled for her phone. It was all she could to do to hit the button to connect her with the one who could help.

6

J ustin stared at her from the monitor as Winter pressed her phone to her ear, trying to hold back the wave of emotions. Noah wasn't answering. This was the third time she'd tried to call and the third time her call went straight to voicemail. The problem was, Bree wasn't answering either.

They're working. What do you expect?

Winter paced the room, trying to think. Given the time required to drive to the prison, chances were actually pretty good that they were in the middle of the interview with Strickland. Busywork. It was all busywork. They were out there following up on the stalest of leads when she was sitting on a gold mine. There was nothing they could learn from Strickland as significant as the video she just watched, and there was no way to let them know that.

"Damn it, Noah!" She swore through gritted teeth as the grown image of Justin…Jaime…stared at her, his lip curled in a sardonic grin. It was enough to make her skin crawl.

Call the Bureau. Report this.

The thought echoed through her mind on repeat. She was

a trained agent. Trained agents didn't hoard intel that might prove valuable. Neither did they keep secrets from their team. She was technically still part of that team...wasn't she?

Maybe that was part of the problem. She wasn't feeling the team thing quite so much right now. Besides, she wasn't ready to lose this tenuous connection with Justin, or whatever he called himself.

So, what do I do?

Her mind wasn't working. Reeling from the shock? She was trained in handling the unexpected. It seemed hardly professional to be waffling now over what to do. Shock, though, would explain her inability to think. One couldn't expect to be rational when one was in shock.

Frustrated, she dropped her phone on the coffee table and tried to ignore it. She needed an activity to engage both mind and hands, a way to busy herself while she waited out however long the interview took. The table was clean now. She barely remembered wiping the tea off the surface, placing the cup in the sink while she'd been waiting for Noah to answer his phone. The apartment itself was spotless.

She growled, pacing from table to door and back. *Think!*

Who else could she turn to? Not someone who worked with her. No, she needed someone who cared for *her* and wouldn't put the job first.

Autumn.

Cars and trucks rushed by on the other side of her window, the sounds of the city muted by the glass panes. For a moment, she let the cacophony wash over her as she thought this through. In the end, there really was only a single choice.

Winter picked up the phone and hesitated, her finger hovering over the screen. One more look at Justin's face convinced her, and she tapped the speed-dial icon. No going back.

Autumn answered immediately.

"Hi." Now that the phone was connected, the words practically flew from Winter's lips. "Uh...I have...I have a problem. Do you think you could come over? Just for a little bit?" As the silence lengthened, she added as an afterthought, "Please?"

"Of course. I can be there in fifteen minutes."

Winter exhaled the breath she'd been holding as emotion threatened to burn her eyes. Damn. It was good to have friends. "Thanks. Be safe."

"Sure thing."

As she disconnected the call, Winter appreciated that Autumn hadn't hesitated or asked a single question over the phone. As if they had a mind of their own, Winter's eyes shifted back to the laptop, searching out the form of her brother within the video's darkness.

She was almost afraid to touch the keys on the computer. It was almost as if touching it would break the spell and destroy the illusion that Justin was still out there, still alive and...well?

She growled in frustration, raking her hands through her hair before pressing her palms against the sides of her head as if desperate to keep her brain from exploding. Memories of her baby brother raced through her mind.

Seeing him for the first time in the hospital, taking off the little cotton hat to see his hair.

Counting his toes and helping her mom give him his first bath.

Being peed on. It had been kinda gross but also very, very funny. And kind of cute. The first time, at least.

Winter smiled, thinking of how many times she or her parents had been in the line of fire. Once, her dad had put on a plastic smock, complete with gloves and protective goggles to change his diaper. Jeanette had taken a picture of the silly getup while Winter stood in the background, her eyes rolled toward the heavens.

The thought of her dad caused the smile to fade from her face. Why had Justin said something so cruel? Bill Black was Winter's father. Wasn't he?

He'd read to her, tucked her into bed, looked into her closet for monsters.

He'd taken her to her school's father/daughter dance, wearing his best suit for the occasion.

Bill Black had taught her to ride a bike and threatened to sit on the front porch with a shotgun when it was time for boys to come calling.

He never got that chance.

She never got the chance to drive him crazy with her teenage angst.

Winter stared at Justin's image, heat rising into her face. Emotion burned up her nose and made her vision blur.

Her baby brother appeared to love the man who had destroyed and divided their family. He called Douglas Kilroy his grandfather. His father. His best friend.

His...sanctuary?

The thought made Winter shudder. The man on the screen loved the man who'd shattered their lives. Loved him how?

Don't think about it.

Which was easier said than done, especially since the only company she had was her own thoughts until Autumn arrived.

Winter stood abruptly and looked around the apartment as if seeing it for the first time. She needed to get busy.

Tea. She could set a pot on and offer tea. That seemed suddenly important. If the kettle shook a little under the faucet as she filled it, it was too small a tremor to notice, as was the rattle of the mug when she brought it down from the cupboard. She tried to busy herself while waiting for the water to boil and eventually began to clean the already spotless counter.

She would stay busy.

She wouldn't think.

She could do this.

Her hands were red and aching by the time the doorbell rang.

"I HAVE TO ADMIT, I haven't seen you like this before." Autumn didn't take her gaze from her friend as she sat slowly on the couch where Winter indicated. "I got here as fast as I could, you sounded...upset."

Winter sat next to her. Her hands looked red and a bit chapped as she poured tea with trembling fingers. Autumn's eyebrow lifted but she said nothing, waiting her out.

"It's that..." Winter seemed to stall out, as though words had simply died in her mouth. That put Autumn on alert. Winter was the rock, the one person she would have said didn't easily succumb to panic or worry. To see her this rattled felt strange. Discordant even. Like discovering your blue-haired grandmother used to be a swimsuit model.

"All right." Autumn found herself slipping into professional mode, acting as therapist, not friend. "Take your time. I want you to try a few deep breaths. When you feel ready, I want you to tell me what's happening in your own words. Don't censor or study them. Let them come out however they do."

Winter just stared at her. Her blue eyes seemed haunted and full of shadows that Autumn had never seen there before. There was pain in those liquid depths that spoke of true suffering, hinting at what exactly? Panic? Fear? Whatever it was caused a chill to crawl down Autumn's spine. A part of her mind decided that she didn't want to hear it after all, but it was a small voice and easily suppressed. This was Winter, one of her best friends. If she couldn't do it for *her*, what good was she to anyone?

As if breaking out of a fog, Winter began to move with jerky movements. Instead of speaking, she reached for her laptop and began jabbing at the keyboard, waking it up. Within moments, she'd logged in and was turning it to face Autumn more fully.

Autumn studied the screen. There was an image of a young man looking back at her, though he was cloaked in an eerie darkness.

He was in shadow, his features obscured, but the resemblance to Winter was uncanny. Autumn looked between the monitor and her friend and found her hand reaching up to cover her mouth.

"Oh my god."

When those were the only three words she could formulate, she turned to Winter, struggling to find something more helpful to say. She settled on a question when she couldn't figure out whether this was a moment of celebration, commiseration, or something else entirely.

"Is this…?"

Winter nodded. "Justin. Jaime. My brother." Without another word, Winter leaned forward over the laptop and hit PLAY, keeping the screen firmly facing Autumn so that she'd get the full effect.

Autumn sat back and watched the video from start to finish without commenting. Winter shifted so that she could watch with her, silent and morose. When it began again and Winter stopped the playback, they sat in silence for long moments.

"I have to ask," Autumn said slowly, trying to gather her thoughts, "did you show this to Max yet?"

Winter shook her head. "No." The single word came out as a hoarse whisper.

"Are…you going to?" Autumn took a cautious sip of her tea and set the cup down again when she discovered it was still too hot. She shifted to straighten her skirt, suddenly uncomfortable as the conflict unfolded on her friend's face.

"Of course. I mean, I have to. This is…" Her hand waved in the direction of the laptop, but the words escaped her. In the end, Winter simply stared at the image on the screen.

"It's evidence," Autumn prompted.

Winter's reply came so long after, Autumn had begun to think she wasn't listening. "He called Kilroy 'Grandpa' and 'brother' and 'friend.'" Winter swallowed hard, as though the words choked her. They probably did. "I know it's evidence. He makes it sound like Kilroy did him a favor by taking him in after he…after he killed our parents."

"What did he mean about you not being his sister?"

Winter shrugged, her gaze finally breaking free of Justin's face. "I don't know." She shook her head. "That…that monster must have made all kinds of things up. Used lies to sever the ties between us. It seems like the sick sort of thing he would do. He probably made the whole story up as part of the indoctrination. No, the part that bothers me is the part about Justin wanting to finish what that sick bastard couldn't."

"And the survivors of the Riverside Mall…?"

"Are being hunted," Winter finished for her.

"All the more reason to contact the Bureau." Maybe Autumn was pushing a little, but Winter seemed to need a little pushing.

"I know that," Winter snapped. "You don't think I know that? I called you because I thought that it was more important to have a friend here who…" Winter clamped her mouth shut and closed her eyes.

"Hey." Autumn reached tentatively for her friend. She placed her hand on Winter's forearm and applied a slight pressure. The feelings of helplessness and guilt that flowed into her made her breath catch in her throat, and it took a great deal of effort to continue speaking. "That's why I'm here. I'm here for you, not for the Bureau or Max or even Noah, as much as I like him. I'm here because a friend asked me to help her."

She had to let go of Winter's arm as her head began to swim. It was too painful, too overpowering for her to continue to touch her friend. Autumn reeled at the intensity of the feelings Winter was holding on to.

Winter seemed to understand and folded her arms over her chest. "Thank you. I just get inundated with people telling me how to be professional and how to do my job."

"And you're feeling like no one is listening," Autumn finished for her.

"Well, Noah listens, but he's torn too. He works in the same place I do, so he can't exactly take sides. To be honest, I tried to call him first, but he's off interviewing Kent Strickland."

"So, Noah is willing to listen, but he's not *able* to. I can help you process everything, you know." Autumn grinned. "That's kind of what I spent eight years of my life learning to do." She nodded in the general direction of the laptop. "I can't imagine what this feels like, and I won't insult you by trying. But it sounds to me like your brother has a head full of lies and falsehoods."

"Yeah, implanted by a serial killer who murdered my parents and happens to be the one who kidnapped my little brother."

"Well, there's little that can be changed about any of that."

Winter looked up sharply at her. Autumn met her gaze without flinching, asking what she knew needed asking. "The question is, what are you going to do about it now?"

"What I already did," Winter answered quickly. "Ask for your help. I know that I can't do this alone."

"I thought you weren't supposed to do anything at all. Didn't Max take you off this one?"

"Yeah, I know." Winter's hand waved that away like so much smoke, dislodging Autumn's grip on her arm. "I'm supposed to stay away, I get that, but this came straight to me. I didn't even know what it was or who was sending the message when I opened it. The video just..." She shook her head.

"Appeared," Autumn offered.

She twisted to face Autumn fully. "Yes, and they won't tell me anything. Max promised they would, and I get little tidbits. It's all bits and pieces but only what they think I should know, and only when they think I should know it. I'm in the dark."

"From Noah too?"

Winter started to shake her head and shrugged instead. "I don't know, maybe. He's not answering his phone, and yes, I know he's busy, but how much is he going to tell me? If he says that Strickland can't answer all of his questions, how do I know he asked the right question in the first place?"

"I don't suppose you do," Autumn countered. "That's trust. Noah is good at what he does. So is Bree. You know this. Trust your partner."

"Yeah. Trust." Winter picked up the teacups and stood. "Like, 'trust me, Justin, I won't let anything happen to you.'" She took them to the sink, rinsing the delicate cups out and setting them carefully on the counter.

"By the way..." Winter turned as Autumn walked into the

kitchen. "I was actually still drinking that." She winked and pointed to the cup next to the sink.

"Ah!" Winter smiled and what appeared to be a startled laugh escaped her. "I am so sorry! I really am. It won't take more than a minute to get some more hot water. I'm just not here." Winter shifted the kettle and slapped the burner back on. "Same as before or do you want to try a different flavor?"

"Anything is fine. So…" Autumn cocked a hip at the door-frame while Winter dug in the cupboard, sorting through packages of tea. "Where do we start?"

Winter turned and smiled at her friend, nearly dropping a box of Chamomile in the process. "Thank you."

Autumn smiled back, the gesture feeling more forced than she liked. "Don't thank me. If I'm helping you, we're going to work with the Bureau. Evidence goes to them right away."

"Deal," Winter said slowly, like she knew it was reasonable but didn't like it.

"But…when we find any evidence, we'll comb through what we have first and *then* give it to the office."

Winter grinned, looking relieved. "That's an even better deal."

"So, tell me about some of what your brother said. Do you think he believes all of this? And what exactly is 'The Path' he spoke about?"

Winter sighed and pressed her fingers to her temple. "Kilroy was insane. As to whether or not Justin believes what he's saying, it's hard to say. If he does, he's as mad as I feared, but if he doesn't, why even bother sending this message?"

"All right." Autumn stretched her arms above her head to get some circulation going. "Let's take another look at that recording and strip it apart piece by piece until we know it frame by frame."

"Thank you." The words came out as the barest of whispers.

"And you can call it in once we're done with it, in case they take it off the server when you do. Though I expect you've already copied the file?"

"They will. I'm sure they will. And you're right, a copy automatically saved to the cloud."

Autumn looked at the design in the floor under her feet for a moment while she searched for the words she needed. When she looked up, she met Winter's gaze and tried to smile. "I shouldn't say this. I really shouldn't because I know you'll hate me for it, but it's very likely they really are the best hope of him getting the help he needs."

Winter blinked. "Help?" She glanced away, staring at the fridge as though it had just come to life and might walk away any minute. When she spoke, her voice was carefully controlled. "There's no hope for him. Not anymore."

"Winter..."

"No." Winter was calm and clear-eyed when she looked back at her. "No. I can't help him. I can't."

"All right." Autumn didn't like the way this was going, but to press harder would be to lose her friend completely. The last thing she wanted was for Winter to feel like she was going through this alone. "What do you want to do?"

Winter's gaze locked with hers. "Stop him." The words were a hoarse whisper, barely audible over the clatter of the tea kettle. "I have to stop him. *Me*. He's my brother, my responsibility. He always was."

7

Stella Norcott's office smelled like old chemicals and gunpowder. No matter how the weapons were fired and how well ventilated the room was, the smell permeated the walls, the carpeting, hell, even the people themselves...or at least their clothing.

In most cases, such as a situation where a single shot was fired, a good airing would solve the problem. In a ballistics lab where constant testing took place, the ventilation simply wasn't up to the challenge. The office had taken on a rather permanent odor that wasn't altogether pleasant, especially if a person wasn't used to it.

Noah Dalton was nearly bleary-eyed from exhaustion. Last night with Winter had been a long one. After seeing the message from her little brother and then having to flag the video by the Bureau for evidence, Noah had sat up with Winter a long time to let her process what she'd seen.

Noah rubbed his nose, but that only increased his sensitivity to the aroma and made his eyes start to water. Where the rubber smell came from was anyone's guess. He resolved to keep the visit brief, the shorter the better.

Stella, on the other hand, was a very nice woman who didn't deserve to be associated with such smells. She probably had very good personal hygiene too, it was just impossible to be sure when she was surrounded by the hazard of her profession.

"Tell me you have something good," Noah started out more brusquely than he had intended. He knew he was reacting to the stench. Especially when Bree shot him a suppressing look.

"And also, hello." Bree smiled at the thin ballistics expert, her version of damage control. "Excuse my partner. He's been watching a lot of *Dragnet* reruns."

"Only cause I'm not old enough to have seen the originals," Noah shot back with a grin. Humor was his saving grace in most things, and when Bree fake scowled at him, he knew it had saved him again.

Stella seemed to be enjoying the exchange, but her smile faded as Noah looked back at her. He was here for a very serious reason, and no amount of humor could save him from this discussion.

"I hear you're working point on Winter's brother?" Stella asked softly, directing the question at Bree.

"On the Jaime Peterson case," Bree corrected her. They'd agreed it was best to distance Justin as far away from Winter as possible, even if it was only through words. "Yes."

"Well, you have my sympathies. I guess it can't be easy tackling a case so close to home. Please give my regards to Winter, I'll be happy to help however I can." She flashed a smile, including Noah in the gesture to show there were no hard feelings.

"Thank you." Bree nudged Noah with her shoulder, reminding him of his manners.

"Yeah, uh, thank you." Why was he tripping over the small talk? It was very unlike him, unable to pull out the charming, easy manner that made him a good interviewer. Maybe the smell of sulfur was getting to him. More likely it was the ghost of that video and the way it had affected Winter, and thus the way it had derailed most of his night.

To her credit, Winter had been reasonably calm by the time he'd gotten home, the press of the moment behind her. But she'd been distant for most of the night. Of course, her mind had been on Justin. Could he blame her?

"Noah?" Bree punctuated her word with a hard poke to his arm.

"Right, sorry. Was thinking about Strickland's interview yesterday." He shook his head when Bree's eyebrow shot up at the obvious lie. "I'm sorry, Stella, could you please repeat that?"

"I said…" Stella replied slowly. She didn't sound angry, but she was watching his eyes now very closely and speaking like he was a reluctant student dreaming of recess. "We took the footprints found at the Black family home in Harrisonburg and compared them to the crime scene of the murder of William Hoult, Jaime's henchman. They match. That puts the same shoe in both places." She indicated a couple of plaster casts that showed a distinctive shoe-tread pattern.

"But it doesn't indicate that Justin is the killer of either of them," Noah pointed out.

"There's only so much you can do with the image of a shoe tread," Bree said, her bright smile somewhat muted as she gave a very unsubtle clue to her partner to lighten up. "At least he didn't leave a stack of dead rats this time."

His arm was going to have a Bree-shaped bruise tomorrow.

Noah gave himself a mental shake. She was right. He was allowing the way this case was affecting Winter to cloud his judgment. It was becoming harder to maintain emotional distance when it hurt the woman he loved so much.

Winter was trying, but he could tell she was chafing at the bit, all the while trying to quietly pry information from him. Information he didn't have. He knew she thought he was just not telling her what he knew, but the fact was there was very little to tell.

According to George Strickland, Jaime Peterson was one of the "trio of terror." Noah wondered what Kent would think of that. The odd thing about this particular teenage-military-wannabe-secret-society was that they seemed to be very polite. At least they had been to the elder Strickland.

The old man had recalled how they'd helped him and Kent around the place, especially as George grew older and less capable of keeping up with the demands of a working farm. He recalled no time in which the boys were drunk, though it wasn't to say they were teetotalers. They just hadn't made a habit of drinking around him.

"Thing you gotta remember," George had said, "is that they wanted to enlist when they was old enough. They wanted to be special forces. No one wants hotheads on their teams, so getting a rep, or going to jail would of potentially ruined that chance."

"Model citizens?" Noah prompted him, his eyebrow raised.

"Well..." Strickland coughed a bit before continuing, "mebbe. I know my boy. Well, he was young and full of hisself. Loved nothing more than the sound of his voice. He got in trouble plenty and I reckon the rest of them got in trouble with him, probably like as not to keep Kent company. They was always good friends." He paused and sipped his tea.

"What else can you remember?" Noah prodded.

"I recall Jaime was a serious one. It was that grandpa of his, I think. That old man kept the boy on the straight and narrow. He had a way of talking, though, that could set a chill down a man's spine, and that's the truth. God-fearing as he was, I wouldn't want to cross him. He probably kept the boy on a tight leash, is my guess."

Noah shook his head to clear the fog. All he was doing was running the same evidence around and around in circles when he should be listening.

"What about Sandy Ulbrich?" The image of her laying in the morgue after she and her husband were assaulted flashed through his mind, and after they'd survived the shooting at the mall.

"We got the saliva DNA samples from the coroner's office." Stella sighed and shook her head. "So far, we haven't found a match on the database. There's nothing to compare it to."

"From where the killer..." Bree wrinkled her nose, "licked her cheek?"

Stella nodded. "Yes. We were lucky to be able to extract a minute amount."

"Could you compare it to Agent Black?" Bree asked.

Before Stella could answer, Noah interrupted. "Maybe, but I don't think so. According to that video Winter turned in, Justin is claiming to be her half-brother. If that's true, the DNA wouldn't be a good match."

"Which half?"

"Mother."

Stella nodded slowly as she thought this through. "That would be less conclusive. On the other hand, we do have the markers in the Ulbrich case so that if you *do* catch a suspect, we can prove that much at trial anyway."

Noah reached back to scratch the back of his neck and thought for a moment. "Thanks, Stella, we won't keep you any longer."

"I'm always here." Stella smiled, though the thrust of the smile was directed at Bree. "If you find anything else, let me know."

Noah winced. He certainly hadn't won any awards with her today. He was definitely off his game, and he didn't like it. *Get your head on straight, Agent.*

"Thank you, Stella." Bree smiled brightly and shook her hand.

Noah followed Bree silently into the hall, deep in thought.

"How do you do that?" Noah turned to Bree as they cleared the elevator.

"What?"

"Stella was about to offer you milk and cookies and a footstool. How do you do that?"

Bree shrugged and turned her mega-watt smile on him. "Noah, it's a matter of listening, of paying attention. When I talk to someone or ask them a question, I listen to what they say. It's important to me."

He was about to protest, to insist that he listened too, remembering just in time that Bree had been chastising him a lot lately for not paying attention. Given the way he'd checked out while Stella had been talking, it was probably well-deserved. Hell, when was the last time he hadn't been lost in thought when he was supposed to be focused on the task at hand?

Thinking quickly, he amended what he had been about to say. "Okay, I *usually* pay attention. I'm a trained agent and know how to look for visual clues if I'm being lied to. I don't think I've missed anything."

"And while you're cross-examining their face, I'm *listening.* You know what happens when someone is listened to? They talk more. The more you listen, the more they talk, and they will tell you what you want to know and plenty you don't."

He nodded. Bree had more than twenty years of experience in the field. He was arrogant enough to shrug that experience off or not drink in the lessons she gave.

"You're saying I need to be more friendly?"

Bree snickered as she held a door open for him, ushering him into the beehive of activity which was the warren of cubicles where the agents had their desks. "Well, cowboy, I don't know many people more friendly than you, so you'd be salivating sugar if you got more friendly." She stopped, grabbing his arm. "You're a good agent, Noah. A damn good one. You're going through some personal shit, and you just need to work on compartmentalizing it all a little more. That's all."

Noah smiled despite himself. The sort of banter and teasing Bree was doing made the day go by a little easier.

The smile didn't last.

He could compartmentalize all he wanted, but that just meant all his worries would be knocking on their little walls, screaming to get out.

8

Winter sat in the car outside of the house. She'd been calmer going into gunfights, and this was the place she'd always felt the most loved, the most protected. This was her grandparents' house, for heaven's sake. Well, maybe that fact alone made it dangerous, after all. Sometimes, it was easier to face a madman with a gun than it was to confront the truth. Especially when this was a truth that had been buried for so long.

Max had been visibly relieved when she hadn't fought him about taking some time off. It was hard not to take his enthusiasm personally, but on the other hand, she needed the time. Going back to see her grandparents, though...

As she got out of the car slowly and dragged reluctant feet up to the doorstep, she couldn't help but think this was a terrible mistake. A horrifying, terrible mistake. As much as she loved her grandparents, this visit wouldn't be an easy one. She almost had herself convinced that it would be better to turn around and go home when the door opened and her grandmother shuffled out onto the porch. The option to chicken out and flee was gone, just like that, as she was stared down by a woman more than three times her age.

She sighed and stopped halfway up the path, feeling the smothering warmth of the older woman's love and concern from where she stood. *I can't do this.* But she did anyway, waving at the woman who'd raised her, who was now waiting for her at the top of the stairs as though she were there for an ordinary, cheerful, your-grandson-is-not-a-serial-killer kind of visit.

"Well, I'm glad to see you," Gramma Beth said by way of greeting. "Even if you're dragging your feet some." Beth offered a wry chuckle as Winter pressed forward over the cracked and buckled concrete path.

"Hi, Gramma." Winter smiled and mounted the steps to kiss the older woman's cheek.

"So, what's wrong?"

Winter opened her mouth to speak, having no idea what to say. Thankfully, she didn't have to come up with anything as the door opened wider behind her grandmother, and her grandfather came bustling through, a big grin on his face. "Well, look who's here. All the way from the city and J. Edgar just to visit us." Winter was swept into his arms and found herself in a big bear hug. "You're looking good, kid."

"Thanks, Grampa."

"Winter was just about to tell us why she was sitting out in the car for ten minutes when she got here," her grandmother said with a hint of reproach in her voice.

"What's this?"

Winter sighed. The fact that her grandmother was right wasn't near so annoying as the fact that she hadn't been alert enough to notice her grandmother had been watching her the entire time. "I have a question for you." Winter turned and opened her purse. She pulled out an envelope and handed it off to her grandmother. "About this."

She took the envelope from Winter and pulled the flap open, taking a piece of paper out and unfolding it. "I don't understand," her grandmother waved the paper toward her husband, "this is your birth certificate."

Winter's grandfather took the proffered document and scanned it thoroughly. "It's the real deal, princess. What's the question?"

Winter swallowed, this was harder even than she was afraid it would be. "The name on it, that says 'father.'"

"William Black," he said, looking to his wife. Winter's training noted the tightness around her grandmother's mouth, the hint of fear in her eyes. "What's wrong with that? That's your father's name."

"Biological father?" Winter whispered, hoping that they would laugh at her, assure her that what she'd always believed about her life was true. They didn't.

"Come inside." Her grandmother turned and disappeared into the house.

Winter stood on the porch for a long moment. The doorway felt ominous all of a sudden, as if it were a portal to a dungeon or cave. The truth lay in there, waiting in the relative darkness and hidden among the doilies and scent of fresh-baked cookies.

"Come on, princess." Her grandfather sounded old, worn out, but he held the door open for her.

You came this far, only a few more steps.

Her feet didn't want to move, they didn't want to hear the answer to her question. But she was an agent, and an agent was trained in how to handle difficult situations. She pulled herself together and walked through the open door, all the way into the front room with her back straight and head held high.

She ignored the way her heart was pounding so hard she thought it might break through her ribs at any moment.

Agent or not, she still had a lot riding on this conversation, and maybe couldn't be blamed for being a touch more…reactive…than she normally would be.

Right?

At least they were taking the question seriously. This was a double-edged sword, though, meaning there was something hidden there that they hadn't revealed yet.

Gramma was already seated on the couch. It was the large white one reserved for company, the one that was never used for day-to-day family needs. The one Winter had never been allowed to sit on until long after she graduated high school.

Grampa settled down beside her, and Winter took one of the chairs that faced the sofa. It felt like being called in front of a review board, or a group of advisors. The old mantle clock's hollow *tock-tock-tock* echoed in the room as her grandmother took a deep breath and smoothed her skirt.

For his part, her grandfather deferred to her, letting the women lead the discussion, but she'd expected that.

"Please tell me," Winter said quietly. "Is William Black my father?"

"Yes," her grandfather said emphatically.

At the same time, her grandmother said, "No."

They looked at each other. Her grandfather spoke first. "He raised you. He helped bring you into this world, and it's his name on the birth certificate. He's your father in every respect that counts."

"Just not biologically," her grandmother offered quietly.

Winter swallowed hard. What Justin had said was true then. She'd told Noah what she'd pieced together from other sources over the years that hadn't clicked until Justin's video, but until this moment had never dared to ask the people she should have gone to in the first place. For a long time, she'd felt it hadn't mattered. Why should it have? Her parents were long gone, and an old journal should have meant nothing to the search for her brother. Except it did.

Winter was fast coming to realize just how sloppy she'd been. Whatever happened to 'no stone left unturned?' Instead, she'd closed her eyes to the one thing that was fast turning out to matter a great deal. "So, tell me," she said finally. "Who's my father?"

"We're not sure." Her grandmother sighed and looked to her husband, who turned away. "And that is the honest truth. We didn't even know…" She covered her mouth with one hand.

"We didn't know either until after Jeanette…your mother…was killed. We were going through their belongings and happened upon a journal of hers. It was in there. That's how we knew."

"What does it say?" Winter's heart seemed unnaturally quiet. It seemed to her that it should be beating hard *now*, now that the truth was out, now that she knew, but she felt only a sense of calm, a dispassionate and strange calm.

"Well…" Grampa started and looked to his wife.

A long sigh escaped Gramma Beth's lips. "Your mother met a man just before she met Bill. They didn't know each other well or for very long. It sort of fizzled out before she and Bill…"

Winter waited, but when it appeared that her grandmother wasn't going to continue that thought, she asked again, "But you never heard his name? Mom didn't talk about my father at all. You never met—"

"John." Her grandmother's lips pressed into a thin line.

Winter blinked. Her father's name was John. "John what?"

Grandpa Jack shrugged. "Well, that's the thing…" He looked helplessly at Beth.

"We just don't know, sweetheart." Beth reached over and took Winter's hand. "Actually, your mother didn't know his last name from what I read in the journal." Beth's cheeks turned a delicate pink. "From what I'm guessing, it never came up."

"It never came up?" Realization hit like a brick. "You mean I'm the product of a one-night stand?"

Jack raised his hand. "Don't put it that way, princess. You—"

"Well, how should she put it?" Grandma turned on him. "It's true enough. I miss our daughter, Jack, and I cherish her memory, but that doesn't make her flawless." She turned back to Winter, looking at her fiercely. "You know she loved you with her heart and soul. You know they both did, but yes, she met a man and one thing led to another and it was a...very brief affair. It lasted long enough to..." She waved a hand to indicate Winter's very existence as being proof.

"I..." Winter's brain was going in too many directions at once. She held up a hand to forestall her grandparents while she thought it through. She replayed the conversation in her head for a moment.

Her mother had conceived after an encounter with a man who was so uninvolved with her, and she with him, that she never even bothered getting a last name. And then Jeannette had met Bill while pregnant. Had he known she was pregnant at first? Had he just offered to raised Winter as his own out of the goodness of his heart. Was...?

"Where is this journal?" she asked.

Why sit here asking herself questions when the answers were somewhere in black and white?

Her grandparents looked at each other. Nearly fifty years of marriage created a sort of intimacy that allowed them to speak volumes with a single glance. Little twitches of an eye, a raised eyebrow, a shrug of one shoulder followed by a careful nod.

Winter watched the exchange, fascinated despite herself.

At some signal she didn't fully understand, her grandmother sighed and stood, leaving the room, and her grandfather looked for all the world like there was just about any place he'd rather be. Including, perhaps, having a root canal.

"Princess…" He licked his lips and visibly forced himself to meet her eyes. "Your father, your *real* father, is Bill Black and—"

"This doesn't take anything away from him," Winter said quickly, trying to reassure him. "He was a rare man. He not only met a woman he loved, he took in her child, made her… made me…his own. There never was a better father." She smiled and leaned forward to make sure he heard the next part. "Except maybe you. You took in a frightened, hurt preteen and built her back up again."

He smiled, though she could tell that it hit him very hard. He didn't answer for a long moment, his hand returning to his nose and mouth repeatedly. To see this strong man reduced to proud tears that he refused to let fall broke her heart, reinforcing the bond between them.

Whatever Grampa Jack might have said in response was lost as her grandmother returned with a leather-clad journal tied with a long leather strip attached to the flap. It looked like the sort of thing sold in fancy bookstores.

"We found this in her desk, tucked away with a handful of photographs." Her grandmother handed over the journal. Winter noticed that her grandmother's hand shook a little, her fingers lingering on the cover as though loathe to give the book up.

"Did the police see this?"

Her grandfather shrugged. "We didn't think it mattered. It was a diary and there were no current entries. We—"

"Were originally told that their deaths were a result of a break-in. That the whole thing was random chance. By the time we knew differently, well…." Her grandmother looked to her husband. Once more the secret language spoke volumes.

"To be honest, we forgot all about the diary," he finished for her. "It was just another piece we had to take care of while cleaning out the house."

Winter looked at the journal she held. How many answers were contained within? What secrets were in there, written in her mother's hand?

"Honey…" her grandmother broke into her reverie, "can you tell me why this came up now?"

Winter weighed the choices in front of her. The situation with her brother was an on-going investigation, so talking about it wasn't exactly a good idea. On the other hand, her grandparents might have withheld information from that terrible night because the police hadn't told them everything either. How much information was lost, discounted as unimportant in an investigation simply because no one knew enough to ask?

In the end, she felt they deserved to know. If nothing else, they were Justin's grandparents too. After all, being related to him might actually put them in some jeopardy.

It was justification at best, but enough so that the decision to tell them came easier.

"Justin's alive." She said the words slowly and held her breath, waiting for the fallout. She wasn't disappointed. The effect of that statement was like dropping a brick into a still pond. They both gaped at her for a moment. Her Gramma clutched the edge of the couch as if seeking something solid to cling to.

"You're sure, princess?" Her grandfather's voice was hoarse. He groped for her grandmother's hand.

"Yes. I am." Winter wanted to reach for them both but worried she wouldn't be able to say what needed to be said if she sank into their comfort. "We've been thinking that there was a possibility that he was alive for a while now, but we didn't have anything really solid until..."

Winter looked into her grandparents' well-loved faces. This was an investigation.

"Until?" Gramma Beth prompted.

Screw it. She was going to be honest and let the chips fall where they would.

"This is confidential information, so I need you to keep this information just within these four walls." When they both nodded, Winter blew out a soft breath. "Justin sent me a video yesterday. He claimed I was a fraud because I wasn't his sister, that I wasn't Bill's daughter."

Her grandfather shot to his feet with more energy than she'd given him credit for. "That little sh—"

"Jack!" Gramma Beth yanked him back down on the couch. "Mind your manners and your mouth. That's your grandson you're talking about."

Jack didn't look very contrite, but he kept his mouth tightly closed.

"We believe that Justin has been living with the man who killed Mom and Dad. Douglas Kilroy groomed him. Changed him."

Grampa's face turned ashen, and Gramma began to tremble.

"Changed how?" her grandmother probed, one hand pressed to her mouth.

"We think he's behind several attacks lately. He's taken to calling the man who killed our parents 'Grandpa.'"

If a man's face could turn to iron, Grampa Jack's face did at the sound of the name. Her grandmother might have cursed. Whatever she said was too quiet and too far under her breath to be sure.

"You take that," Beth pointed to the journal in her granddaughter's hands, "and you use that in any way you have to in order to get him help."

Winter glanced at the journal. That was a lot of faith to put in an old diary.

"I don't know, Gramma. I think it's too late for—"

"No!" Winter jumped at the vehemence in her usually sweet grandmother's voice. "No! He's still your brother! He's still *family*. I don't care what he's done, you get him help. If it's in prison or not, whatever you need to do, he's *family*. And he needs your help."

"Princess." Once more, her grandfather sounded a hundred years old, his voice a dry rasp. Winter's head came up at the air of defeat in his voice, the resignation. "Read the diary. Go through it. Every word."

"It's evidence, Grampa. I don't know if I'll be allowed to." The journal suddenly felt heavier, as though the weight of her entire past, the death of her parents and her brother's life rested in its pages.

She looked once more to the old couple who raised her, who supported her all those years.

"And we're *family*," he said firmly, his eyes flashing fire.

Family.

Funny how a single word could become both plea and promise.

Winter bit her lip and swallowed hard, fighting down the bile and bitterness that wanted to rise. "I'll do my best."

9

When Autumn knocked and Winter opened the door, it was immediately apparent that her friend's mind was somewhere else. Her gaze was distant, unfocused as she greeted Autumn. "Oh, hi."

Autumn grinned at her friend. The smile might have been more than a little forced, but Winter clearly didn't notice. But there were a lot of things that Winter apparently wasn't noticing anymore. Bathing, for example, given the greasy look of her hair.

"Hi, yourself." Autumn tried to keep the conversation light, though this was fast proving to be more and more of a challenge. "I thought I would come by and take you out for the evening. When's the last time you went to a club or a nice restaurant? Seeing as how you're already dressed for it…" She bobbed her eyebrows, hoping a bit of humor would break through Winter's heavy mood.

Winter looked down at her heavy sweatshirt to examine the word VARSITY on the front. She brushed at what appeared to be a pizza sauce stain. She looked back at Autumn, her face a mask of confusion.

"Never mind. If this is a bad time, I'll just go."

Before Autumn could take a step away, Winter seemed to suddenly come back to her body. With a shake of her head, she rubbed her eyes and put out a hand in mute apology. "I'm sorry." She smiled and stepped back, gesturing for Autumn to come inside.

One step over the threshold and Autumn stopped in her tracks. The usually immaculate apartment looked as if a hall of records threw up in it. Papers were everywhere, stacked neatly into smaller piles and separated by knick-knacks that looked shoved between them to mark their places.

Even the chaos was organized, each crumbling pile held apart from the others, porcelain figurines desperately trying to stem the avalanche of pulp and not get buried. A glass unicorn rode the top of a gathering tsunami of papers holding official-looking seals. This was not the most impressive thing she saw, though. It was the debris placed within this set-up straight out of *A Beautiful Mind* that stole her attention.

In strategic locations around the room, piles with dirty plates were set precariously on tottering stacks, held apart Jenga-style by various cups, spoons and even one open pizza box with three slices left. Autumn wrinkled her nose at the rather desiccated pepperoni and sausage. It was at least six hours old from the look of it.

Don't ask me how I know that, Autumn found herself thinking as she dodged the odd display with a sudden flashback to her college years.

"So, you're um…redecorating?" Autumn asked, taking off her coat and looking for an unclaimed space in the room to lay it down. She failed, not that Winter noticed. She'd already returned to the couch and was shuffling through a stack of papers there. "It's only been what, a couple of days since that video? You work fast."

Winter waved her over. "It's amazing what you can get with the Freedom of Information Act, a badge, and a ton of quarters for the copier."

Autumn picked up the paper nearest her and glanced over the image. "This is a birth certificate."

"It's a copy." Winter nodded, not really looking. She was busy reading.

"Who is Randolf Wagner?"

Winter looked up at the name and took the page from her. "No idea. Would you put that on the pile on the breakfast nook, please? It doesn't go here."

Autumn did as she was asked before turning to her friend. "Winter, what's going on? Talk to me."

Winter's head bobbed up like it just crested the surface. "What?" She blinked a few times and looked around the room as if she hadn't seen it before. "Oh. Wow." She took a breath and pointed to the box. "You want some pizza? It's probably cold by now, I don't remember how long ago I—"

"Winter!" Autumn snapped. "What's going on? Talk to me!"

Winter looked at her, eyes large and filled with so much pain that Autumn's breath caught in her throat. At first, she didn't think her friend would speak, then Winter pressed her hands to her face and took a deep breath. After a few moments, she sank onto a chair. She looked better. Marginally.

"I went to see my grandparents. After my parents were murdered, Gramma and Grampa raised me, so they're as much parents as grandparents."

Autumn nodded patiently. She already knew all this. She'd been in Beth and Jack's home a few times and had personally witnessed the love the couple felt for their granddaughter. But she said nothing, letting Winter say whatever was haunting her however it came out.

"Anyway, what Justin said in his video…it's true. I'm his half-sister. His father was not my father." She frowned, shaking her head, almost like she was trying to rattle the words around in a more effective manner. "Bill Black is my father, just not biologically." A single tear brimmed and fell down her pale cheek. "I love him, and I miss him, and he raised me, and his name is on my birth certificate, but I don't carry his blood."

"I'm sure that was a terrible shock," Autumn said, reaching out to touch Winter's hand. She closed her eyes against the pain that flowed from her friend and into her at the touch. It was why she so seldom touched others. But this was Winter. Her friend. She would carry her pain, both emotionally and physically.

"Yes, it was." Another tear fell. "I can't understand why Mom and Dad never told me."

"Maybe they were waiting for you to grow older," Autumn suggested. "Waiting for the right time."

The saddest smile Autumn had ever witnessed appeared on Winter's mouth. "They never got that chance."

There was nothing Autumn could say. Winter was right. Time and chance had been ripped from them one brutal night.

Instead of trying to understand that which could never be understood, Autumn indicated the piles of paper throughout the apartment. "What's all this about?"

Winter blinked and looked around. As if lifting herself from a fog, she stood and reached for something in one of the piles. "I got this from my grandparents. They've kept it all this time. The rest just kind of multiplied from there." She held up a slim leather-bound volume, the long string that would have held the book closed had uncoiled and wrapped itself around Winter's wrist. "It's my mother's diary from before I was born. From when I was conceived, actually." She flipped through the pages until she found the one she was looking for. "Here, read that." She thrust the journal into Autumn's waiting hands.

"John brought me back to..." Autumn pointed to a word and turned the journal so that Winter could read it.

"...*his hotel,*" Winter translated after a moment of squinting at the text.

"...*his hotel. It was a wonderful night, but in the morning, I had an early shift so went to work wearing the dress I wore at the club...*" Autumn looked up. "The walk of shame into work? Wow. Been there, done that. Not my grandest moment."

"Look at the date." Winter pointed to the scrawl at the top of the page.

"June 17." Autumn understood instantly. Simple math didn't lie.

"I was born in March," Winter confirmed. "Nine months later and...tada."

Autumn looked back at the page, then flipped the pages over, glancing at the entries that came before. "You're sure it's not a coincidence? Babies can be born anywhere from thirty-six to forty-two weeks without the timing being considered out of the ordinary. And even preemies born at thirty-two weeks can do okay with the right care."

Winter took the book from her again and turned to a page a few farther in. She handed the volume back, careful not to lose the place.

"I'm pregnant," Autumn read out loud. *"It can only be John's baby. I don't know how to contact him or let him know..."* Autumn handed the book back to Winter, choosing her words carefully. "I'm guessing your mother didn't know your biological father well."

Winter snorted at the understatement. "Well, in the biblical sense, maybe. But apparently, she never got a last name. She certainly never told her parents. As far as they knew, Bill was the only man in her life and he...he accepted me as his own. Gramma and Grampa didn't know the truth until after she...they...were gone."

Autumn smiled at her friend. "It sounds like Bill was a good man who loved you very much."

Winter nodded, another tear threatening to escape as it lingered on her bottom lashes. "Yes, he was, and at the same time, I can't keep from wondering who this John is. Is that wrong?"

"No, it's not wrong. It's being human." Autumn gestured at the piles that had gone somewhere past idle curiosity into the identity of an unknown father and ventured into the realm of creepy obsession. "At the same time, be careful of how much time and energy you put into this search. Your mental health is more important than your curiosity."

"She met this John at a college mixer," Winter said, completely ignoring Autumn's statement. She fished through another pile of papers. Autumn was surprised to watch her pull an open book from the pile with all the flourish of performing a magic trick.

"What's that?"

"Her college yearbook." Winter flipped the book over to show her the front. "I went through and found all the Johns, Johnathans, and Johnnies in here, trying all the different spellings."

"He might not have been a student."

"Right. That's why I included faculty as well. It's less likely that someone from another college or a non-student was at the mixer, though it's possible. If that's the case, there's not much I can do to find out, unless I want to start investigating other colleges in the area in case he was someone's date that night. I can look at who the local employers were in the area at the time. Maybe I can find employee rosters from the older, more well-established companies." Her eyes glazed over, going unfocused. A moment later, she shook her head sharply, snapping herself back into the here and now. "Maybe later. I have plenty of other leads to search. If nothing comes up, though, I'll—"

"Winter." Autumn closed the yearbook on some very self-satisfied photos of young men and women poised to take on the world. "Why?"

Winter looked blank for a moment or two. Then the question clicked. "All this?" She waved at the piles of paper. "You saw the video." Winter's hand went to her temple as she took a deep breath. "Justin knew. He *knew*, Autumn. How? Did Kilroy tell him, and if so, how did that monster know?"

And just like that, Autumn understood the rabbit hole her friend was crawling through.

How did Justin know such personal information? The question lifted goose bumps on Autumn's skin, and she crossed her arms over her chest to ward off the sudden chill.

"That psycho probably told him many lies that—"

"Yes, but this happens to be *true,* doesn't it? That kind of makes a difference. This isn't just some random lie he made up to make Justin feel off-balance and uncertain." Winter's hands swept out to grasp her friend's. "He *knew!* There has to be a connection I'm not getting. You have to see that. Something that would tie my biological father to Kilroy? Maybe to Justin? If I can find this guy, I can follow that thread and maybe find my brother."

Autumn tapped her lip, thinking through the possibilities. "She might have eventually met him or seen him again somewhere and told him the truth."

Winter shrugged but didn't look excited or convinced. "I guess. If she was pregnant with me, it might have caught her off guard or he might have demanded to know or something, but why wouldn't she put that in her journal?"

Autumn flipped to the last page. "Because the last time

she journaled was right after Thanksgiving of that year, unless there is another journal we don't have."

Winter frowned. "Gramma didn't say anything about a more recent journal, and I don't remember Mom ever journaling when I was a kid."

"So, it's a possibility?" Autumn prompted.

Another shrug. "I guess."

Autumn leaned forward. "We might have to accept that we might not ever get all the answers to our questions."

Winter's entire visage darkened as she frowned and crossed her arms over her chest. "Which would truly suck."

Autumn smiled. She could almost envision how this pouty, forlorn version of the Winter she had grown to know so well would have looked as a child. "It is what it is."

Winter flipped her the bird but smiled as she did it. "Maybe."

"Speaking of 'maybe,' we have a lot of maybes on our hands, don't you think?" Autumn eyed the piles of papers. "You're putting a lot of work into a tenuous connection at best. You don't even have a last name, no idea what he looked like. It's just a line in a diary and…"

She didn't know how to finish. She knew right away that, had she been in Winter's shoes, nothing would have stopped her from crawling down the rabbit hole too.

"And…?" Winter prompted.

Autumn caught the look in her friend's eyes and sighed, rolling her head to release the tight muscles in her neck. "All right." Autumn shook her head and laughed at herself, glancing at her watch. "It's still before six, so hang on a moment." She dug in her purse for her phone.

"What are you doing?" Winter asked.

Autumn held up a finger after hitting the speed dial and waited as the phone connected to that of her boss, Mike Shadley. After the brief hello, Autumn launched into the purpose of her call. "Something has come up, a personal issue. I won't be available for a few days, but I can work on my files at home."

"Anything I can help with?" Autumn smiled. She liked Mike. Her other boss, Adam, not so much.

"No, but thank you. If you need me, don't hesitate to call."

She gave him a brief update on her cases to make sure he knew she had everything handled, which she did. She always did. After saying their goodbyes, Autumn grinned at Winter. "I'm all yours. Personal assistant Autumn Trent, reporting for duty."

If her smile wavered a touch, could she be blamed? But someone had to represent at least an element of sanity, seeing as how Winter seemed to have lost hers.

"But…" Winter looked at Autumn's phone as if she had never seen one before. "Won't you get in trouble?"

"Nah." Autumn waved a dismissive hand. "I'm actually ahead of schedule on my cases, and there's nothing with a tight deadline right now, so the timing is perfect."

Winter leaned in and gave her friend a hug. "Thank you."

Autumn returned the squeeze and reached down to take off her shoes. At least Winter keeping busy meant less tension and guilt in her friend. It wasn't nearly so painful to touch her now.

"I *do* have some personal time accrued, and I can't think of a better way to use it. So, what's the deadline?"

"Midnight," Winter said and gave her a sly look. "Noah should be home by midnight, and I want to have the papers stashed away someplace before that happens. Tomorrow, I'll send him on his way with a kiss on the forehead, a piece of burned toast and a note pinned to his jacket in case he gets lost. All this comes out again the moment he leaves."

"All right." Autumn stood and stretched. She didn't like going behind her other friend's back, but she wouldn't argue right now. "Midnight. But if we're staying here that late, I'm making tea." She looked at the pizza dubiously. "What the hell…" She snagged a piece and carried it into the kitchen to heat. Still shaking her head and wondering how in the world she'd gotten sucked into this, she filled the teapot and set it on the burner to boil. Some hunting unearthed a plate for the slice of pizza which she placed in the microwave.

A vibration from her hip pocket caught her attention. She'd forgotten that her phone was there. She pulled it out as the microwave began its countdown, opening a text from Aiden.

Heard you're taking some time off. Hope this means you're taking care of her.

Autumn stared at the phone, reading the message twice. The microwave dinged, but it wasn't until the kettle began to whistle that she felt calm enough to answer the text.

Are you spying on me? And how the hell did you learn about that so soon?

She hit send and took the protesting kettle off the burner and fished out two cups. The microwaved beeped again.

She pulled out the pizza and found two teabags in the cupboard that she dipped in the hot water. She managed to take a bite of the pizza before her phone vibrated again.

You haven't reported in. And I have my ways.

Autumn clenched her jaw till it hurt. What was the old expression? "Make a deal with the devil and you pay the price?"

Autumn grabbed the tea and set the plate with the pizza on it, balancing both in one hand, leaving the other free for the second mug as she returned to Winter.

"Tea!" she said brightly as she tried to find a blank surface to set the mugs down. Eventually, she set them in the cardboard remains of the pizza box, all the while formulating her reply in her mind. Though sending something along the lines of, *Hell, if you know everything anyway, why should I?* probably wouldn't exactly send the right message.

Or it might send the right message too well.

Make a deal with the devil, indeed.

"All right, were should I start?" she asked Winter. Her phone buzzed again, but she ignored it. Let the devil deal with himself for a change.

10

Noah set the last box he was carrying down with a thud on the conference table. The sound echoed in the cavernous meeting room. "That's everything we have on The Preacher." Noah stretched, flexing his muscles. "I carried it all up from the archives. I should have gotten a forklift."

Noah rolled his shoulders back and forth, rubbing them as Aiden rose from the chair, handing Justin's file back to Bree.

The latest file was becoming thick; more than an inch of papers and photos and various bits of information about Justin/Jaime. The boxes, on the other hand, were heavy-duty storage files filled to the top. They contained evidence on all the victims of one Douglas Kilroy.

Aiden pulled off the top of the standard file box, one of many that had yet to be converted to electronic media. Nor was it likely to be. Like most of the archives, it contained things that couldn't be converted. A knife in a plastic bag with the word EVIDENCE emblazed across it, for example. Aiden carefully set the weapon on the desk and pulled out a file folder stuffed with papers nearly as wide as his hand was able to grasp. There was a lot of Kilroy there. The worst cases always generated the worst paperwork.

And nightmares.

And regret.

"All right." He randomly took a third of the papers and handed them to Noah. "Look through these, and Bree…" he handed the next third to her, "look for any addresses. I know we found the house and the church, so I want us to find anything that wasn't followed up before. I want any indicator that he owned property or had a place he liked to go to, someplace he might have wanted to hide away or land he had that wasn't disposed of. Someplace that he would have taken Jaime to, or talked about to the kid."

Noah nodded, taking his papers to the table. "Maybe we'll find something obvious like the Unabomber cabin," he said, already flipping through the pages.

"Isolated cabin in the woods?" Bree shook her head, her face screwed up in distaste. "Those places don't always have the best paperwork. Most seem to belong to some cousin's third wife's father." She caught Aiden's look and held up a hand. "I'm looking, I'm looking."

"Just find me anything that might give a hint on Jaime Peterson's location. Did Kilroy have a link to someone that none of us felt a need to follow up on? He was a preacher. Did he have a follower we can ask about a supposed grandson? Nephew. A boy he raised in any way. Hell, I'll take anything at this point."

Aiden sat down with his own sheaf of papers, silently agreeing with Bree. Everything in that file had been gone over twice and then twice again, but once the killer had been caught, there'd been no need to pursue other clues. Something might have been overlooked if Kilroy had been killed before it was followed up. Honestly, it was about as likely as finding a needle in a haystack at this point.

Bree set her papers on the table and divided her attention between the men. "I think we've been thinking about Justin calling Kilroy 'Grandpa' in a figurative sense. Is there any possibility that there might be some actual familial merit to that? Maybe there's an actual DNA connection between them somehow?"

Aiden turned to Noah, who only shrugged. "Maybe." Aiden scratched his chin as he pondered this. "It's certainly worth looking into. Stella has the DNA sample from the Ulbrich case, right?"

Both agents nodded, Noah somewhat absently. "There is DNA on file for Kilroy," Bree offered. "Maybe she could run a—"

Noah held up a hand, looking up from his sheaf of papers. If he had been wearing glasses, he would have been looking over the top of them like a disdainful grandmother. "I don't know if there's much of a point." He shuffled a page to the bottom of the pile. "Even if they are related, it doesn't change much."

Bree's expression spoke volumes. "I think it would change a great deal."

"Does it?" Noah relegated another sheet to the ignominy of the bottom of the pile. "We still have to figure out *where* Justin is, and fast, before he kills anyone else. His blood relations are inconsequential to that end." He hefted his stack and lifted the top sheet again. "But if the old man did have a grandson we don't know about, family who weren't contacted, something that came up in the original investigation, then it's worth diving through all this garbage to find it. This claim about him being Jaime's grandfather hit us from the blue, I don't want any more surprises."

Noah didn't add the words "for Winter," but then again, he didn't have to. It was like a rider with every sentence since he took this case. For a while now everything he'd been doing was *for Winter.* But in a greater way, weren't they all doing that? Winter had touched each and every one of them.

Even though things hadn't worked out in the direction he once hoped, Aiden would still do nearly anything for her. Just for the sake of the friendship as well as supporting another agent.

He wondered how she was. He had heard nothing from her for days, not surprising, but...worrisome.

He hadn't heard from Autumn yet either. There was another relationship that could have gone differently. She was the whole package, both stunning and a very intelligent woman. The fact that he'd been attracted to her was no surprise. So, he'd sent one woman he was attracted to out to spy on the health and well-being of another woman he was attracted to, all while he worked with the boyfriend of...

He shook his head at the strangeness of it all. And that was before he even added in the fact that Winter's own brother was a suspected serial killer. Half-brother.

Hell.

"It might not matter," Aiden said finally, "but it might end up being used by a lawyer in court if we ever are able to bring him in. Personally, I would rather not be surprised by some last-minute courtroom dramatics." He turned back toward Bree. "Contact Stella. Have her run a comparison between the sample she has from Ulbrich and whatever they have on file from Kilroy." She nodded and he returned to his sheaf.

"We won't be able to get a judge to buy into that," Noah warned from farther down the table. "In order for us to compare the sample we have on Ulbrich, we need a viable one from Kilroy."

"That should be in the database." Aiden raised an eyebrow at Noah. This was standard procedure. DNA evidence was logged and filed with the case.

"It's not." Bree shook her head, her mouth a tight line. "When we saw that tape and heard the word 'Grandpa,' we checked." She glanced over to Noah, who leaned back in his chair and looked up at the ceiling as if looking for guidance from some higher power. "There was no DNA entered into the records for Douglas Kilroy."

Aiden dropped the papers on the table, trying to ignore the way they scattered in all directions. In truth, he wanted to hurl them across the room, but he prided himself on keeping his composure. "Well, why the hell not?" he asked, hearing just how flat and tight each word dropped from his mouth.

Noah shrugged. "Maybe it didn't seem important in the wake of his death. Maybe someone forgot. Who knows? Stuff happens. You know that as well as I do. But in order to make a good comparison, we—"

"We have to dig up the body of Douglas Kilroy," Aiden finished for him, dropping his head in his hand. "That's just the best thing I've heard today." What a fuck up. They needed that DNA because they still, to this day, had no idea of the total number of people Kilroy murdered, and without a DNA sample, it would be that much more difficult to link a murder to him. It was sloppy as hell that this was never entered properly, and somewhere, a head would roll for it. Hopefully not his.

The problem was, it was Aiden who was now left hanging. It should have been a simple matter of running samples through some mysterious lab procedure and getting a result that pointed them in the right direction. Nothing should be this complicated. If the samples had been preserved in the database like standard procedure required, it would be a much simpler process.

Noah cleared his throat. "And that would mean comparing Winter's DNA as well."

Aiden's hand fell. "Tell me that her agent DNA didn't get lost too."

"No, we have it." Bree said quickly, looking up again from her stack of papers. The Bureau maintained a record of agents in case an agent had to be identified after death but accessing someone's DNA records while they were alive was more tricky. "Of course, we'll need—"

Aiden nodded and waved off the rest of what she was about to say. "I'm aware of the legalities involved." It didn't matter how many pieces of paper an agent signed to allow their records to be accessed in the course of duty, the fact was that they could rescind that permission at any given moment under a half-dozen privacy acts, so legal always wanted clear and informed consent from an agent *before* such an investigation involving personal records. There were few things more personal than DNA records. "Do you think she would refuse to cooperate?"

"No." Noah and Bree spoke at once.

"At least, I don't think so," Noah added, one eye on his partner. "Winter wouldn't have an issue with it...under normal circumstances. But right now, she's so shut down and withdrawn, I'm not sure what she would say or how she would react."

"And despite what Stella says, that sample they got from Sandy Ulbrich..." Bree gave an involuntary shudder. "I'm sure the researchers know exactly what they're doing, but it is hard for me to imagine that the bit of saliva from where the poor woman had been licked would be viable."

Aiden closed his eyes and counted. The fact was, they were right. They were very right. Once hailed as the be-all-end-all of forensic investigations, DNA matching was coming under more and more scrutiny as case after case of malfeasance and outright foolishness on the part of labs and collections were reported across the board.

Recently, a wild chase for a rapist was spent on a man who matched every DNA swab taken, only to find that he worked in the place where the swabs were created and had tainted the swabs before they ever shipped out to be used. One man was arrested for murder based on DNA, only to discover that the same EMTs who brought that man into the ER had later brought the victim into the hospital using the same oximeter on the victim's finger to measure pulse as on the first man, thus putting DNA on the murder victim.

DNA was messy. Not the cure-all it looked to be on the crime shows on TV.

Worse, digging up a corpse, especially one as high-profile as The Preacher would become a media circus no matter how clever or discrete they might try and make it. Driving a backhoe into a cemetery and lifting a coffin with chains drew attention. When the media labeled that freak with the name The Preacher, he'd gained a fan following of sorts. Anything to do with him was pretty much guaranteed a great deal of unwanted attention.

Aiden sat back. What was he missing?

This case *couldn't* be allowed to be thrown out of court or dismissed on a technicality. Cutting corners or taking short-cuts on this could mean that a serial killer was set free. This had to be by the book. That meant delays, both in getting the appropriate orders from the appropriate judges, and delays in gathering other hard evidence to present to a judge to get the okay to proceed. It also meant getting enough hard facts to hold up against media frenzy when Kilroy's body once more saw the light of day.

"No, you're right," Aiden said to them, sitting up and starting to collect the scattered papers, putting them again into a neat stack. "But we need all the evidence we can get, and if that involves getting enough of a case for a judge to sign off on opening that bastard's grave, then we get all the evidence we can for a convincing argument. All that we have to work with is here, so something in this file has to be strong enough to make our case. Find it." He didn't wait for a reply but dove back into the pages that lay on the table, flipping through them to make sure they were in the right order before picking up the top one.

He did not add the words, 'for Winter.' But from the grim expressions on the faces of those who loved her best, he really didn't have to.

11

Sitting forward like this in the chair, the edge cut into my legs. I could feel the pressure shutting off the circulation, but I didn't dare move. I knew better. Grandpa always wanted me to stay still, to not move, to not make any noise.

"Obey your elders, boy. There is a purpose to everything, and you'll realize that purpose one of these days."

Of course, I knew he was gone. He was dead and buried deep in a hole underground, but that didn't mean the rules had changed. He didn't like me to move. He didn't want me to make a sound.

I didn't always obey.

The chair flew through the room and smashed against the wall. "Damn her!" I screamed at the top of my lungs, hoping my dear sister could somehow hear me through the miles and through the years. "Damn you! Damn you to hell!"

I kicked the table, rage and frustration coursing through my veins. I didn't realize I'd kicked it as hard as I did. I thought it would bounce, or maybe flip over and spill the things off the top. But the old table came apart with a deafening crack. The screws that held the top to the legs pulled free all at once. In slow motion, I watched as the scarred top folded and splintered. Shattered wood flew in all directions.

Stupid boy! Bad boy! Horrible terrible spoiled-rotten bastard. This is how they raised you? This is how you behave?

His voice. Grandpa's voice. I could hear it as clear as if he stood in the room with me. Maybe he did.

I stared at the floor, not wanting to look and find out for sure. I had to punish. I had to be punished. Grandpa taught me that.

I wet my lips with my tongue, struggling to get the words out, hearing the pathetic whisper of sound. "I tried. I tried. I *really* tried. We followed you. We finished what you began. The mission, the path, the Holy Way…we were there. Tyler, Kent, and me. We cleaned up what you couldn't finish. We believed, and we were faithful. We were true to the path, Grandpa, but…but…but…but…"

But you make excuses, you fail, you always fail. You were raised as failure by a failure and you're weak.

I sank down, haunches on heels, hands coming up to cover my eyes.

He was dead. He was dead and he was buried and he was rotting in the grave and he was still in my head, and he was talking and he had fingers on me, burning, hurting, mean fingers.

I could feel them on my skin. It became hard to breathe, and I choked, trying to find air. Even *that* I was getting wrong. I was supposed to be sitting quietly. Maybe he'd leave me alone if I just sat quietly. Sometimes it worked and he'd forget I was there…

Lazy, useless little shit. There's work to be done, there are things that need to be done, you need to finish what I began, and you sit there cowering on the floor like you have all the time in the world? I need you to finish the work.

He was right. I needed to finish the path. The ones from

the mall, the ones he couldn't finish, they needed to be finished. I shouldn't have wasted so much time on Winter. I shouldn't have tipped my hand. I shouldn't have sent the video. When would I ever learn?

But Winter shouldn't have let me go. She shouldn't have slept in the hall while his fingers dug into my flesh, while he grabbed my arms and hurt me and took me away. I saw her again in my mind's eye, the child-woman Winter lying in the hallway sleeping while he'd taken me away.

Stupid vixen.

She never came for me. Never once. She left me and then she killed Grandpa and she took him away from me just like he'd taken Mother and Father away.

Everyone was taken away. Every last one of them.

That's when the true hellishness of the situation came clear in my mind. I couldn't finish the work. I couldn't walk the path. I couldn't because there was something in my way.

I got up on trembling legs and forced myself to pace around the room, kicking splinters viciously as I worked the thoughts through. It was all coming clear, so bright someone might as well have walked into the room and turned on the light. There was always something keeping me from finishing the holy work. Something else.

Not me.

No, this wasn't my fault. That belonged to someone else entirely. I had been locked down. Weighted down and kept from my cause. I could feel the weight of it, like it pressed on me now. My sister. My sister, the millstone around my neck, the albatross, the leaden weight I had been forced to carry my entire life.

I had ties, and all ties did was bind and restrict and cut off circulation like chairs that were too big, but you had to stay still anyway, even when the blood stopped flowing through your legs and you couldn't feel them anymore.

I stopped to sit, realizing belatedly that no one had said I could get up. *I'm sorry, Grandpa. I'm sorry I didn't see this sooner.*

To keep to the path, I would have to go through the last of the obstacles. Winter. Winter was the last obstacle. If I could get around her...no, not around, *through*. Go through the barrier. Nothing could stop someone on the true path.

I leaned forward, balancing my weight on elbows that dug into my knees while I cradled my chin on my palms. *Think.* Winter was an FBI agent now. Such a big deal, stopping The Preacher. Grandpa hated that word, such an ignoble word for such a sacred task. But he knew, he'd known that he would never be understood. Never appreciated for all the good works he did.

Good works.

No. He was bad. He was evil.

That was what made knowing him so confusing.

He was good and he was bad. He was righteous and he was evil.

But he was Grandpa, and since he was killed, there was no one else to take care of me. He was dead. He was dead and buried. That probably made him angry. He was always angry. Always.

My head was starting to hurt from all the thoughts racing through it.

I couldn't sit still, I couldn't. But I couldn't leave the chair. It was broken. I'd slammed it against a wall, and it hadn't been the same since, one leg tilted crazy askew.

But if I sat still, maybe Grandpa wouldn't notice how confused I was and he wouldn't get mad.

I couldn't sit still, though. I rocked back and forth, back and forth.

Finish the work, boy. Finish the holy path.

I couldn't.

I balanced on the edge of the broken chair, shivering in the dark. The chair shivered with me.

You can do this, boy. Do it for me. Do it for God. Follow the path and get your rewards.

Beginning to calm, I let his words echo through my mind. Yes, I could do this. I was born to do this. Grandpa was killed so that I could take over and receive the great reward.

After forever, I stood. A bright clarity washed over me, and suddenly, I could see Grandpa's path clearly. I could finish the work after all. I could be there for him. I could please him.

Or not.

The man didn't matter anymore. Only the mission.

At least that was what I told myself.

The chair quietly fell apart at my feet. One chair, one table. Grandpa couldn't be mad, not anymore. He was dead and the worms feasted on his soul. Only the mission remained, only the right way, the holy way. That was all that was left. But before I could walk with the righteous, I had to clear the way. I had to sever ties and free myself from the bonds that held me down.

The bastard. What was the name for a female bastard? *Bitch?* Appropriate. She'd left me. She'd napped while I was taken, not even the blood of my fathers. My sister, the get of a whore who slept around without remorse. No different then. My mother was no different than any other woman. And my dear sister? No different. They were all alike, and they were the reason for the holy path.

With the clarity came calm. I saw the damage around me, but this time, it was only analytical. Just broken pieces of wood, cast off, cheap, sluts and whores, not worth restoring. There were more of them I could pluck off the streets and dispose of.

Winter. Winter had to die. Once she was dead, I could be

free, I could fly. I could continue the mission. I would walk the holy path and there would be no one left who could stop me.

Keep to the path, boy.

Shut up, old man. You died. It was my turn now. I decided the shape of the path.

I gathered my knife, the weight filling my fist like cold rage, like divine purpose. I already could feel my half-sister's blood warming my hands as I sliced into her belly.

Grandpa would be proud. I would make him proud. If I had to call him up from the very depths of hell and rub his face in it. I would see the pride, at last, in his eyes.

So like the ones I saw now in the reflection of the steel. So like the ones I would see fade away when I buried the steel in her heart.

I called my sister, yelling at her to come to me. Hoping to wake her from her long slumber.

Wake up. It's time to die.

I laughed all the way to the car.

12

Winter jerked awake. The morning sun streaming in through the window missed her by a good foot, putting her in the shadows just enough to lull her back to the edge of restless unconsciousness.

Late nights and obsessing about Justin were taking their toll. Her mind refused to let anything go, but her body needed sleep, and she found herself dozing off in the chair more often than not. Her back ached from the position, and she stretched, grimacing at the pain. Still somewhat disoriented, she picked up a sheet of paper that had fallen from nerveless fingers into her lap and puzzled over it, trying to make sense out of the words printed there.

The fact that Noah was working so hard on finding answers, on finding Justin, endeared him even more to her, but it didn't help that he came home late and left early. She suspected no one would be getting any sleep until her baby brother was found.

She rubbed the back of her neck, trying to wake herself. What time was it? She fumbled for her phone and considered making something to eat or walking around to keep going.

In the end, she did none of those things. Leaning back in the living room chair, she took a deep breath and closed her eyes against the sunlight streaming through the window and blocked out the traffic noises from outside.

A quick glance at her phone told her there was still time before Autumn was due. Cross-town traffic at this hour wasn't going to be pretty. Her eyelids felt heavy. Maybe a twenty-minute power nap would refresh her, at least well enough to get through the day. She settled in, the printout of an old newspaper clipping still in her hand.

Local Woman Lynn Williams Deceased.

As it turned out, a nap was not what her body had in mind.

The vision came quickly, and she panicked, fighting the images thrusting their way into her mind. The newspaper crackled between her fingers, and the sound settled her enough to still and let the vision take over. Within moments, she fell into the unfolding scene.

Her visions brought her strange images. Things she knew and didn't, everything out of context mingling with memories she'd long since forgotten.

A young boy played in and around farm machinery. In a mud-stained shirt and jeans that were more dirt than denim, he crawled around the big tractor like it was a jungle gym. Perhaps to him, it was. He treated it with a familiarity that spoke to his roots, to his heritage.

He turned to her, deep brown eyes flashing with unrestrained mischief and enthusiasm. Every blade of tall grass was a toy and the vast open expanses were all his playground. With a little wave, he ran as fast and as far as he could, dodging rows of growing corn, leaping deep troughs where water irrigated the plants.

He ran to a building, sun-bleached white, and if the paint was chipped a bit here and there, it was at least clean and honest, like a good farmhouse should be. A transistor radio belted out rock and roll, straining its speakers as it swayed from its tether, swinging like a hanged man on the clothesline where it had been brought to give music to the day's chores.

A woman reached into the basket on the ground at her feet, rising and pulling out a man's shirt in one fluid movement, pinning it to the line beside the others. Shirt to shirt, pants to pants, towels and sheets marched up and down the string, socks stuck between them. The whole menagerie swayed and rotated as summer winds lazed about the clothing, picking at it, playing with the fringes.

Winter tried to think who this woman might be, why she was important enough to break into her thoughts, but it was a face she'd not seen. The dream-vision continued, heedless of her desire to stay a moment and linger here in this peaceful interlude.

The woman smiled a secretive affection. "Little boys running under summer skies are noisy beasts, and this particular one loves to surprise a body," she told the white shirt she was currently pegging to the line. Indeed, Bill seemed to make little use of whatever stealth God granted him. His sneaking up on her was about as silent as a clatter of colts. "Such a wild boy."

She turned her back on his approach, and Winter could tell she was enjoying the game of waiting for him.

"Auntie Lynn!" the boy yelled, jumping into the air with excitement.

For her part, Lynn acted as if he'd suddenly popped from the ground in front of her and gave a squeak that made the boy laugh. "You're a sneaky little monster."

His grinned widened as he made his hands into claws and gave a big, raucous roar. "Auntie Lynn! Guess what!"

Aunt Lynn?

The name triggered memories, stories told to her long ago. Recognition flared. So, this was Winter's great aunt, a woman Winter would have liked to have known. She looked quick, friendly, and open. But there was a world of pain hidden in her eyes. Heartache, trial, and sorrow marched hand in hand with her sweetness. Maybe it only made her all the more beautiful, the pain nothing more than a frame to showcase her uncommon grace and courage.

"William Black!" The woman scolded the troublemaker with mock fierceness and knelt down to the boy's eye level. "I swear, you will be the death of me, you surely will. Sneaking up on a body like that. That's just rude."

Winter drew in her breath quickly, feeling the pain flutter in her chest at the name. Bill Black, the man who raised her, the man she'd been proud to call 'Daddy.'

William looked properly chastised, digging one bare toe in the grass, his head bowed under the onslaught of her words. Lynn grinned and flicked the boy's nose with one long finger. "Now, what is it that I am supposed to guess?"

"I caught a snake!" The boy raised his head, puffing out his chest with all the pride and self-confidence of a great hunter.

There was nothing fake or pretend in her reaction this time. The shudder and contempt for such a pursuit were clearly genuine. "Good heavens!" She shook her head. "You need to let those things be, William. Someday, one of them will take a big bite out of you for your trouble!" She demonstrated by pretending to take a bite from his arm.

Bill giggled and pulled his arm away.

Aunt Lynn opened her mouth and took a breath to continue, but the words ended before they began. From the other side of the house, a door slammed. A screen door, by the empty rattling sound of it.

A male voice boomed through the empty farmhouse. "Dammit, woman!"

Winter caught her breath. In the logic of dreams and visions, the voice was as familiar to her as it was foreign. But the effect it had on Lynn was remarkable.

The woman froze, a panic-stricken look running over her face.

Winter knew that was the voice of Arthur, her husband, in the same way she knew the boy was her own father.

"Where the hell are you?"

"You run along home now, you hear me, William?" Lynn's voice went quiet and cold. The fear in her eyes held weight. "Hurry! And don't come back again until morning, you hear me?"

"Lynn! Dammit!" It was Arthur, all right. Winter had seen family photographs, knew that fearsome countenance, all the more terrifying come to life. The fear came off Lynn in waves. He didn't sound drunk, as he did most of the time. Now, he sounded weary and angry. "Get your ass in here!"

Lynn's thoughts ran through Winter's mind. A sober and angry Arthur was much worse than a drunk and angry Arthur. And a drunk Arthur was bad enough.

The boy lingered.

For a moment, Lynn stared at him blankly, her eyes distant and strange. What did she see there in her mind's eye? This much of her thoughts was a mystery. A memory perhaps, of something she couldn't quite figure out how to escape. She blinked finally, seeing the boy still there. He was plucking at her arm in concern.

"Go now!" She shooed the boy off, shoving him forcibly from her, and stood, smoothing her skirt and apron. She picked up the clothesbasket and walked into the house, her head held high and her back straight.

Winter swallowed hard, realizing Lynn wasn't as beaten

as she'd first supposed. She felt the fierceness of Lynn's resolve. The woman refused to enter the house already beaten down. It was a small defiance, but she clung to it hard.

Arthur didn't even wait for the door to close before attacking her verbally. "Well, *there* you are! Where the hell have you been?"

Winter couldn't hear the reply; her thoughts had gone back to Bill. She could see the child, half hidden behind the curtain of laundry on the line. He was already backing up, a look of abject terror in his eyes. Turned out that he had a right to look so afraid when the sound of flesh hitting flesh echoed over the fields, as did something that sounded suspiciously like a wooden chair being smashed into kindling. At the sound, Bill turned and fled to the edge of the cornfield.

Blinking back angry tears, Winter watched the door to the house open and Lynn stumble free, holding her hand against her mouth to muffle her sobs.

Bill watched her from the shelter of the cornfield as she fell under the starched white shirts and the bleached sheets that were still playing in the breeze, and the tiny radio that still spewed tinny rock and roll. A passing cloud obscured the sun, and the boy shuddered in the sudden darkness.

She watched as Bill Black ran through the cornfield and back to his home like the devil himself was on his heels, his legs pumping, all thoughts of being the great snake hunter gone in a puff of fear. Arthur's voice still echoed through the crops, as did the tears of Aunt Lynn. They seemed to follow him through the corn and past the tractor and all the way to his bedroom and under the bed.

Lynn had died of natural causes, according to the archived newspapers, but it might be that the 'natural" causes weren't as natural as they were made out to be.

Daddy.

Her mind cried out against that thought. No. He was still

her father. It didn't matter what some journal said. Bill Black had been her father in every way that counted.

Knock. Knock. Knock.

The fields and the house all vanished as the door behind her rattled. Winter jerked awake, disoriented, not sure where she was. The door rattled again. In a rush, it all came back to her, riding the memory of the dream.

Autumn. Autumn had come.

"Hang on!" she called to the front door and levered herself from the chair to answer the summons. For a moment, she caught her balance against the wall as dueling images of her apartment and the farmhouse fought for her attention. It was as though she had to choose which reality to follow. She longed to comfort that boy. For a moment, she hesitated, lingering there, not quite ready to let the image go.

It was too late. The dream boy wavered in her gaze, dissipating, an unsettled ghost drifting back to the netherworld. She shook her head and opened the door to see Autumn bundled in her coat, shivering in the icy December wind.

Autumn's smile evaporated when she took in Winter's expression. "Winter? Are you all right?" She searched Winter's eyes as though for some clue or reassurance. She dug into her purse and pulled out a small pack of tissues. Winter didn't need to be told that her nose had started bleeding. She took a tissue and pressed it under her nose.

"I..." Winter looked back to the chair, unsettled under such tight scrutiny. "I had a...dream...a vision."

The farmhouse had faded, but the apartment hadn't yet taken on the solidity of the real. The last tendrils of the dream clung to her like the smell of smoke from a fire. The enormity of the vision struck her as she pulled Autumn into the apartment. She spoke quickly, desperate to get the words out before the images were lost to her completely, before dream sense was replaced by cold hard logic and reality.

"I think I know how Kilroy was related to my father...to Bill, not to me." She turned and headed back to the living room and grabbed her coat. "Something in the old interviews, a connection that no one put together or maybe it didn't matter...I don't know." She clung to that farmhouse, that woman under the wash who wept and hid her face from her vision. She tried to pull out any detail, any idea, but the images were too faded and becoming less and less real by the minute.

"Winter!" Autumn snapped to get her to pay attention. "What are you talking about? What's going on?"

It took a long moment for Winter to recall her thoughts. It only occurred to her belatedly that Autumn hadn't shared the same vision with her. "Right. Right. Sorry. Bill Black was related to Douglas Kilroy. Ah...Arthur and Lynn...dammit..." The vision hadn't added a last name, and she couldn't remember what it might have been, either from family history or from the investigation into The Preacher. Yet, it seemed the most obvious thing, as if she'd known it all along, but it wasn't there for her to hold on to.

She quickly outlined what she remembered, stripping the emotion from the dream, trying to recall the details the way she'd been trained to as an agent. She wasn't entirely successful in her efforts because tears pricked at the corners of her eyes as she finished, her body longing to weep for this stranger who'd died so senselessly years before she'd even been born.

"Have you told anyone this?" Autumn asked her when she finished.

"No. It just happened now. Besides, I can't enter a vision into evidence, and until I can remember the last name and connect the dots, it's not worth much. But it gives *us* a lead of sorts." Winter shrugged on her jacket. "And it gives us a starting point."

"What starting point? It's a vision..." Autumn rationalized, then subsided at the look Winter gave her. "I know, I know, I'm the last person to cast doubts considering what happens when I touch someone, but that still doesn't clarify a starting point."

"Dream or not, it at least gives us somewhere to look," Winter argued as she headed for the door. She stopped, her hand on the knob, twisting to meet Autumn's gaze. "We're going to look at the time around when I was born, or when I was conceived. If we can nail down the family connection and maybe figure out what my mother couldn't...who my father was, that should be enough to pursue and take to Max."

Arthur might very well be still alive too.

Only she didn't say that part out loud. Some things were better left unsaid.

13

Noah's finger hovered over his phone while his mind worked on ways to delay making the call he needed to make. What was it, that old story about someone tying a sword with a single strand of hair from the ceiling and letting it hang, point down, over someone seated in a throne? He couldn't remember the whole story, something he'd heard in high school or college. Now here he stood, finger poised over a tiny picture of Winter's face on the screen of his phone, wondering what that story felt like from the point of view of the sword.

He punched the screen and the phone obediently called the woman he loved.

In the years he'd worked in law enforcement, he'd had to make tough calls before, but this one was personal. Aiden had offered to deliver the punch, but this was Noah's load to bear. The phone rang, and Noah shrank even farther into the corner where he huddled, not quite far enough away from everyone else, and far too conscious of the words he needed to say. With the amount of foot traffic in the hallway, privacy was going to be a relative thing, but at least it wasn't the closed and confined space of the conference room where Bree and Aiden were buried in papers and keeping an ear out for whatever he was going to say to Winter.

The phone rang again. And again.

For that matter, what was he going to say to Winter? He should have thought this through before dialing. Usually, it was better to just state the bad news, and not try to lead into it. Especially with Winter. She preferred the direct approach, her attitude being to just let it out and deal with the fallout as it came.

Another ring. *Where are you?* Noah gripped the phone harder.

"Hang on." Winter's voice barely registered, it was so quiet. She sounded distracted, like she wasn't all there.

"Hello?" Noah called into the phone. He listened as background white noise and silence echoed back at him. He checked his volume control, but he had it at max already. He could tell that the connection to her phone was strong. It sounded like the phone was in motion. Was she driving?

"Hello?" he called into the phone. When there was no answer, he strained to pull out the slightest sound that might give him an indication of where she was. All he could hear was traffic in the far distance, muted. She could be anywhere.

"Noah, I'm sorry. I can't…"

He pressed the phone harder against his ear, trying to hear her words.

"Winter!" he called into the phone. What was she doing? He hated how frantic he was beginning to feel, but he supposed such feelings under the circumstances would be normal. Her lunatic brother had sent that video to her, by name. Finding her wouldn't be difficult. He glanced down the hallway, noting he was still mercifully alone as he leaned into his corner, listening to Winter say nothing at all.

Suddenly, on the other end of the phone, the background silence became the usual life-blood sounds of the city on full volume.

"Hi!" Winter's voice seemed bright and almost...cheerful, the single syllable blasting out his eardrum.

Noah hadn't realized how hard he'd been straining to hear what was going on until she'd come back. For a moment, he had to hold the phone away from his ear. What the hell? Not that he wasn't happy to hear her sound upbeat and more her old self. It was just...well...that she was upbeat and sounding like her old self. Not the same Winter he'd seen only hours before.

What the hell was going on?

"Sorry about that. I was in a library and they don't much like cell phones there." Okay, yes, she sounded better than she had been for a while. Something was up.

He stiffened and the breath he'd been holding left in a long, weary exhale. "It's okay. Having any luck?"

Her tone was making him nervous. Her independent investigation wasn't on the books. In fact, Max would only turn a blind eye just so far. Up until now, Winter had been limiting her involvement, keeping her digging to public records and doing research anyone else would be able to do without being a member of the FBI. While that was still a little gray, it was certainly legal, and frankly, she'd been saving him and Bree some time. Even if she ended up with dead ends, they were dead ends he could avoid.

"Maybe." Winter's tone felt elusive. She was holding something back. He knew her too well.

"What have you got?" he asked carefully, shooting another glance down the hall, noting a figure at the end, who'd appeared and was talking through an open doorway to someone he couldn't see.

"Nothing yet," Winter said a little too quickly, "but I

might have an angle to figure out the relationship between Kilroy and…" Winter paused so long Noah thought that the call might have dropped, "and my brother."

Noah blinked. This was new. "Really? Anything definite?"

"Not yet, but we're looking into it. How are you doing? I haven't seen a lot of you lately."

"I know, been working on this, might not make it home tonight."

Winter sighed. He hated that sigh. The past weeks had been particularly hard on their relationship, and he could tell her patience in this regard was starting to wear a little thin. How much of that was hidden resentment that he was still on the case and she wasn't, or how much was the simple fact that she missed him? He wasn't sure anymore.

When she spoke, her tone was muted. "I understand, and for what it's worth, I know a lot of what you're doing is for me, and I'm grateful. I just hope we can get this all finished and get our lives back."

Noah nodded, even though she couldn't see him. In the meantime, he still had a purpose to this call, one he'd been trying hard to ignore. He took a steadying breath, trying to work up the courage to jump in and say what he needed to.

"I'm working with Bree and Aiden, and we're working up enough evidence to try DNA testing on Kilroy."

There. It was out.

"Okay." Winter sounded confused. "Why not just get into the database? If it's official record, it's—"

"There isn't any." Noah interrupted her before she could wander down the same rabbit trail he and Bree and Aiden had been on half the day.

Silence. Dead silence. God, he wished he could see her face and know what she was thinking.

Desperate to fill the silence, he tried to explain. "No one filed DNA evidence after The Preacher was caught."

"But…t-there was a *ton* of DNA involved, t-that was the whole…" Winter tripped over her words before her voice faded mid-sentence.

"Yeah." Noah took a deep breath. "There was. There seems to have been some kind of screw-up. None of it was kept."

"Great. That's just…" She blew out a long breath that created static over the line. "So, now what?"

"You know the procedure as well as we do. We need enough evidence to convince a judge to let us dig up the old man and take a fresh sample."

Winter swore. Some of her word choices were particularly creative. When she wound down, she huffed out a breath, gathering herself before speaking again. "Can I help?"

He smiled. While the words were laced with heavy frustration, he loved how she was able to pull herself back on task even after being hit out of the blue with one more thing going wrong.

"Yeah, you can. I'm sending you a file for an e-signature. We have your DNA in the agent death files."

She sucked in a breath. "Don't call it that."

"Sorry." Noah was genuinely sorry. It had been a long and arduous few weeks, and his sense of tact was failing fast. The 'death file' was a maudlin gallows humor way of dealing with the idea that every agent risked their death every day on the job. The files that stored DNA for potential identification later were a constant reminder of that mortality. "We're going to run your DNA against the sample we found in the saliva on Sandy Ulbrich. That should at least tell us if we're on the right track. If that comes back as a positive match, maybe we can use that for an exhumation."

"Yeah. I understand." Her tone had chilled considerably. While Winter may have understood, she wasn't happy about it. "Send it over, I'll sign."

"Thank you. I know the timing is bad." *Atrocious* might have been the better word choice, but since when had murder ever been convenient?

She hesitated. "No, it's okay. I mean…it's already on file. I gave my permission to use it if necessary. Might as well."

"Just making sure all the bases are covered."

Another pause, this time longer. "How long before you have an answer?"

"Twenty-four hours or so." Noah tried to soften his voice. "What is it?"

Winter let out a breath. It sounded loud in the phone, like a tornado brewing. "Nothing, it's just…I know that Justin is responsible. You know probably with more certainty than I do, given your access to the files. But there's always a little part of my mind that clings on to the hope that somehow the killer isn't him, that it's someone pretending to be him, or… something. I guess I'm afraid that after we test the DNA, that little hope will die off and I'll know for sure that my little brother is a killer."

Noah pressed the heel of his hand into his eye. "I'm sorry, but so far, everything is pointed in that direction. All the evidence we've gathered to date indicates Justin."

Noah's heart went out to her. Winter knew that. There hadn't been much doubt for days that the chief suspect was Justin/Jaime.

"It's one thing to know it intellectually," Winter breathed out softly. He tried to ignore the catch in her voice. "But to have to admit it to yourself, to not be able to deny it even on an emotional level…it's hard, Noah."

"I know. I mean, I can't know like I've been there, but I can't imagine this is at all easy." There was a long silence between them. Oddly, though it could have been a difficult and alienating silence, there was also a healing factor to it, a refreshing and soothing affability in which Noah felt as though they were able to reaffirm their mutual support. Noah broke into the silence first.

"Sweetheart, whatever happens, remember that you were a child when he was taken, and you were injured badly. You couldn't have done anything any more than your parents could have."

"I know." The words came out in a rush. "I've heard that a hundred times. I've said it myself over and over. Maybe someday I'll actually believe it. But you'll have to forgive me if all I can *feel* right now is that my baby brother has transformed into...into The Preacher. He's..." Winter's voice drifted away.

"We'll find him. If we can get him any help, we will." It was a promise Noah didn't mind making.

"Help? Noah, he's already killed people. Even if you do find him, it's too late."

Was it? He wasn't sure. It bothered him to hear her write off her brother so quickly. The happiness in her voice that had been there when he'd first called had disappeared completely. His heart ached with the need to comfort her.

"Do you need me to come and get you?"

"No." Winter spoke the word with quiet vehemence. "No, I'm a grown-up. I can handle this. You need to get back to work, and so do I. Good luck to you."

"I'll make it home tonight," Noah promised. Even if he had to quit his job just to be with her, tonight he was going to hold her for as long as she would let him.

"Bye."

"Goodbye."

Noah disconnected the call and switched over to the forms app. He sent the form legal had prepared for her and dropped the phone back into his pocket. Mission accomplished. The deed left a sour taste in his mouth.

There were days when he hated this job. This was one of

them. But getting Justin off the streets would make it all worthwhile.

He swore it would.

14

Winter dropped her phone back into her purse. What else had she been able to say? *No, you can't use my DNA?* Of course they could. They had to. It was all right because it had to be. Plain and simple.

She took a moment before going back into the library, feeling the cold brisk air against her face, watching as people ran up and down lighted sidewalks, bags of merchandise slapping against their legs as they ducked under ribbons and holiday décor festooned on doorways. People dashing from one store to another to get presents for their families.

Their families. Noah could reassure her all he wanted, and intellectually, she knew that what happened to Justin wasn't her fault, but regardless, she was a federal agent. Wouldn't a good agent…a good sister…have tapped into those resources before now? She might have gotten to him in time to…just in time. What she might have been able to accomplish, she couldn't say, but the feeling that there might have been *something* she could have done for him lingered in her mind.

The DNA was going to prove that the killer was related to

her. Her records would condemn her own flesh and blood. That too was not the mark of a good sister.

It was, however, the mark of a good agent.

She took herself firmly in hand. People were dying. The reason they were dying was her little brother. The part of her that tried so desperately to deny the truth was getting smaller and smaller as the evidence mounted. The video he'd sent had put the final nail in the coffin, so to speak. Despite herself and the desperate need to believe none of this was happening, she wasn't able to deny it any longer.

An icy wind sliced through her jacket, promising colder temperatures on the horizon. She pulled the coat tightly around her. The chill was as much from Justin and Kilroy as the December iciness. Ghosts of the dead sent tendrils of condemnation around her, turning her blood to ice as though hoping to draw her down to the grave with them.

She mentally shook herself, drawing herself back to reality, listening to the desolate song of a Salvation Army bell ringer from a shop nearby. Standing on a street where every lamppost sported silver and blue snowflakes, and the gaiety of the holidays in every storefront, it was impossible not to feel disconnected and lost.

She discovered that her right hand had fisted so tightly that her fingernails were burrowing divots into her palm. She looked at the imprinted half-moons in surprise. There was some anger there, clearly, but most of the emotion sweeping through her was the pain of letting go, the pain of knowing that whatever happened now, her little brother was lost to her in a way he'd never been before.

This wasn't a difference of opinion, this wasn't just different values, this was murder, repeated. Her baby brother was a serial killer, and the best outcome for him now was a long time in prison. Maybe in a psych ward. The outcome she most feared for him was the same thing that had happened to Kilroy or Haldane, a cold hard death at the end of a long chase.

And if it came down to it, if she had to shoot to save a life, had to kill her own brother to ensure he couldn't hurt anyone else ever again, she would. It was that cold certainty that sent the hairs on the back of her neck to attention. She would have to. That was why she wasn't allowed to work on this case. She might hesitate, might wait too long before acting. She might hesitate when the time came to point her gun straight at her little brother's head.

I won't hesitate.

The thought surprised her in its ferocity. Of course, Winter was a good agent. It was what a good agent would do. There was nothing personal in it. She would always do what was necessary.

No matter what.

Sometimes, I really hate my job.

She leaned against a corner of the building, indulging in the windbreak created by the entrance to the library. Her phone vibrated. A quick glanced showed her it was Autumn inside the building, no doubt wondering what had happened to her. Winter ignored it, figuring to go back in momentarily. She just needed a few more minutes to...what exactly? Freeze? Deny the facts? Watch parents with small children walk past her on their way to hot chocolate and toy stores and all the things Justin never had a chance to have?

There's no point in standing out in the cold.

The library wasn't exactly the best place to meet, even if it was just her and Autumn, but it *did* have resources she desperately needed and access to a hundred other libraries. Right now, what she needed more than anything was information. The problem was, she still wasn't sure what the right questions were to ask. That was something they were still working on.

For example, was "The Preacher" related to Bill and thus to Justin? It mattered. Even now, it mattered. Noah could run the DNA for all she cared. Let the tech gurus and scientists sort out the whatever markers they needed to link her to him. For her part, she preferred old-school detective work. There was something satisfying in digging through the past to find the present.

As she watched a mother holding her toddler's hand as she crossed the street, Winter reminded herself that, in the end, it really didn't matter if there was a Kilroy dangling from the family tree. The only reason it made a difference at all was to figure out where Justin would likely be hiding.

*Right. Like you don't want...no...*need *to know this too, for the sake of your own peace of mind.*

Winter pushed off from the corner of the city where people jostled each other and mumbled Christmas greetings. She'd had enough of the holiday bustle for one day. She turned her back on the cheerful decorations and headed back into the library, her head down against the wind. The part of her that felt hope that this wasn't Justin after all stayed out in the cold. Let it freeze there, and shatter into a million pieces.

She walked as quietly as she could, but her footsteps echoed in the vast emptiness of the library. Rows of books in every corner did their best to muffle the sound, but the place was too large, and for a library, it seemed to have excellent acoustics. Every rustle of paper, every scrape of a chair over carpet or tile echoed from a thousand places, despite the seemingly fanatical attempt to keep the silence perfect.

It was like a grand mausoleum, the lives of a thousand people nestled away on shelves in neat matching containers only awaiting to be opened to tell their tales and then slid back into the wall for the next supplicant to the wisdom of the dead.

It wasn't a cheery thought, but there was little to cheer

about today. If the day was productive and Winter and Autumn found everything they searched the records hoping to uncover, Justin would be caught—or killed. With a hope she couldn't explain, though, Winter discovered that her determination to get him help only increased. If she could get to him first, talk to him, get him to surrender without anyone else getting hurt, then maybe there was something to be thankful for.

Autumn was at the same workstation she'd left when Noah called. Libraries used to carry large piles of old newspapers going back a hundred years or more. Then they spent a fortune converting all that newsprint to microfiche. The vast amount of data still wasn't done being converted when microfiche was replaced by electronic media.

Now, the entire venerable history of the great state of Virginia had been put into the care and safekeeping of a hard drive somewhere. Somehow, the reduction of the world to only so many pixels on a screen made New York seem more fragile, as if the entire past of the state would simply disappear one day. What happened then?

"Winter!" In her excitement, Autumn spoke a bit too loud for library protocol. She covered her mouth and glanced around, but other than a couple of curious glances from those around them, the *faux pas* simply rolled off. "I tried a different approach," she said in a stage whisper that was not much less in volume. "I wasn't getting anywhere with your birth date, so I thought about it a bit. After your vision, I thought that instead of looking at *your* birthday, I should start with your father's…" she waved a hand at the computer, "I mean, William Black. Look, I found his parents' marriage certificate."

Winter took a chair and looked over her friend's shoulder. "I never met them," she whispered. "I was raised by my maternal grandparents after my folks were killed, but his folks both died before I was born." She studied the record of two people she'd never met. "What am I looking at here? I can see that it's a marriage certificate, I guess what I want to know is why I'm looking at it."

"I took Bill's parents and started creating a genealogy for them." She reached to a stack of papers on the desk beside her. A quick glance showed Winter they were a collection of printouts of different documents, including several birth and census records. "One of Bill's relatives…" Autumn shuffled through the pages until she pulled one free, "is an Arthur Williams. He—"

Winter's head snapped up. "Arthur?" It was the same name that she'd heard in the vision. A strange feeling came over her, like the moment before a shudder, when the body was about to react but hadn't quite reached the point of release. It was a strange feeling, all build-up, as though she'd suddenly created a distance between the mind and what the eyes were seeing.

"I know, right?" Autumn grinned. "Before you ask, Arthur was married to a woman named Lynn, who died at the ripe age of forty-one. I can't get a cause of death since there's nothing official listed, just the newspaper clipping, and that by itself says a lot. Arthur remarried, but his new wife left him a few years later, citing cruelty as a reason for divorce. I take it that divorce was a taboo subject where they lived, and the story was that she was sent away to live with relatives, but I found the divorce decree fairly easily. Anyway, they had a place that was recently sold at a bank auction in McCook."

"McCook?" Winter echoed the name. A cold chill ran up her spine. McCook was an area she knew too well. Nestled near the Virginia-North Carolina border, McCook was where The Preacher/Douglas Kilroy had honed his preaching style to mostly empty pews every Sunday. It was also where his own father had taken his life. As an added curiosity, it was very close to the town where Kilroy was killed.

Full circle.

"Excuse me?" Autumn replied.

Winter blinked, because she hadn't thought she'd said the words out loud. She flushed, wondering how much else she'd been revealing unintentionally. "It comes full circle, doesn't it?" She retrieved the papers from the desk, shuffling them to cover the awkwardness.

"I would say that this needs to be brought to the attention of the authorities," Autumn reminded her.

Winter's head came up sharply. "I *am* the authorities, remember?" She sighed and held up a hand. "I know. I'll talk to Noah about this. He knows about my visions. At least he'll believe me, even if a judge won't."

The mention of a judge reminded her of something Noah had said earlier. What was it?

Oh yes. The details came back to her in a rush. The news felt distant and unreal now.

"I think they're going to dig up Kilroy," she whispered.

"What?" Autumn's green eyes were huge in her face. "Why?"

"Because some incompetent asshole forgot to add his DNA records into the central database. They can't make a match without some fresh samples."

Autumn shuddered. "I was part of an exhumation once, long ago. It's not something I want to repeat." She rubbed her eyes as if trying to get rid of that vision. "Is it that important? To get the order and go through all of that? Does it matter about his relation to…that man?"

Winter knew what her friend wasn't saying. *The phrase is serial killer. Like Justin.*

She bit back the retort that had risen to her lips, reminding herself that Autumn was only trying to help. How was she to know her carefully couched words were more cruel than just coming out and speaking the truth? As though Winter were too fragile to hear the truth.

In the end, she only nodded, staring at the papers scattered around the workstation. "Maybe. It would help, I think, in linking Justin to the Ulbrich killings. I don't know."

There were a lot of things she didn't know anymore.

15

For Autumn, driving her own car through the city was taxing at best.

There had been a time when she'd been more likely to take advantage of mass transit to get from point A to point B, but the novelty had worn thin quickly. And while Autumn could handle herself in a fight, she'd learned the hard way that, when outnumbered, it was still difficult to come out uninjured. Besides that, even if the locals were behaving, the trains often smelled of old beer and fresh urine.

Definitely not her style.

The problem was, there weren't a whole lot of alternatives. A girl could go bankrupt fairly easily riding around in taxis, and the bus line was tedious and held several of the same issues the subway did. In the end, she'd caved in and bought a car, which sort of obligated her to use it. After all, what was the use of having a car, paying for insurance, paying a small fortune for the privilege of parking it someplace overnight, if it never got driven?

In any case, she was thankful for her car tonight, as it gave her the privacy to think as she made her way home. The day had been long, and helping Winter was starting to take a toll mentally. Autumn pulled up to a stoplight and tapped her fingers on the steering wheel as she considered everything that had happened.

Idly, she glanced at the three cars going the opposite way across the intersection, waiting impatiently as nothing crossed the road while everyone waited for the light to change. The traffic signals seemed unimpressed by the lack of need for them and maintained a bright, challenging red that seemed to last forever.

Autumn yawned, stifling her impatience.

Her mind tugged at the research she'd done at the library and the way Winter had greeted the news that she'd been right on so many levels. Friendship aside, the whole dream thing was a little freaky, especially when it was verified through the old records. For Winter to have figured out the names of two of her father's boyhood relatives still felt odd and a little too easy.

A pair of headlights from the car behind her blinded her momentarily as her side mirror reflected the glow right into her eyes. She moved her head, using the rearview to check out the newcomer. It looked like an older model truck if the shape of the headlights was anything to go by, though it was impossible to make out the make or model in the dark using only square points of light as an identifier.

She edged her car up a few inches to escape the reflected light and decided that this was probably the nicest driver in the city, or he wasn't entirely sober when he made no move to close the space and blind her again. Not only that, the lane beside her was empty and open. Most would take that lane and whip around or use it to try to vie for lead, but he was behind her, keeping a respectful distance now that she'd moved, and for a wonder, he didn't even have his brights on.

In front of her, the light shifted to a green arrow for

traffic turning left. There was none, which only served to annoy her even more.

Her attention returned to Arthur and Lynn. She hadn't found any indication whether Arthur was still alive, though he would be rather old by now. From what Winter had told her about the vision, it didn't seem as though he would be very cooperative, even if he was still around. He wasn't exactly citizen of the year.

The light changed, for a mercy, and she checked the intersection and eased out, staying in the left lane. The pickup behind her stayed well back and in the same lane as her as they moved forward.

Arthur seemed like he wasn't going to be particularly friendly, especially if Winter's vision was at all accurate. Autumn had no reason to doubt it wouldn't be. Spooky or not, Winter had been proving her accuracy in her visions. Besides, it wasn't as though she were one to talk, given her own unique gift.

She went through a green light that changed to yellow as she crossed the intersection. To her surprise, the pickup behind her pushed the yellow light. While this wasn't exactly the same thing as running a red light, it caught her attention. Pushing a yellow was something everyone did once in a while, but usually when late or in a hurry. Oddly enough, the driver gave no other signs of being rushed. He didn't try to pass her or go around but seemed content enough sitting way behind her and going every bit as slowly as she was.

Thoughts of Winter and Arthur and Lynn vanished, and she began to concentrate on the truck behind her. She put on her left turn signal. The next street took her into a minor, residential street that wound through stacks of houses with carefully maintained trees and salted roads. The idea of some random driver belonging in this particular neighborhood was as remote as Autumn being there.

He turned with her all the same and cozied up behind her as she waited for an oncoming car to turn in front of her. She watched him carefully in the rearview as she coasted down the street, parked cars on either side narrowing the available roadway. If someone had been coming the opposite way, it would have been a tight fit.

Still, her new friend was behind her at a respectful distance. Coincidence? Not likely.

There was a small offshoot of a road to her right that went deeper into the darkness of crowded houses and brittle grass waiting for the first snow to hold onto the frozen ground. She spun the wheel at the last minute—no turn signal, no warning—making it look like she had almost gone past her turn, something anyone would do. The question was, would her shadow come with her?

He did.

Frowning now, Autumn hit the gas, speeding through the darkened roads, praying it was late enough at night that no one would be walking across the street. The headlights behind her chose the same street, and the gap between them closed.

There was no longer a question that she was being followed. Who it might be remained a mystery. She couldn't get a clear enough look at the truck to tell what kind of pickup it even was. Streetlights were sparse through this neighborhood, and he was too far back to get a clear look. Regardless, whoever it was, he or she wasn't exactly chasing her down to tell her something quite so innocuous as a warning that a taillight was out. Whoever it was meant business.

All right, then. She could deal with this.

This wasn't the first time Autumn had been on the wrong end of a creepy stalker. For that matter, she had a list of people who wouldn't mind seeing her suffer in some way.

Such was a hazard of her profession. Her work and testimony had put people in jail, and she was still fairly new at her job.

But for some reason, her mind kept turning back toward Justin. Was it because he was the bogeyman of the hour? She and Winter had been so buried in that research, she could easily be projecting. There was no reason to think the two were linked. The important thing now was to get rid of her tail.

She raced the car at twice the safe speed, turning on the brights to forestall any confusion about a crazy woman driving at high speed down a sleepy road. She took the next right, praying that it wasn't a dead end, and gunned it when she saw the opening of a road in front of her. To her surprise, she'd circled back to the same road she'd been on when she first spotted the tail.

She hit the corner on two wheels, counting on the fact that it was late and traffic on the surface street was spotty. If she sideswiped another car, then at least she would have some relative safety in the form of another driver to keep her company while waiting for the police to come and make out a report. The road was empty, though, and she wound up pushing her own car faster, running the red light in front of her.

The creep not only stayed with her, he was moving closer.

She pushed the car up to fifty and then a little past that. If someone crossed in front of her, she would T-bone him. Not one to pray, she called on a few deities anyway. The last thing she wanted to do was kill someone. As it was, if she hit a pothole wrong, or misjudged a turn, she would have to put some heavy-duty trust in her seatbelt and the airbags.

More pissed off than frightened, Autumn looked around wildly for a chance to escape. No way was she letting the bastard get to her. Whoever he was, he had more than just tailing her in mind, or he would have stayed back in a position where he could watch her without notice. This was someone who meant business. Someone who had something malicious in mind.

Which meant that this wasn't the time to try and get him under the lights to look at his face. A move like that would only give him a clear view of her as well. Damned if she was going to give the bastard a clear shot at her head. It was time to lose him. Fast.

The only options she could see were unpleasant ones. There was a furniture store ahead to the left. The parking lot was generous enough to accommodate several delivery trucks, all of which seemed to be put away for the night. She careened off the street and into the driveway of the lot, the tail following closely behind.

Autumn tucked in close to the building and whipped the wheel around hard. The car jumped and ran for the curb. Autumn aimed for the concrete posts, each one bearing a sign for handicapped parking that marked the spaces closest to the building, trusting her little car wasn't too wide to fit between. She shot through the space, the mirror on her right folding inward as it hit the pylon. She made it through, but her car bottomed out on the sidewalk as she rolled over the curb, sparks flying from the undercarriage, covering the road with glowing confetti.

The pursuit vehicle wasn't as small as her little car. The lights from the store lot had shown her something larger than she'd expected, some kind of large truck or SUV. The wheelbase was wider and the narrow passage that her car barely made it through turned out to be too much for him. He hit the brakes hard. She held her breath, her eyes more focused in her mirrors than on the road ahead. She swore when she saw he hadn't hit hard enough to get stuck. She sped along as fast as she dared, leaving his lights behind her.

It bought her some time, but the delay wouldn't hold him for long. He'd make up the distance quickly enough. She suspected he'd had to reverse and go back out the driveway he'd come in on. She had only seconds in which to vanish.

She found her solution quickly. A drive-thru liquor store. It was closed, as the hour was late, but it was also lit up brightly, vapor lights streaming off every corner except one. The very back of the store ended at a brick wall, unbroken, lacking doors or windows. While the lights showed the back of the lot in high resolution, there was a hole in the light behind the building, leaving the space in shadow.

She whipped the car into that pocket of darkness and killed the headlights at the same time. Furious now, she reached into her purse for the little gun she always carried, and waited. By this point, she wasn't entirely sure whether she was hoping he wouldn't find her...or that he would. She adjusted her grip on the cool metal, relishing the feel of the weapon in her hand.

She didn't have to wait long. An old green full-sized pickup truck raced past the liquor store at high speed, too fast for her to make out the driver or the license plate. The tires squealed as he turned a corner and then she sat in a growing silence as traffic sounds from far away drifted through the darkness, filtering through the closed windows, punctuated by the sounds of her own breathing, coming fast and hard. From the sound of her, one would imagine she'd been running at a sprint.

Autumn held her gun, willing her breath to calm. It took a long time before her heart was willing to slow down again. Minutes passed before she felt like she could put the car in drive. In silence, she eased out of the parking lot.

It's not going to be there. It's long gone.

Despite her brave thoughts, she couldn't help but think the truck would eventually find her again. It was out there, waiting for her in the shadows, much the way she'd waited for him. At any minute, it would pounce.

But the street remained deserted.

For an extra measure of safety, she placed the gun on the seat beside her and turned left, the opposite direction, away from home, at least from any direct route there.

The twenty-minute drive to home took more than an hour as she traveled the most roundabout way she could think of. The sparse traffic offered only the normal rudeness, the drivers more often than not half-drunken fools who wanted nothing more from her than for her to get the hell out of the way.

By the time she pulled into the covered garage, her breathing was back to normal and the adrenaline was out of her system.

Still, she walked to her apartment holding the gun. If her hand shook a little, that was fatigue, not nerves. She repeated that statement over and over again until she believed it.

16

She was gone.

That was all there was to it. She'd vanished in front of me like so much vapor. I sat at a stop light while it turned to green, but I didn't move. I had no idea where to go anymore. The bitch was just gone.

I backtracked my steps, followed the road back to that damn furniture store. Nothing. She was probably in Timbuktu by the time I got turned around.

The light changed back to red again, and the color only magnified my anger. Damned mindless timer with no care for its usefulness. Not a single mindless government official seemed to have any idea how completely unneeded that light was at this time of night. It didn't add a single thing to the world.

I sat there, hands drumming the steering wheel impatiently as a car pulled up next to me. The guy behind the wheel stared straight ahead, minding his own business, trying to be invisible to the night. Trying to not be noticed by people like me.

Where did she go?

I couldn't wrap my head around the idea that she was better than me. She was smarter, discovered that I was following her, knew it, knew it, knew it...

Slamming my hands on the steering wheel, I forced the thought from my mind. I needed to focus on a solution instead of beating myself up for the past.

Where did that leave me? I didn't even know which way to turn. Left? Right? Forward? Turn around? Every moment I sat still was another moment she got farther and farther away.

I felt the scream building within me, fueled by rage, frustration, even a little fear. Damn it! I slammed the steering wheel with my fist, the dashboard, my clenched hands bouncing off the vinyl, rocking the vehicle back and forth. I imagined her in front of me as I took out the impotent rage on the truck.

The dashboard was unmoved by my futile efforts. The truck didn't care. I hit it hard, solidly, until my hands stung. My fingers throbbed, yet the dashboard was still unmoved by my display. I took my knife and slashed the vinyl, stabbing the blade deep into the dash to make the truck see me, to make it hurt the way I did. When I stopped, it would wear my mark, would wear it forever.

I pulled the knife free, the blade held upside down, ready for the killing blow. The hair on the back of my neck stood up, and I turned to look into the car beside me. The guy was staring straight ahead, but I could see his eyes cheating, looking at me with naked fear. His car edged forward, his foot coming off the brake as he considered whether breaking the rules and running a red light at an intersection where there was no traffic was worth his life.

It was funny. I saw myself as I must have looked to him,

crazed and out of control. I was a denizen of the night, a lone killer loose on the street, and here he was, locked next to me, frozen.

For all he knew, his life was in the balance, and the only thing keeping him in danger was an automated light spreading a red glow across the pavement like so much blood. Useless and stupid, and there he was, transfixed by it, willing to risk his life by waiting for the light to change, regardless of what was beside him.

It was *funny*. I looked at the knife in my hand, at the sideways glances he hoped I didn't see, and I laughed. Really laughed. I pointed it at him, made little jabbing motions with my knife, and laughed so hard I nearly wet myself.

There were no other cars. There were no cops, no one, nothing, just him and me. I waved to him as sweetly as I could, and the fool *waved back*! How insane could one person be? The idiot actually waved back at me, his fingers moving jerkily on the end of his hand as though he were Miss America trying to woo the crowd.

Maybe I needed to show him that he didn't have to wait, he didn't have to obey a light, the rules the old fat men in government created. He was a man, right? He could make up his own mind.

I drove out into the middle of the intersection and stopped. *See? See? I can do* anything!

Giddy with my own power, I turned around as the light cycled and the nonexistent cross traffic got the yellow. I drove back into my own lane, facing the wrong way and stopped. Now, our doors were even with each other.

Didn't this man understand? Couldn't he see? Laws were up for grabs. He was a man, wasn't he? The law was his to follow or disregard, yet here he was, sitting in the middle of danger simply because a little law said he couldn't go.

The light was still red when the man finally understood. He took off so fast he left rubber behind him on the pavement, a stinking streak of black that smoked in my headlights. It felt good being able to help a man think for himself, to let go of the confines of his mind and act as he saw fit. It was part of my holy mission. A sacred quest. The path of the righteous.

It occurred to me then that even this was part of the holy path, the sacred mission that Grandpa had begun, the work that I needed to carry on. Everything all made sense.

I had been pursuing the wrong car. The wrong woman. I had tried to hurt my sister. Hurt her like I was hurt. I'd started by trying to take her friend away. I'd wanted her alone. Isolated.

But doing so meant I'd left the path, the true path, just to make her hurt. That was where my mistake lay. That was why I'd lost the redheaded bitch. Because she was a distraction I didn't need to bother with.

I drove down the wrong side of the road for a while. It felt good. This was freedom. Liberation. This was what the true path was, breath and life and being someone useful. Powerful even. No more stoplights. Ignoring the signs on wooden sticks that got in the way of a man driving the way he wanted.

But as I retraced the way I'd come, I couldn't help but wonder about the redhead again. I wondered how that bitch had given me the slip. What had she done? How had she gotten away? I'd been right behind her. That furniture store parking lot only delayed me for a moment or two. That hadn't been enough time for her to vanish.

I stared at the torn vinyl on the dash.

Oh no. What had I done?

My heart began to hammer as I examined every tear. Grandpa would be pissed that I'd damaged the truck. Even though it was old and falling apart and there was as much rust as paint on the body, one scratch, one dent, and he would be angry. Very angry. He would yell, and the next thing I knew, he'd have his belt off so I could feel the taste of repentance on my back.

"I'm sorry, Grandpa," I cried, terror wrapping its icy fists around my throat.

Follow the path, boy. Stop being stupid.

The words sounded to loud and so real that I looked over at the passenger seat, sure Grampa would be sitting beside me now.

Pulling over to the side of the road, I placed my hands over my face until I could calm down. I'd gotten distracted, then distracted some more. I needed to focus. Be still. Concentrate.

Follow the path.

When my breathing was calm again, I realized where I was. After a few more deep breaths, I put the old truck into drive and whipped it over into the correct lane—the correct path. Driving the correct speed, I kept my hands at the nine and three positions, eyes firmly on the road in front of me.

Doing it right. Doing it the way Grandpa would want me to.

A police car with flashing lights ran past me in the other direction, heading toward where I'd just been. I'd bet all the bitcoin in my account that the bastard at the light had ratted me out. I had made it my mission to liberate him, to empower him, and he'd called the cops on me. If I saw him again, I'd have to use the knife. Some people just couldn't be taught.

The cop didn't have his siren on. Maybe he didn't want to wake anyone. I was driving through a nice neighborhood, after all. He ignored me because I was driving like an old lady, stiff and unnatural, but in a way where I couldn't hurt the truck.

Would Grandpa like what I was doing? I thought I was being good. He said God didn't like when I was bad. When God didn't like something, Grandpa had to punish me on His behalf.

This was the holy path. This was the legacy Grandpa left for me, to carry on his holy works. I needed to be more like him. I needed to *be* the wrath of God.

"That's right, sonny boy."

Grandpa nodded at me from the passenger seat, the flap of his ravaged skull flapping as he agreed. Dead eyes sought passage to my soul, and his mouth curled up into something that might have been a smile.

But I was going about it all wrong. Hurting Winter had been my idea, my personal vendetta. It wasn't God's or Grandpa's, but mine. I'd strayed off the path for the sake of petty vengeance. I didn't need to hurt her. God didn't want me to hurt her. I only needed to kill her.

The thought of watching the life drain from her eyes was pleasing, and I felt better as I imagined it. I could still whet my desire to see her suffer, but I needed to see her suffer at the end of my blade, skewered through the heart. I needed to feel the heat of her blood on my hands as it pulsed from her body.

Grandpa looked away, revealing the hole in his skull the bullet left behind. He stared out at the street and then reached a cold hand to the dashboard to the place I'd stabbed the knife. His gaze raked over me, promising punishment. It was a look of pure hate, though he didn't speak.

That was God's mission. Grandpa's mission. I shouldn't have stopped hunting the people he couldn't finish, the people on the list I'd made, who had cheated their preordained deaths the day Tyler and Kent and I tried to reveal to them the truth at the mall. I reminded myself I would continue that mission in due time.

Winter was what was important right now. She was the only one who could stop me. It made sense then that she was the one I needed to remove so the holy work could keep going.

And I already knew where she lived.

17

Dammit.

Aiden slammed down his office phone, hoping SAC Max Osbourne felt the true extent of his irritation with him.

A damn press conference? Now? With so little warning?

Had Max lost his ever-loving mind?

Slapping the file he'd been reading before the call down on his desk, Aiden closed his eyes to make all the stacks there disappear, if only for a moment. There were times when Aiden felt as though he spent his entire life flipping through carefully assembled file folders and reading reports. Sometimes, the enormity of that and all it involved was so…ridiculous.

This report would have to be broken apart and the pieces reassembled inside a larger file. That would then be broken apart, scanned in and the original destroyed while waiting for the hard drives to fail so that all the information could disappear forever. In the meantime, what's one rainforest, more or less.

"We don't actually work law enforcement," he told the

papers he was going through. "We just kill forests and reassemble them in cellars and call it 'archived.'"

"Sorry?" Bree asked as she came through the door of Aiden's office. Noah was right behind her, nursing a cup of coffee and trying not to let out a yawn. It showed. Yawning and suppressing yawns looked remarkably similar. He also looked as though he'd slept in his suit and forgotten to shave that morning. If Aiden had to guess, he'd bet Bree had skipped the shower part as well. That should make Aiden's announcement all that much sweeter.

"Rough night?"

Noah grimaced and pulled a long drink from the coffee cup. "They're all going to be rough until this is resolved." He sat heavily in a chair facing the desk, his shoulders slumped. "This mess has been rough on Winter."

"Well," Aiden waved the newest entry into the ever-growing pile that was Justin's file, "I don't know if this will help or harm, but we got the DNA back from the saliva on Sandy Ulbrich's cheek. It looks like a good partial match for Winter's. It's not exact, only a twenty-five percent match between half-siblings, but it's consistent with half-siblings, about what we expected."

"Is it enough?" Noah took the papers from him and set the coffee on the edge of Aiden's desk. "Is this enough to dig up Kilroy?"

Aiden shrugged. "Max thinks it's enough to go public."

"What do you mean?" Bree asked as she tried to read over her partner's shoulder. Aiden wasn't sure what she'd see that he didn't. The details listed were helpful for tracking their findings, but only if you were a qualified expert on DNA research. Unless you knew what 18S rDNA was, or Triploblastica, Mesozoa, Eutriploblastica, or any of a hundred buzz words, it might as well all be in Greek. At least the conclusion paragraph at the end was pretty straightforward and written for the layman. The samples were enough of a match to indicate that Winter shared several markers with the...sample.

But was it enough?

"Max wants to go to the press with this," Aiden informed them both.

"Shit. When?" Noah handed the papers to his partner without looking. His eyes were firmly glued on Aiden to the point where a lesser man might have backed down. Aiden met the intense gaze square on. He could take it, though he noted the banked fires in those eyes, and the pain Noah was trying so hard to hide.

The concern for Winter was obvious. Hell, Aiden shared it, though Aiden wondered if a small part of Noah's reluctance to have a press conference soon was because he looked like shit. A man liked to look his best when getting his picture taken a million different ways. Especially when knowing your image was about to be disseminated around the country. Noah looked about as appealing as reheated leftovers with his scruffy jawline and bleary looking eyes.

"It's being assembled now." Aiden took a deep breath and debated sending Noah out to shower and find a clean shirt. "Sorry to spring it on you, I just found out myself."

"This is a bit premature, isn't it?" Bree asked, slipping the report onto his desk. "We're making progress on this case, so I—"

"There is a killer on the loose trying to recapture the glory days of some bastard with the name 'Preacher.'" Aiden crossed his arms over his chest. "People are dying. Justin is either the killer or he came along Sandy Ulbrich and thought he'd give her a lick as she lay dying." It wasn't like Aiden to be so sarcastic, but right then, sarcasm felt good. "Either way, we can't leave a murderer out there. If we can get the public to turn him in, fewer people get killed in the long run."

"I need to call Winter and warn her." Noah was already reaching into his jacket pocket for his phone.

"You don't have time," Aiden said. "As lead on this case, you two will be fielding questions. You need to be up there with us."

Noah was fully awake now. "I can't go on TV and tell the world that Winter's brother is a cold-blooded killer without warning her!"

"Make it quick," Aiden said, standing and heading for the door, "and see if you can manage talking to her on the run without tripping over your feet. We need to make our appearance."

He didn't like taking the extra time, as they were on a tight timetable, but it was the decent thing to do. God only knew he could use some good karma about now.

Bree looked like the proverbial deer in the headlights of a Mac truck, but she shook that off and rose, smoothing her pants as she stood. Aiden wasted no more time on conversation, and assuming that they would follow, headed out of the office and toward the elevators.

Noah arrived with his phone by his ear as they waited for the car to arrive. They piled inside and Aiden pressed the button for the first floor when Noah started talking.

"Winter? Damn." His shoulders slumped and he leaned against the railing in the car for a moment. Aiden could hear the familiar sounds of a recording stating that the owner of the phone was unavailable. "Winter, I need to get a hold of you. There's going to be a press conference. In fact, we're on our way down there now. I wanted to warn you before you saw it."

Well, that was a hell of a thing. Nothing he could do about it now. Aiden cursed himself for not thinking to call her himself as soon as he had the news. It would have been the respectful thing to do.

The elevator doors opened, and Aiden strode through the hallway to a door marked "Press Room." He stopped and looked back at the other two and tapped his watch at Noah. Time was up.

"Gotta go. I...I'm sorry." Noah hung up the phone and shoved it into his pocket, his expression that of a man wishing like hell he'd had a chance to talk to her directly. He caught up with the others just as Aiden opened the door, surprising Max, who was standing on the other side and watching the press assemble in the room past the curtains.

"Looks like a full house," Max grumbled, looking at the grim-faced men and women finding seats and the two cameras set up in the back of the room. If their intensity had anything to do with their announcements and a genuine desire to take a threat off the streets, none of the agents would have minded doing the press junket half so much.

As it was, all of the major networks were in attendance, lined up beside the locals. Serial killers were all the rage and boosted ratings. Everyone else was a third-tier reporter, either in the process of scrambling up the corporate ladder, or in the case of one graying reporter in the corner, someone on their way out. This particular individual had been coming around ever since a scandal minor enough to shunt him to the side had broken last month. Of all of them there, he was the only one worth his salt as a reporter, if he was sober enough to put the story together.

Not exactly the cream of the crop. It would have to do.

Max checked his watch and nodded to the others. "Time's up. Everyone ready?"

Aiden nodded in return, and the four of them trotted out on the small raised stage, Max heading for the podium, Aiden directly behind him and to his right. Noah and Bree stayed in the background as flash after flash of cameras left them all blinded.

The room lapsed into silence as the fourth estate waited breathlessly for the point of the meeting. Or more likely, they recognized the sooner this was over, the sooner they could get all the gory details on the air.

"Ladies and gentlemen." Max held up his hands. Not only did the gesture create full silence in the room, but it at least gave the illusion of the feds being the ones in control of the meeting. After he finished the customary introductions, he jumped right in. "There is a suspect in the murder case of the Ulbrichs and the Danville shootings." He picked up a remote and pressed a button. The screen next to him sprang to life with an image of Jaime Peterson. Jaime, not Justin. Until this was over, it would be easier for Aiden to think of him as Jaime. Noah wasn't the only one struggling to distance himself from the case.

This particular image was a screen capture from the video Winter had received. In the video, Justin had sat in shadows, half sunk in blackness. The tech team had worked for hours to enhance the photo, using visible lines to more clearly outline the face. Then, an artist had taken the photo and created a composite sketch that they were now using.

Unlike television shows, law enforcement couldn't take a shit picture and make it look like a daisy. But this was pretty close, Aiden felt sure. And if it was as close as he believed, Jaime Peterson was a strikingly handsome young man with ruffled dark hair and a strong chin that made him look like a Hollywood version of a homecoming king.

Instead of a menacing, dark threat, the sketch looked like a high school graduation picture, something posed and worthy of a yearbook entry. There was even a smile of sorts, if you didn't look at the eyes. They weren't smiling at all. Aiden was reminded of a shark as he stared into those cold, lifeless eyes.

"This is Jaime Peterson," Max was saying. "Also known as

Justin Black. Jaime is possibly related to Douglas Kilroy, also known as The Preacher. We have reason to believe that Jaime was raised by Douglas Kilroy after Kilroy killed his parents and badly injured his sister."

Faced by cameras and a half-dozen major outlets ready to report anything they saw, Aiden kept his face impassive and his emotions in check. Despite the fact that Max was detailing more than he'd expected him to, Aiden was able to hold his face neutral. He just hoped the two behind him were able to do the same thing. The most important thing in press meetings like this was to show a sense of unity. Any division or altercation in the face that the Bureau showed would be exaggerated and rebroadcast.

"The suspect is a childhood friend of Tyler Haldane and Kent Strickland, who were the principle shooters at the Riverside Mall in Danville, Virginia. The suspect may or may not have had prior knowledge of the shooting and is wanted on suspicion of conspiracy to commit murder. The two shooters, Tyler Haldane and Kent Strickland, were intimately acquainted with the serial killer Douglas Kilroy, also known as The Preacher. It is for these reasons and others that the FBI has declared Jaime Peterson one of America's Most Wanted."

What the hell?

Aiden couldn't hold his reaction. His head shot up, and he looked at Max. Remembering where he was, he turned his gaze to the press, wondering if they'd noticed. The old guy was poised, interested. Sober enough to understand what just happened. Thankfully far enough away that he couldn't hear the sudden intake of breath Aiden had heard behind him. He didn't know if it was Noah or Bree who had lost control, nor did it matter. They'd been broadsided every bit as much as he had.

Why hadn't Max warned him? Keeping them all in the

dark was a shit move. The fact that he'd dropped this bomb in front of the press was unusual for a tenured SAC. Max liked a cohesive department, and this was close to being a violation of trust.

America's Most Wanted was how Douglas Kilroy came to be called The Preacher. Just being on the list brought the suspect into a harsh spotlight where half the country lived in terror of him and the other half wanted to hunt him down for the reward, even if no one ever said anything about there being one in the first place. With this one sentence, they'd just dramatically increased the chances of Justin not being taken alive.

I should have delayed the press conference until Noah was able to get a hold of Winter. Hell, I should have called her myself. If this was such a surprise for us, it's going to be devastating for her. God, I hope she's able to talk to Noah before she sees this.

Max continued with the boilerplate speech, the whole "asking for the public's help," and "do not approach" phrases which were standard at this point. All the crap you had to say when what you really meant was, "don't let this man rest." A suspect with no safe place to hide would often turn himself in just to be done with running. That was the best-case outcome. Aiden had his doubts that it would apply in this particular case.

That done, Max introduced Noah and Bree as the agents in charge and opened the floor to questions.

The Danville shooting was like tossing chum into shark-infested waters. The press fired question after question at Max, who sidestepped them with the aplomb of a master dancer.

"Was he there at the time of the shooting?"

"How many have died?"

"Are we looking at a copycat killer?"

"What is being done to apprehend the suspect?"

"How is he related to the two mall shooters?"

Questions that had already been addressed as well as probes for new and juicy bits of information peppered the air.

Everything was part of "an ongoing investigation" and therefore "could not be discussed," one of them said over and over. Noah and Bree carefully sidestepped the relationship between one of America's Most Wanted and one of America's Finest Agents. That too was a well-done dance, close enough to the truth without actually entering it. Noah, it seemed, had a gift for saying nothing at length.

Aiden began to grow resentful, waiting until the conference was over. The fact that that bastard Kilroy could still be headline news even after his death was revolting. It was bad enough that these boys were following him and shooting up malls, but to keep him in the spotlight with the cute little names the press were calling him made Aiden more than a little nauseous.

The best curse for that son of a bitch was obscurity, to be forgotten and spend eternity as nothing more than a footnote, not rehashed over and over again. This madhouse of questions and press interest showed him what would happen if Kilroy was exhumed.

A feeling of dread lay heavily on him as he looked at the swarming mass of reporters. This investigation needed to end. And quickly.

18

"Gotta go. I'm sorry." Noah sounded harried and worried.

The voice prompt asked if Winter wanted to delete the message or save it in the archives. She hung up on the recording, throwing the phone on the bed and grabbed for the TV remote, fumbling in her haste and knocking it under the nightstand. Cursing, she fished for it, flipping the TV on before she even turned around, hearing canned laughter behind her as a sitcom came up, startling her in its intensity.

Still on her knees, she flipped through channels. There were few enough stations that cared about press conferences anymore. Soundbites were usually extracted and dangled on the evening news like sugar plums. There were a couple that still played them live, cable channels mostly, ones that didn't care overly much about ratings.

She couldn't remember which number would find her the news and wound up flipping through a dozen movies and infomercials frantically, wanting to scream that the world cared more about tight abs than things that went bump in the night. She gritted her teeth in frustration.

Mouth dry, she got up and sat on the edge of the bed, tightening the towel around her and vigorously drying her hair with another. The timing had been remarkably bad. She'd just stepped into the shower when Noah called and didn't hear her phone. By the time she found the right channel, the press conference was already in full swing.

Max took the podium, Aiden at his side. The handsome and debonair Aiden looked dyspeptic, as if something he ate wanted back out again.

Bree, on the other hand, looked like she'd just walked out of a beauty spa. As far as traits went, it was irritating to say the least. Winter had spent the first week of their acquaintance feeling like the frumpy friend whenever the two of them were in the same room. Had they not been good friends and Bree not an absolute joy to be around, Winter would have had to hate her for that magical ability.

If Bree looked perfect, then Noah was Bree's painting of Dorian Gray. Every wrinkle her clothing avoided, his took on. Her hair was styled and neat, his was...something between pillow hair and Einstein in an electrical storm. She stifled a laugh seeing them side by side like this until it registered with her exactly what Max was saying.

"It is for these reasons and others," Max stared directly at her through the television, "that the FBI has declared Jaime Peterson one of America's Most Wanted."

Winter gasped, her hand flying to her mouth. *Most Wanted?* Max had just declared that Justin was wanted dead or alive, and it didn't really matter which. Of course, that was never the intent of such a designation, but it was the net effect. Being on the Most Wanted was an invite for every nutcase with a deer rifle to go after Justin and claim self-defense in hopes of fame or fortune, or both if they could get it.

Justin. Her baby brother.

She'd said it was too late to help him. He was too far gone, had done too many crimes. But this brought it home in a way that she never would have believed. The horror that someone she knew and loved, someone from her own family could have reached such a terrible point in his life, was beyond painful. What made it worse was that he deserved it. Justin had earned the name of Most Wanted. She hated it, but she also couldn't disagree.

Her heart ached.

If she hadn't been watching so intently, she might have missed Bree's reaction to Max declaring that title on Justin. The agent covered it quickly, but it was there. Max hadn't told her, that much was clear. That meant he hadn't told Noah either. She stared at Max, seeing only his grim iron stare, and tried to suppress a shudder.

Even if Max was justified in declaring this, the news still hit her like a cold wave. She watched numbly as Noah stepped to the podium, the remote falling from her hand to the floor, and thudding against her foot. She left it, too intent on the drama playing out on the screen to care.

A small part of her mind took in the stubble and the rumpled suit, and she risked a tremulous smile that he would go on TV in such a state. It meant he cared, that he'd worked all night just like he said he would. If he'd slept at all, it was on a couch somewhere in the Bureau. Winter knew that when Noah said he was working late, it was the job that called to him and nothing else. Here was her proof. He looked like shit. On national TV.

Remembering the towel, she lifted one hand to blot moisture from her hair, trying to bite back a wave of emotion. How lucky was she to have someone in her life who was working around the clock to solve this case?

Oh, she knew he was doing it to protect future victims and not let anyone else get killed. She also knew that the extra effort he expended every day was as much for her sake. He wanted her to be able to put this behind her, to let her bury her past and not have to deal with the reality that her little brother with the sagging SpongeBob pajamas and the stupid broken giraffe dragging on the floor behind him was…America's Most Wanted Serial Killer.

She gave up on her hair and put the towel over her mouth and nose, breathing in the fresh scent of soap and fabric. For a moment, the towel became her security blanket, a tie to her mommy and daddy and a night before the bad one, the night before she found them dead in their bedroom, throats slit and blood everywhere.

That old bastard. That son of a bitch.

Why did he have to do it? Why couldn't it have been enough to kill her parents, as horrible as that was to even think. But to take her little brother and turn him into…into a younger version of himself? What kind of anger fueled something so vile, justifying the action in the killer's mind?

Douglas Kilroy had twisted an innocent child and bent him past redemption. If there was a hell, it wasn't deep enough or bad enough to suit the damage the preaching bastard had done in Justin's life.

She sent out a prayer and message to whatever gods were out there, giving every angry, injured thought to the universe. *Let The Preacher writhe in pain for eternity. Amen.*

On the screen beside Noah, an image of Justin stared, mocking her. The image was washed from the video he'd sent, but it was done professionally, illuminating his face, defining it through a very talented sketch artist. She took in the hard line of his mouth, the tightness around his eyes, and searched hard for the little boy she once knew. She gave up, unable to see him. Maybe the boy with the giraffe wasn't there anymore, as dead as her parents.

It would have been better if he had died. Kilroy should

have killed Justin. At least then she would have grieved alone. How many more families would suffer at the loss of a loved one before this was over?

Stop. Just stop. She couldn't think that way.

Something occurred to her as Bree spoke briefly about DNA and evidence on the Ulbrichs. Looking at Justin's image, larger than life, she wondered why.

Why would a mad man and killer abduct a child? For that matter, he killed my parents and left me in a coma. Why hadn't he finished the job and killed me too? Why hadn't my blood been used to write scripture on the walls?

Through the intervening years, she'd often asked why she'd been spared. Sometimes in wonderment, sometimes in impotent rage, often demanding answers from her grandparents or from God.

But for the first time, she asked that question not with rage or guilt, but with the keen analytical mind that the FBI had trained and honed in her. It was a valid question and one she needed to understand.

Why had she been spared?

Why was Justin taken?

What would make a mad man want to adopt a boy then raise him as his own?

And why this particular boy?

She got up and paced around the room, thinking hard.

Typically, men like Kilroy were lone hunters, running through the night and causing death in their wake. What made Justin so special? Was it just the blood relation? That seemed thin, a stretch, and even then, it didn't make sense.

The press conference ended. Winter stared at the screen as the images faded and the commentators stepped in to discuss what had been said. Their words felt meaningless, nothing more than a repetition of what they'd just been told, worded slightly different to make them seem astute and insightful.

Then they began speculation, hurtful accusations about Justin's family and the way he was raised. News commentary turned to idle gossip and each word twisted in Winter's heart. Sick to her stomach, she turned off the TV and went to get dressed.

The phone rang again. It took her a minute to find it, as it had gotten lost in the bunched sheets on the bed. As she fished it free, she saw Noah's picture on the screen. She couldn't deal with him right now. He was concerned for her, he cared and that was wonderful, but in order to get through the day, in order to force herself to be able to respond to the stress, she had to be cold. Professional.

Having him asking her if she was okay wouldn't help. There would be time for tears and comfort later. For now, she was Agent Black, not Winter, not Justin's sister. She was a member of the FBI, and she was proud of that.

Besides, she was unreasonably pissed at him. It wasn't logical, she knew. She was projecting her anger and helplessness onto the person closest to her, which wasn't right. Better to stay silent than say something she might regret later.

She pulled on her underwear and had her pants belted when the obvious struck. If she needed to know what a psychopathic killer like Kilroy thought, then she needed to talk to one. What would make him want to take and raise a boy? What would force someone like that to do something so different?

She puzzled these questions through, turning ideas over in her mind as she finished dressing and paused to quickly make the bed. By the time she finished she was calmer, more ready to face the world. Her phone waited for her on the nightstand, where it had been dancing in silent vibrations for the last ten minutes. When she picked it up, she saw Noah had called three times since the press conference ended. She would have to call him back, but first, there was something she needed to do. She searched for a phone number and punched it in.

"Hello," she said to the operator answering the phone, surprised that her voice could sound so calm and natural when her stomach churned and her head still spun with a thousand thoughts. "This is Special Agent Winter Black, FBI. I would like to request an interview with one of your inmates."

"Of course, Agent Black," the woman on the other end said more cheerfully than she maybe should have sounded. "Which inmate are you looking to interview?"

"Cameron Arkwell."

The silence at the other end of the phone was telling. Winter wondered how many people requested visits with the young serial killer she'd helped to bring down.

"I'll process your request, Agent Black, but I must remind you that it will ultimately be up to inmate Arkwell if he will talk to you or not."

"Tell him it's me." Winter smiled bitterly into the phone. "He'll see me just out of curiosity."

"Yes, ma'am." The woman's tone was dubious. "I'll call you back with a decision and set up a time for your interview."

"Thank you." Winter gave the woman her cell number and went to the closet to find the purse that matched her shoes. The phone rang in her hand. Noah again.

"Hi," Winter said and didn't wait for his question. "Yes, I saw the press conference. Might I suggest keeping a razor and a fresh suit at the office for such an occasion?"

She smiled more genuinely when he barked a laugh, and she could almost see him raking his fingers through his hair.

"I guess so. It was very last-minute. I'm sorry I wasn't able to warn you."

"You tried. I was in the shower and didn't hear the phone. Thank you for letting me know." She felt a rising surge of annoyance at Max and the Bureau, but the image of Noah with his rumpled suit and wild hair gave her a moment's pause and the anger ebbed a little. "I have to say, it was quite entertaining to see you all scruffy like that. I'll have to see if I can get a print to frame from one of the photographers there. To remember the occasion."

"Max suggested I go get a shave and change of clothes."

"I hope you suggested he give you a bit more notice before pulling you into the circus ring like that."

Noah took a deep breath, and she flinched, knowing what he was going to say before he even said it. "I thought I'd come home for lunch. I've missed you."

She pondered this a moment. She wanted to see him. She always wanted to see him. Would he be her undoing? Maybe not. So long as he didn't expect her to weep on his shoulder. "Can you get away? If you can, give me some warning. I'll order in."

"Deal. And Bree already said she'd cover for me. Apparently, I have a certain aroma."

"Oh yeah." Winter chuckled and the laughter felt more genuine now. "Bring that home. It'll add to the occasion."

Noah laughed too. It was good to hear. It only occurred to her then how long it had been since either of them laughed or even smiled at each other.

"Please," she said seriously, surprised at how much she meant it, "bring that home."

"I will," Noah promised. Those two words were filled with intimacy and promise, and they cut straight to her heart. There was nothing he could have said more endearing, more important than those two words.

"I love you," Noah whispered over the phone. She was wrong. That was so much more.

"I love you too."

It felt like they had been apart for a long time, and in a way they had been. She hung up and walked to the living room where yards of papers were in neatly stacked piles. She began picking them up and filing them into boxes. Each paper was neatly set in orderly rows, separated by orientation so they could be extracted and the pile recreated quickly when Noah left again.

She was going to make it up to him, make up the time she'd been obsessing on Justin. Noah was the important part of her current life.

She was *not*, however, going to tell him about Cameron Arkwell.

Not unless he asked.

19

Noah walked through the door feeling better than he had in weeks. He was still exhausted, and one of the things he was hoping he'd be able to do today was shower and change. It wouldn't replace a good night's sleep, but it was the next best thing. Right now, he'd take what he could get.

Primarily, though, he wanted to see Winter. This investigation had been a strain on their relationship. The stress wasn't just the long hours and the occasional physical distance between them, nor was it only the strain of the suspect being her brother. All of those contributed to the tension between them, of course, but the frustration of her forced inactivity was beginning to tell in different ways. It showed in the way she held herself, in the tightness around her eyes and the pallor of her skin.

She was conscientious enough to put away the boxes of papers when he got home, but she didn't try to hide them from him at least. It was as though the apartment was neutral territory when he was there, though what the place looked like when she released the cyclone of paperwork and spread it out to truly work, he didn't want to guess. Every day, it seemed the boxes multiplied, adding more documents to the mix.

He never looked to see what the boxes contained, though. To do so felt like an invasion of her privacy. She'd tell him when she found something, this much he knew. Even in those moments when she woke from feverish dreams from which she would rouse shaken and confused, he didn't appease his curiosity.

Not that it wouldn't have been easy to. When he walked into the kitchen for a glass of water or a small glass of wine, he could have very easily peeked into the boxes to find out what had left her so rattled. But somehow, he couldn't come to disturb the sanctity of her obsession.

He had to consider what he would do in her place, though it was hard to imagine what she was going through. More than anything, he had to trust her. Maybe this case was pushing her over the edge a little, but she was a highly trained agent and an intelligent, capable woman. He had to allow her to go a little off the rails now and then or she might go *very* off the rails and not be able to come back. That was true for anyone.

Still, he'd warned her that he was coming home for lunch. That warning was fair, but it was also a way to tell her to get her papers in order and covered so that the illusion of her keeping her actions separate from him, from their relationship, could be maintained.

Even with that notice, he hadn't been sure what he was going to walk into when he'd opened the door and thrust his head into the apartment.

The place was clean and tidy, with the boxes carefully placed under the table. A part of him was glad to see that. Maybe they could spend time together over lunch and *not* have Justin hanging over their heads for a while.

On the other hand, and quite perversely, there was a deep part of him that was disappointed that there was a part of her he couldn't touch, a part of her that had no intersection with him. A part that was deliberately kept separate.

A part of her that didn't trust him.

I'm not being fair.

He stepped into the room and heaved a sigh. The truth was, she couldn't trust him, not to keep evidence from the Bureau, if that was what she was doing. Those boxes, whatever they were, might contain vital clues, or they might be full of old newspaper coupons. If he didn't know, he didn't have to act on it. He preferred to not know, for her sake.

"Hi!" He stalled inside the doorway, waiting for her to realize he was there. A moment later, Winter entered the room from the bedroom. She'd showered and dressed. Not just the sweats that had been the ubiquitous uniform of the week, not even in the jeans and t-shirt she'd worn when she announced that Autumn was stopping by the other day. She was in slacks with a white shirt and a blazer. It was the sort of thing the Bureau loved their agents to wear: professional, smart, and stylish. This seemed a good sign, and he found himself hopeful that she was finally coming through the chaos back to normalcy.

She looked like she was back on duty.

Noah blinked. Not sure he liked where that thought was going. "You're looking good?" Noah made the statement a question, hoping she would tell him the reason for the sudden shift in attire. So far as he knew, Max was giving her time off until Justin was found. As unusual as that was— normally, she'd be sent to other duties—the stranger thing was that she hadn't fought it.

"Thanks." Winter smiled. She looked as though she was going to kiss him but took a step back as her eyes scanned him from head to toe. "You're not." She winked to take some of the sting out of her words. "And you're right about being ripe." She stepped aside and gave him a clear shot to the bathroom. "Why don't you take a shower, and I'll get our lunch ready?" Without waiting for a reply, she turned to the kitchen and left him standing in the living room.

Noah sighed. Still distant. He headed for the shower. It wasn't like he'd thought that they would have sex or even make out, not when she'd been so wrapped up in a decade-old grief as she'd been. But after talking to her on the phone, he'd thought she'd be back enough to greet him with a kiss, perhaps. Hell, right now he'd settle for her being willing to talk to him about her day.

On the other hand, he might have been reading too much into it. He *did* smell strongly. Of course, he'd wanted to come home for lunch and spend time with Winter, but it was Bree's and Aiden's desire for him to go home and clean up. Preferably, as Bree'd said with a wrinkled nose and wave of her hand, "In boiling bleach. And burn the clothes. They're beyond saving at this point."

He stripped in the bedroom, assuming that her remark about his clothing was a joke, but as he stripped off the shirt, he wasn't so sure. It was going to take some effort to get the suit back to fresh and pressed, the way the FBI like their agents to present themselves to the world.

The shower was hot, and the water pulsed from the showerhead, giving him an impromptu massage. He took a little extra time buried under the spray and let the heat untie his muscles and warm him from the chill of the December air.

Even drying off involved a vigorous toweling to get the circulation going. He walked back into the bedroom and gathered his dirty clothing, and was immediately repelled by the aroma. Ah, so that was what Bree meant. Of course, she had worked as long and as hard as he had, but she had this knack of always being freshly minted and pristine, no matter what she was doing. Somehow, he had only to look at a shirt for it to crumple and become ripe.

He dressed in a different suit, this one a light gray to distinguish from the dark blue. That too was refreshing and made him feel a little better.

When he walked back out into the living room, Winter was drinking a cup of coffee and searching her laptop. What had involved her on the screen, Noah couldn't tell as the laptop was turned away from him and she closed the lid as soon as he entered the room.

"Hungry?" Winter asked and with a brisk swipe of her arm gathered the computer and put it on a shelf. She then walked into the kitchen. "I thought about making us some sandwiches, but I wasn't sure what you wanted so I waited."

He forced himself not to frown. Hadn't she said she would take care of lunch while he showered? She really was distracted.

"I could take you out to lunch," Noah called after her. She turned around and came back.

"What?"

"I said I could take you out."

"Oh." Winter blinked. Yep, she was definitely distracted, her focus on something he couldn't see, but he was pretty sure he knew what it was. The unspoken agreement that he wouldn't acknowledge her independent investigation if she didn't confess to doing an independent investigation had never been more strained than it was now. He knew that look on her face, that determined, slightly distracted look. It was the same look she'd had when she was working on The Preacher case.

"Thank you." She seemed uncertain about the offer and finally shook her head. "Autumn is coming over. She called while you were in the shower. She'll be here any minute."

"She can come too," Noah offered. He had hoped for a little time with Winter, a way to reconnect and rekindle things between them, but if that meant that Autumn was part of the equation, if that was the price for being with the woman he loved, it was worth it.

"Thank you." Winter reached up on tiptoes and kissed his cheek. "But we're...we've got things we need to do."

Noah took a breath and held her gaze with his. Unspoken agreement or not, this was getting out of hand. Winter wasn't on this case for a reason, and she was endangering herself, him, and Bree by carrying on independently. He formulated the words in his brain to tell her that, to tell her that this couldn't go on this way, that she needed to leave this one in his care, but before he could get out a single word, her phone rang.

Winter looked at the caller ID and held up a finger. "Sorry, I need to take this." She was already out of the room before she answered. "Hello...this is she. Excellent, what time..." The door to the bedroom closed on the rest of the conversation.

He actually considered pressing his ear to the door, but that was petty and rude, not to mention a little childish. It was also beneath him. In any event, before he might have done such a thing, the doorbell rang.

Noah opened the door to find Autumn poised to ring the bell again.

"Oh!" Judging from the surprised look on Autumn's face, it seemed he wasn't the only one a little off-kilter. Apparently, Winter hadn't told her that he was home. "Noah! What are you doing here?"

"I live here," Noah reminded her. The words came out a little more sharply than he'd intended, but she seemed to take his tone in stride.

"Since when?" Autumn smiled to take the sting out of her words. "I thought you'd moved into the office full-time."

"It feels that way," Noah admitted ruefully. He stood aside to let Autumn into the apartment. "So, what are you two up to today?"

Autumn's face froze for a moment before she shrugged. "Honestly, I'm not entirely sure. This is Winter's day and her call, so I'm just here for the ride."

Noah nodded. So much for lunch. The selfish part of him wished that Winter would have asked Autumn to come over later in the day. It stung that she hadn't, but he was careful not to let it show.

He reached for his jacket. "Please tell Winter that I'm going to grab something on the way back to work."

Autumn looked surprised. "You're leaving?"

"Yeah, back to it." He opened the door and hung back a moment. "Listen, Autumn." He turned to look at her from the hall. "I'm glad she has someone who…" He cleared his throat. "I'm glad she has you for a friend." Noah left, closing the door softly behind him.

It hurt, but dammit, what could he do? Winter…well, Winter obviously needed her space right now. Even from him.

He might as well move into the office. Let Autumn keep an eye on Winter for him.

The best thing he could do for her was catch her brother.

Alive.

He didn't think she'd ever forgive him if he brought Justin in any other way.

20

Winter looked out through the car window as the city crawled past. Autumn was silent. She'd been silent a lot lately.

Winter pressed her lips together, seeing her reflection in the glass, grim-faced and determined. She was starting to wonder how she hadn't scared Autumn away completely—she'd become such an ogre. It seemed that she had frightened away Noah, though she'd tried to be friendlier and more loving with him.

He'd only been back a short time but had left as soon as Autumn showed up. She'd tried to call him, but there'd been no answer. Thankfully, her friendship with Autumn seemed up to the strain. The point was, she *was* there. It helped knowing someone had her back. Especially today.

Going to see Cameron Arkwell was testing the limits of that friendship. Autumn had played an important part in stopping him and saved a lot of lives in the balance. Autumn still felt the effects of being in too close of a proximity to a cold-blooded killer, though. Winter had no doubt Autumn still felt that madness that came off Cameron in waves, her special gift not even necessary for that one. The man positively emanated evil.

"It's like I can't ever get that part of me clean again," Autumn said when Winter had told her that Cameron had agreed to meet.

Autumn pulled into a parking space in front of the prison and turned off the car. They crossed the parking lot, going straight into the reception area where Autumn turned off and headed to one of the benches in front of security. This was as far as she could go.

"I won't be long," Winter promised.

"It's okay." Autumn shot her a smile, though it seemed a rather sad one. "I've got a book to read," she held up her phone to show Winter the app, "and it's warm in here. Festive even." She laughed and pointed her thumb to the corner of the room where a desolate-looking Christmas tree stood, dropping needles on the floor. "And look... there's a coffee machine. I'm good. Do what you need to do."

"Thank you." Winter felt like she should have said more, should have been able to tell her friend how much all this effort meant to her and what a good friend Autumn was being, but there were no words she could think of that would adequately express that.

Instead, she turned and took off her coat, placing it on the conveyor belt. Her badge and keys followed, and she stepped through the metal detector and waited on the other side of the x-ray machine for her items to clear.

The man behind the machine stopped the belt for a moment and stared at his screen for so long Winter began to feel a curiosity over what she might have forgotten in her coat pocket, but as she was about to ask, the belt started moving again and the coat slid free, followed by the plastic bin with her badge and keys.

She carried the coat and the badge. A guard met her at the next checkpoint.

"Agent Black." Winter handed over the badge and waited as the guard checked the clipboard in his hands. His gaze shot up to hers and then back down again, and Winter surmised that he'd seen the name of the man she was visiting. Cameron probably didn't get that many visitors. The guard handed the badge back and pressed a button. A buzzer indicated that she could proceed through the next door.

This was replayed twice more, each time the guard in question seemed surprised at her destination, but none of them said a single word to her. They simply buzzed her on to the next checkpoint, and presumably, someone else's problem.

After the third door, she was met by another guard, this one a large man who had once likely had an athlete's body but had begun letting himself go. He was still physically intimidating, even if his waist was a little thicker than it maybe should have been. She handed the badge to him, but he waved it off.

"No need, you're past security." His smile was warm and generous, and Winter took a liking to him immediately. "I'm Sully." He offered his hand, and she switched the badge to her left so she could shake it.

Some men, especially seeing an agent and a female at that, tried to overpower her at moments like this. When his hand engulfed hers completely, she braced herself for a painful squeeze, but he was surprisingly gentle, though his handshake was firm.

"You're here to see Cameron Arkwell?"

Winter nodded. "That's correct."

He hesitated a moment, like he needed to think about her answer. "May I ask why?"

Winter's eyebrows crept upward. That wasn't a question

that was generally asked at this point. The fact that the Bureau wanted to talk to a con and that con had approved the meeting should have left little room for questioning from a guard.

He held a hand up to forestall any complaint she might have. "The reason I'm asking is to know if we need to have more than one guard. Arkwell is generally easy to manage, but when he gets upset, it's best to have more than one guard present. Just as a precaution."

Winter considered that for a moment. It was the first time this option had been presented to her when dealing with a prisoner. Typically, she went where they set up the meeting, without thinking a whole lot about why she'd been sent one place or another. Her input had never actually been asked for before. "I don't believe there's a reason for extra security."

Sully nodded and waved his hand past the next door, suggesting she should continue walking. Winter looked inside briefly as she passed. There was a series of tables and chairs about the room. One table was occupied by a nervous looking young man in a prison jump suit and a distinguished if tired looking older man who was shuffling a large number of papers. Winter identified him as a lawyer, likely a public defender based on the rumpled suit and resigned expression.

The next room was a typical sterile room with a single table bolted to the floor with an eye hook built into the top.

"Tell me something, Sully," Winter said as she took a seat. She scanned the room while waiting for Arkwell. "Why are you asking about extra guards?"

Sully shrugged. "A day or two ago, one of the inmates took a tumble while being questioned. His public defender is trying to make a big deal out of it. He won't get anywhere with it, but the warden doesn't want it to become commonplace."

Winter shot the large man a questioning look, but he appeared to have said as much as he was going to. He glided back unobtrusively to the corner and vanished into the background. Winter had noted that there was no other guard watching when they arrived, but Sully looked like he could handle himself well enough. Judging by the way his nose looked like it had been broken more than once, Sully had proven his aptitude.

She had no time to consider that. A buzzer sounded and then the steel door ratcheting on its tracks announced the arrival of one Cameron Arkwell. If she hadn't known better, he would likely have been startling to her. As it was, even remembering the innocent baby-faced expression, she was surprised by just how much he looked like an overeager college student.

He was the pleasant young man next door that people just naturally trusted. He was one who everyone said "kept quiet" and "kept to himself" and "was no trouble at all." It seemed almost cliché, but people truly were shocked to find out he was a mass murderer. Which was exactly how Cameron's previous neighbors did speak of him.

His wrists were chained, his ankles too. There was another chain that ran from the cuffs to the ankles, hobbling him into taking small baby steps. Winter found breathing harder, her pulse picking up. The man had killed several women and looked as innocent as a glass of milk. If it weren't for Justin's sake, she wouldn't have come within a mile of the man. She kept her face expressionless, but she felt like her pulse was throbbing so hard that a vein in her neck had to be pulsing visibly.

"Thank you for seeing me." Winter stood. Cameron extended his hand for a shake. Sully and the guard who'd escorted him into the room grabbed Cameron's cuffs and locked them to the eyebolt in the table.

"I'd shake your hand, but…" Cameron looked at his restraints and lifted a shoulder in resignation.

Winter sat and tried to unobtrusively rub her right palm on her pants. She was nervous, on edge from being so close to him. She hated that her body betrayed her nerves and forced herself to relax.

"I don't get many visitors, so this is a treat." He sounded as if that was a mystery to him, a slight frown creasing his smooth brow. "Even if my visitor is the same one who put me here."

Damn right I did, you murdering bastard.

"I need to ask you a few questions." Her voice was calm, pleasant even. She couldn't sound too eager or he'd just play with her.

"Sure, but I have a pretty good alibi." He gestured to the walls, a self-satisfied expression on his face. "Whatever it was, I can guarantee I didn't do it."

"That's not why I'm here."

"Then can these be taken off?" Cameron rattled his chains. "I'm not violent." He said it with the straight face and conviction of a talented actor. Winter flashed onto the snuff movie Cameron had made for his father. The girl he'd murdered on camera.

"I can think of at least several young women who would disagree with that," Winter reminded him, "but they're dead."

Cameron had the grace to look ashamed. "I mean, I'm not violent anymore. Not in here. I do what I'm told, when I'm told, and we get along. Besides," he looked past her at Sully, "I know better in here. I heard about someone that was questioned, and he came back bleeding."

Rumors like that were the bread and butter of prisons; rumors that were often helped by the staff to grow in the telling. They helped hold the population to a peaceable status quo.

"We're looking for someone." Winter got to the point quickly. Her visitation time was limited. "I need some insight into the mind of a killer."

"You're a killer, Agent Black." His voice was soft, almost a singsong. His pupils dilated in excitement as he watched her closely, almost as if waiting for her soul to squirm. "I nearly died because of you and those you work with. Tell me you haven't killed in the line of duty."

She stayed in tight control. "Yes, I have. Someone has to take the maniacs off the street."

"You say that like it makes you different."

"As different as night is to day, yes," she agreed.

"But you're still human, Agent Black. In the moment, your blood is pumping in your ears and you're only acting to stay alive." His gaze dropped to her lips, her throat, her breasts. "Well, that's what it's like on this end too. We're not all that different."

Winter leaned forward, taking up a bit of the space between them. She refused to cower or back down. She smiled, almost seductively. The smile grew as his breathing grew heavier. "Let's not quarrel, Cameron. We don't have much time together. Will you answer my questions?"

His Adam's apple bobbed as he swallowed. Yes, Cameron Arkwell was a killer, but he also was still just a man. A young man who would never fulfill his fantasies again...except by his own hand or one of the inmates who offered a bit of release.

"What do I get in return?"

She smiled again. "The satisfaction of doing the right thing."

He snorted, clearly amused. "Go on."

"Why would someone who thought and acted like you want to capture and raise a child? Why would he bother?"

Cameron's handsome face split into a grin. "Oh. Baby Preacher."

Winter blinked at that name. "Excuse me?"

"That's what they're calling him, in here, anyway. Baby Preacher. That's who you mean, right?"

Winter considered the question. "His name is Jaime Peterson. We have reason to believe that he was taken as a child and raised by The Preacher, yes." She couldn't stand to hear Justin called Baby Preacher again. "Why would Douglas Kilroy do that?"

"Well, even people who kill have a desire to procreate." Cameron spoke with all the authority of a legal counsel. He might as well have been addressing the judge and jury, making an imaginary case. He'd clearly picked up a few things from his father, a former judge. "Most people want their legacy to continue on past themselves. Sometimes, it's a matter of wanting the name passed on, or there's work yet to be done."

Winter schooled her reactions. *Work yet to be done.*

The phrase sang through her. Justin was trying to complete that madman's legacy? Kilroy had babbled on about a lot of things; he wasn't called The Preacher for nothing. But could he have so infected Justin that her little brother was trying to finish what that bastard had begun?

"It's a bit of a stretch, isn't it? Thinking that someone with no training can brainwash a child into being something he's not?"

Cameron smiled at her and leaned back. Sully shifted in the background and Cameron slowly raised his hands to keep them where they could be easily seen. Cuffed or not, any change in position made Sully twitch. "Tell that to my father," Cameron said. "You may need to remind him that he has a son first. I guarantee you he won't be happy that you brought that up."

She refused to be driven off topic. "If you were him, if you were this…" Winter gritted her teeth, forcing herself to say the phrase, "Baby Preacher, where would you go to hide?"

Cameron considered this for a long time. Eventually, he shrugged and looked at Winter, bright eyes dancing in amusement. "Someplace significant." Cameron's voice was almost wistful. "Someplace I could feel closer to a dad who loved me enough to take me away like that."

"And you believe Douglas Kilroy loved Jaime?" Her throat tightened. "Do you also believe Jaime loved Kilroy in return?"

Cameron nodded. "Without a doubt. The Preacher probably fed into all that little boy's fantasies, let him know how powerful he was. Words like that from a father are like a drug." He looked wistful now, his voice softening. "An addiction. A son would do anything for the man who made him feel like the king of the world."

"But why would Kilroy choose this particular boy?"

Cameron laughed. "You're the federal agent. You figure it out."

"I will," Winter said with a certainty she didn't feel. "But I'd like to know your thoughts."

Feed the ego, she reminded herself.

"Maybe Baby Preacher reminded Daddy Preacher of someone he'd lost at some point."

"Is that why Jaime's family was targeted? Because he reminded Kilroy of someone?"

Cameron lifted a shoulder. "Maybe. Why do you keep calling him Jaime?" His gaze grew sly. "Don't you mean Justin? Justin Black? Also known as your baby brother?"

She should have known.

Prisoners had very little else to do than watch TV or read the news. While their internet searches had restrictions, all the news sites were open for any of them to view whenever they got access.

Winter refused to be baited. "Do you believe that is why he was targeted?"

"Do you mean why *your* family was targeted, Agent Black?" He chuckled when she just stared at him. "That is a very good question. One I bet you've been asking yourself for, what, thirteen years." He raised the tone of his voice, attempting to sound like a woman. "Why my mommy? Why my daddy? Why my sweet little innocent baby brother?" He laughed again, his voice going back to normal. "And the biggest question of all…why not me, right, Winter Black?"

The laugh grew louder as Winter pushed to her feet. She turned to Sully. "I'm done here."

Cameron wasn't. His laugh was crazed now, almost hysterical. "Don't you wonder why you weren't special enough for him to take you with him too? You weren't even special enough for him to make sure you were good and truly dead."

The door clicked open, and Winter strode calmly through the opening, keeping her back straight and her hands by her sides, even though she only wanted to run.

"He didn't even take the time to kill you," Cameron shrieked. "You didn't matter enough. Weren't worthy enough. You didn't even—"

The door slammed shut, cutting off the terrible words.

"You okay?" Sully asked as he jogged to keep up with her long stride.

Okay?

She almost laughed.

She hadn't been okay for thirteen years. And she didn't think she'd ever be okay again.

21

W inter shrugged her coat back on and pulled it tight around her. It wasn't the chill in the wind that made her feel frozen to the bone, it was the chill of having spoken to Arkwell. He'd seemed reasonable, personable even, and then suddenly there would come that flash in his eyes, and she could see the monster that dwelt within him.

But that was why she had wanted to talk to him, wasn't it? Precisely to probe the mind of a monster. A monster like Kilroy. A monster like her brother?

Autumn stood as Winter entered the lobby and slipped her coat on wordlessly, taking her cue from Winter. The silence was a welcome part of the friendship, a soothing balm to the phrase "Baby Preacher" that still rankled in Winter's head.

She braced against a brisk winter wind that brought a bone-chilling cold on its teeth and walked quickly to the promise of a warm car without guards or madmen or noises of any sort. It was kind of a mobile sanctuary, a refuge behind glass windows and steel.

Autumn was barely keeping up with her. Winter suddenly

realized she was setting a grueling pace and slowed down, giving her friend a chance to catch up.

"Went rough?" Autumn's face was flushed, her eyes worried.

Winter paused in the parking lot, letting the wind whip around her, and looked back at the heavy building behind them. Thick walls and bars on the windows couldn't keep Cameron's words contained inside. The memory of what he'd said swirled around her, the words winding themselves through every fiber of her being and echoing in her mind until they became part of her.

"There's work yet to be done."

The phrase stood between them. When Autumn spoke, her voice seemed guarded. "That's what he told you?"

"That Justin was trying to finish Kilroy's dream. Not in so many words. But yeah. Kind of."

Autumn considered this. "Was he cooperative?"

Winter snorted out a laugh. "I'll tell you in the car."

"Good." Autumn glanced up at the leaden sky, the wind tugging at her hair and blowing strands into her eyes. She pushed them away with a gloved hand. "It's *cold* out here."

Winter followed Autumn to the car, letting her choose the pace. She tried to talk, but the air was too cold, so she hunkered down in her jacket and tried to cover her ears with the upturned collar. Getting into the car was a welcome respite from the blowing ice winds that had sprung up since she'd been inside with Cameron.

She shivered a bit as Autumn started the car and they both sat and waited for the car to warm up a little. "Yeah," Winter said as if they hadn't been interrupted, "he was cooperative. He had some insight, but not a lot. He thought that Justin might be hiding out in someplace 'significant.'"

"Significant?" Autumn barked a laugh. "Well, that narrows it down. Wish I'd thought of that."

"You know..." Winter said slowly, her thoughts falling into place. "Not that we haven't already considered that, but the way he said it kind of triggered something. It just might narrow things down if we can get a good idea what we're looking for. I think maybe there's someone else we should be talking to."

Autumn tapped her hands on the wheel as she thought. The engine was warm enough now for the heat to be useful, and she turned it on full before turning back to look at her. "Given I have no idea where I'm driving right now, it would be helpful if you would share what you're thinking. Just who are you thinking of?"

"Arthur Williams. You said he was still alive."

"No." Autumn turned back to look out of the windshield. It didn't escape Winter's notice that she was suddenly avoiding her, refusing to make eye contact. Hiding her reaction. "I said I didn't see a record of his death, and I assumed he was still alive. But he'd be in his nineties by now."

"Eighty-seven," Winter corrected. "I got his age from the marriage certificate you uncovered. Eighty-seven isn't all that old these days when people are routinely getting past a hundred."

"Where do you expect to find him?"

"That clipping you found of Lynn Williams was from McCook. We start there."

Autumn nodded but made no move to put the car into reverse.

"What?" Winter asked. "You know you can talk to me about anything. You're obviously upset about something. Did I say something that up—?"

"No, it's not that. It's...well, it's *Cameron*." Autumn whispered the name, as though even voicing it was difficult. "I felt him when he was captured. His emotions, his...madness. I can't shake that, it's like something rancid and sticky. Just the thought of him makes my teeth on edge."

"I'm sorry I dragged you down here." She should have thought. Winter felt horrible about putting her friend into such an uncomfortable position. It really hadn't occurred to her what it would mean to bring her back into close proximity with the murderer. "Take me back. I'll go and find this Arthur Williams. This is—"

"No."

"Yes." Winter spoke louder over her friend's objections. "This is *my* problem. Justin is *my* brother."

"No!" Autumn said again, shouting this time. "This place…*he* wouldn't bother me so much if I wasn't good at reading other people's emotions. You *need* me. Who else can be your private lie detector?"

"You really don't need to do this," Winter said softly. It wasn't that she would mind the company, but Autumn's reaction to just being in the same building as Cameron surprised her. From the look of things, it had surprised Autumn too, or so it seemed. "I'm just heading to talk to an old man, I think I can manage that safely.'"

"Eighty-seven isn't all that old, remember?" Autumn shot back and turned her head to meet Winter eye to eye. "Besides, old man or not, pulling a trigger doesn't take a lot of youth. You need backup."

Winter opened her mouth to protest and closed it again. "Maybe I do. Just…if you're sure."

"I'm sure," Autumn said, looking more confident this time. "It was just bringing up the memories of Cameron, it was…I was back there again, and it'll take a while for that to go away." Autumn slipped the gearshift into reverse and backed out of the slot. "So, where to?"

"Let's get something to eat." Winter pulled out her phone. "You found a record of some property that was sold. There has to be documents, escrow or something involved. A paper trail. Let's see if we can get someone who knows where Arthur is. I'll start making calls while you find us a place to eat." She looked back at the prison, watching it recede in the mirror as the road ran straight from it. It felt like they were making a break from the penitentiary.

Winter busied herself with the phone as Autumn drove. *Someplace significant.* She'd put that off as being obvious, but something about the phrase stayed in her head, something that she wasn't seeing. She was missing something important, something that should make sense and wasn't.

"Someplace I could feel closer to a dad who loved me enough to take me away like that."

That chilled her. More than the phrase "Baby Preacher." More than anything else he'd said. As if kidnapping and murder were expressions of love. The bastard murdered her parents, murdered *Justin's* parents, and that idiot called it "love?"

Yes, Cameron had his own issues with his father. It was a strange and unwholesome relationship to say the least. But to think for a moment that Kilroy *loved* Justin? That was enough to make Winter want to throw up.

A cooler, more professional part of her mind took over. What Winter thought of that idea really wasn't the issue here. It wasn't her they wanted to find. It was Justin. What if Cameron's point of view—no matter how strange, no matter how twisted—was the same point of view Justin had? What if that was what *he* believed? After all these years...he had been so young when it all happened. Could he have forgotten? Could he truly believe that psychopath worked from a sense of love?

She reminded herself that Justin called him "Grandpa." That was telling enough alone.

My god. What if it's true? What if Justin does love his so-called grandpa? And if so, what is he trying to prove to him?

She looked up from her phone to watch as the scenery flew by the window. It looked cold and empty out there, every field barren and brown. The chill of winter had its cold hands on the landscape, but there wasn't any snow, not yet. There was no cover to protect the ground from the artic winds that scoured the earth and withered the plants. Dry leaves rattling in the wind.

She was already looking forward to winter's end.

Shivering, Winter dove back into her phone. She needed to find Arthur Williams. She only hoped he was still lucid enough to remember when she did.

22

Winter stared at her phone in consternation, then looked through the windshield again at the house. The address on the phone matched most of what was on the farmhouse just over the front door, but one of the black plastic numbers had fallen off. Were it not for the figure eight shown in paint that was slightly less faded than the rest of the house, she would have thought she was in the wrong place.

As a home, it needed a great deal of work. As a relic, it was loaded with what could charitably be called *personality*.

"I guess this is the place." Winter sighed and shook her head.

Autumn seemed fixated on the house. She'd been a little jumpy since Winter had found an address for Arthur...no, since they'd left the prison. She still hadn't shaken off Cameron's influence. Winter inhaled deeply, trying to push down her worries and concerns and let her breath out slowly.

She'd been taught various ways to calm herself over the

years, although none of them seemed effective lately. It was getting harder and harder to pull herself together, and right now, she had a role to play.

Autumn and whatever angst she was nursing would have to wait until after they were done.

It was getting late in the afternoon, and Winter wondered how he would react to having a couple unannounced visitors drop in. She considered coming back tomorrow when it wasn't so close to dinner, and would have, had time not been running out. She needed to find Justin and quickly.

"Maybe I should do the talking," Autumn said, catching Winter off guard. Winter's face must have shown her surprise because Autumn hurried to explain. "I can get a read on him. Think about it. If I can touch him, I might be able to pull more information than you can. And you are a little close to the case."

A little close to the case? How could she be anything but close?

Winter bit back an angry response, struggling to appear reasonable. "No, I think it's better that I do this. I'm Bill's daughter. Even if it's not biologically, I'm still family of sorts."

"I get that." Autumn nodded in agreement, a little forcefully maybe. "I just think you're…too close."

Winter debated asking her friend what the problem really was, why Autumn was acting so unnerved. Frankly, it was something that needed to have been talked about earlier, why Autumn was willing to go through with this when she was already on edge. "Reading" someone like she did would only make it worse. She opened her mouth to say something when she saw the flicker of a curtain at the window. They had been spotted.

Well, that decided it then, didn't it? They were out of time.

Winter opened the door and got out with Autumn close behind. All the way across the yard, Winter was wary. Between the disrepair of the home and the unkempt aspect of the yard, the entire place put her back up. Several over-grown evergreens crowded the house from the left, long sweeping branches reaching out to embrace the structure as if holding it up. For a moment, she found herself thinking how anything could be hiding back in those trees and longed to pull her weapon.

Look at me. I'm actually jittery.

Winter forced herself to breathe, to let go of the anxiety and get the job done. She and Autumn stepped onto the wooden porch at the same instant. Perhaps it wasn't the best approach, given the way she felt one of the boards give way under their feet with an ominous sound. She pointed the cracking wood out to Autumn, who stepped around it dain-tily to take the lead.

That should be me...

Holding back never felt so hard.

Winter kept her distance as Autumn knocked on the door, which creaked open almost at her touch. A thin, elderly man blinked at them through the doorway as though he hadn't seen daylight in some time.

She knew him. Just as her mind had taken her into the vision, her mind now knew this was the terrible man in that dream.

In front of her, Autumn took a breath, but the jolt of recognition Winter experienced from her vision was too much for her. There was no way she could stay silent. Winter plowed ahead before Autumn could so much as get a word out.

"Hello." Winter smiled as brightly as she could. The years had not been kind to Arthur, but she could still see the younger man of her vision in his eyes. These were suspicious eyes, unfriendly and cold. They seemed to bore a hole through her.

"My name is Winter Black," she said through the open door. "I'm Bill...William Black's daughter. My parents were killed when I was still young, and I don't really know any of my relatives, so I'm now trying to make connections to their extended family, and I wondered if I could talk to you?"

She ignored Autumn, who was shooting silent daggers into the side of her head. Not only was this completely contrary to the plan, but it was an entirely different approach. To be fair, the family thing had only just occurred to her as the door began to open. She would apologize to Autumn later.

The old man glared at each in turn, giving one assessing gaze at a time. It was as though he was looking at a couple of horses for sale and found them wanting. It was a wonder he didn't ask to check their teeth.

His upper lip curled, and Winter was convinced that he was going to slam the door in her face. She was reaching for the badge in her back pocket when the old man backed out of the doorway, disappearing into the depths of the house. He left the door open behind him.

Winter and Autumn exchanged glances. Arthur didn't seem like a cooperative witness, but the silent welcome was probably as good as they were going to get.

They stepped into a front parlor that had seen better days. Old tattered furniture and stacks of random auto parts and old pizza boxes lined narrow walkways. Arthur swept his hand over the couch and sent bolts, screws, pens, paper-clips, stale-looking M&Ms, and other small bits of garbage to skittering under an old chest of drawers that had more than one drawer missing, giving it a toothless grin.

"Have a sit." Arthur fell into an easy chair, dark brown

with random silver lines where peeling duct tape held the upholstery together. Winter balanced on the edge of the couch and Autumn perched next to her. Arthur peered down his nose at them both.

The glasses that balanced precariously at the end of his nose indicated that he was trying to get her in focus, probably through bifocals or progressives. The thickness of the lens indicated it was likely a fruitless endeavor. The look he gave her was narrow and more than a little disapproving.

"You're Bill's girl?"

"I am." Winter smiled, trying to give off a harmless, even innocuous vibe.

"And who's this?" He turned the basilisk gaze toward Autumn.

"This is Autumn Trent." Winter made the introduction awkwardly. Autumn was beyond pissed off right now, she could see it in how she sat ramrod straight.

Still, she had to give her friend credit for being a professional. She only nodded and even smiled as she looked around the room. "Hello. Lovely place you have here." To her credit, she only faltered a little on the words.

"It's a shithole," Arthur growled. "Too damn old to clean, too damn old to do much of nothing anymore. No one comes by to help, so I get to live in this filth. If I was a dog, people would be coming from all over and throwing money at me to get me out of the squalor, but an old man, more or less," he waved off the world at large, "no one gives a good damn."

Winter swallowed hard, thinking hard how to best get what she wanted. So far, this wasn't going at all how she'd thought it would.

Maybe that was the problem.

She leaned forward, elbows on her knees, hands clasped. "I was hoping you could tell me a little about my family."

"What about them?"

"Well, like I said, my parents were killed when I was young."

"Yeah." Arthur made a hand gesture indicating she should get on with it. "You did say that. A couple of times now. Something you want me to say about that? Offer you a tissue?"

"No." Winter shook her head. "No. I just want to know about my family. The other members of it. The ones I haven't met."

"Not many of them worth knowing about." Arthur crossed his legs and reached for a can of beer at his side. "No one's got any money, no one gives a damn about anyone but hisself. Don't know what you'd want out of any of them."

Autumn raised her hand. "Do you have a restroom I might use? It was a long drive."

Arthur gave the impression that he was debating whether or not to allow Autumn to use his bathroom. "It's no good," he finally said. "Water pipes burst 'bout a month ago. Too damn old to fix 'em." He considered her a moment longer and relented. "There's one upstairs, second door on the left. That one still works. You can use that."

"Thank you." Autumn stood and smoothed her pants, rubbing her palms on the fabric. Autumn's special talent involved touching someone to read them, but there were those who didn't need to be touched, people like Arthur who emanated their personality so much that even Winter could feel it. It must have been very difficult for Autumn to be in the same room.

"Bill adopted me when I was a baby," Winter began. It didn't matter so much what she said, as long as she kept his attention on her and not Autumn. She was giving Autumn the opportunity to explore and dig around Arthur's house unencumbered. "I don't really know anyone on his side of the family."

"Not surprised." Arthur took a healthy pull on his beer can. "Bill always did think a great deal of himself. Too good for the family, he was. At least to hear him say it."

"Too good?" Winter knew she was being sidetracked, but her father had taken on near mythic proportions in her heart after his death, and to hear someone like this man denigrate him got her back up, and she seethed at the accusation.

"Sure. After he married that knocked up woman, he never kept in touch, ignored his family. Even kept you and your brother away." He gave Winter a hard look. "If you want to know the reason we've never met, he's it. Got hisself a city job, started making decent money. A year or two later, he bought a fancy house in the city. None of his kin never heard from him again."

Well, she'd gotten that question answered at least. This side of the family somehow knew that Jeannette had been pregnant with Winter before she met Bill.

"Was there a relative named Douglas Kilroy?" Winter tried to keep the question as light as she could but knew she'd failed the moment she saw Arthur's eyes go black and cold.

Arthur looked as though he'd been kicked. He sat bolt upright, the beer can crashing to the floor, spraying its contents on the bottom of the chair. "I think it's high time you two got the hell off my land." Arthur levered himself out of the chair and headed for the steps much more quickly than he'd been able to walk earlier.

Autumn's up there.

Winter was hard on his heels, not sure what she was going to do, but she'd do whatever it took to get Autumn safely out of that house.

"Mr. Williams," she called to his back. "We'll leave. I just—"

Need to get my friend.

The words stuck in her throat as the old man reached behind a door. Within seconds, he turned, and she was staring down the long black eye of a rifle.

23

Autumn took one look at the toilet and decided that even if she did have to use it, she probably wouldn't. It was a bright orange-red, probably a result of rust in the pipes, and it looked like it hadn't been cleaned in her lifetime.

She shook her head. There are some things that needed to be done no matter how old a person was, and apparently, Winter's long-lost relative was unaware of this. Or simply didn't care.

This is one long-lost relative who should never have been found.

Her sensitivities were driving her mad just by being in close proximity to the man. The feelings he gave off were bitter and hard. He struck her as a man who lamented his lot in life and comforted himself with the knowledge that it was all someone else's fault.

Realizing just how little time she had, Autumn got straight to work. She started by looking in the medicine cabinet above the sink. It was filled with prescription bottles, the sort of pills one might expect to see in the house of a man pushing ninety. Most of them were medicines she was unfamiliar with.

Then there was Pipamperone. She knew that one. It was an antipsychotic, used to treat schizophrenia. The bottle looked full, but the fill date on it was over two months ago. Which meant only one thing in her mind. The man wasn't taking his pills, and his schizophrenia was being left untreated.

Not good. Better hurry.

She looked around a bit more, noting the rag on the towel rack, the evidence of mice in the small dots of droppings around the base of the sink. The sink itself had a brown stain down the back of the bowl where the water had dripped, the rust and iron in the water wearing away and staining the porcelain. The threadbare bathmat in front of the sink had an aroma when she stepped on it. She winced and retreated hastily, trying hard not to breathe in too deeply.

He's right about one thing. If I had seen a dog living like this, I would have taken it to a shelter.

The room next to the bathroom was the master bedroom —at least that was what she presumed. It held a queen-sized bed, though the sheets were in disarray and needed a good washing with a gallon or two of bleach. The rest of the room was clean, a stark contrast to the rest of the house, though she spotted the remains of a mouse still caught in a spring-loaded trap behind a dresser. It was difficult to guess how long it had been there, so mummified were the remains.

A small wooden box sat on the bedside table. The box and table were polished and shone like they were brand-new, which made her think they, at least, received some attention. She looked over her shoulder to be sure no one was coming and crossed the bedroom to the box.

The box was an ornate thing, carved of wood so rich the

grain gleamed as she held the object up to the light. Autumn didn't know one wood from the next, but that piece could have been oak or walnut, or more likely given the ornate beauty, something more rare and expensive. Mahogany maybe.

She slowly opened the lid, and her eyes widened at the contents. Inside was an old, faded picture that looked like it was taken in the sixties or early seventies. A slim, beautiful woman stood in front of a car, a large tank of a vehicle with raised fins. The car was definitely fifties, but the woman wore a halter top and shorts. That put it late sixties or so.

The woman had a kind smile, though her eyes were sad. She leaned against the driver's door of the car, her bare feet crossed at the ankles. In the background was the house Autumn was standing in now.

She could feel an immense sadness with the woman's picture, a heaviness that made her want to weep with the weight of it. Under the picture was a necklace, a fine gold thread from which hung a charm in the shape of a heart. There was a single stone in the middle of the heart, a bright stone like a diamond, though it might not have been a real one. The woman in the picture was wearing that very same necklace.

"You put that the hell down!" A snarl tore through the bedroom, and Autumn dropped the necklace into the box. She raised her hands and turned to see the wrong end of a rifle pointed directly at her head. Arthur had the gun butted up against his shoulder, his finger on the trigger. "What the hell you think you're doin' in here?"

Autumn spread her arms, showing she was unarmed. The box was in her right hand, the photo in her left. "I'm sorry, I just..."

"You just what?" Arthur snarled. "You just thought you'd

rifle through my house? Looking for drugs? Looking for money? Answer me, damn you!" He rattled the gun, and Autumn could see his trigger finger turning white on the knuckle.

"That's enough." Winter's calm and clear voice was a counterpoint to the barrel of the pistol she placed against his head. She cocked the hammer and Autumn could see the sound registering in Arthur's mind. Even so, he held the rifle on Autumn for such a long moment that she honestly believed she was going to die in this shithole.

Arthur let go with the right hand, letting his left grasp the barrel as he lowered the rifle. "I ain't got nothing worth stealing. That bauble you got, it's not real. It's a fake stone. I only got it for personal reasons."

"Yeah, I could tell you were a real sensitive guy," Winter spat, her voice cold as the wind outside. "Wanna get his rifle?" She nodded in Autumn's direction.

Autumn set the box on the table and put the picture back inside of it. She left it open and carefully took the rifle from Arthur's grasp.

"Ain't nothing but a .22." Arthur gestured at the gun. "I use it for rabbits and the occasional coyote. Wouldn't have done nothing so long as I didn't hit her head. Just hurts like a sommabitch."

That wasn't true, but most country folk considered that gospel since that type of rifle was underpowered and the bullet was small enough to be stopped by bones or muscle. At close range, however, with a careful shot, the results could be lethal.

Winter relented a bit on her pistol, pulling back far enough to allow her room to walk around Arthur. "This will hurt a hell of a lot more than that." She reached across her body with her left hand, the gun never wavering. She pulled out her badge and flipped it open. "Agent Black, Federal Bureau of Investigation."

"Ah hell." Arthur spat on the floor. "A damn Fed? I should have knowed that bullshit about you being Bill's daughter was nothing but a lie. You told it well enough, though. I can usually spot a lie."

"It's not a lie." Winter closed the wallet, gripping the badge in her left fist. "I am Bill's daughter. I also happen to be an agent."

Autumn returned to the box and grabbed the picture to show to Winter. She carefully lay the rifle on the bed.

"That's Lynn." Winter let out a low whistle. "Just as I saw her."

"That's my wife," Arthur spat, hunched in on himself now that he'd been disarmed. "How is it you know her name?"

"Dad was very fond of her." Winter was making it sound as if Lynn had been a common topic of conversation between her and her father, though Autumn would bet her next paycheck that Auntie Lynn hadn't been brought up around the Black family dinner table.

"All I remember about your old man was a noisy little brat who got into everything. Left a raging mess wherever he went."

"Charming." Winter frowned, her weapon still trained on him. "Now, tell me something I don't know." Autumn could tell that her friend was losing her patience with the old man. He reminded her of Kilroy and had about the same respect for others as The Preacher did.

"Like I'm an old man and don't give a shit what you do to me, *Agent* Black?" He put as much vitriol and bitterness into her title as he could. After eighty-seven years, he had a great deal to put into it.

"You're not so feeble as you like to pretend," Winter countered. She spoke to Autumn, but never took her eyes off

Arthur. "You should have seen him running up the steps. He took them like a man half his age."

"Half my age?" Arthur laughed. He dropped his hand to his side, seemingly no longer concerned with the gun pointed at his heart. "Half my age is still twice yours."

The math was a little off, but his point was made. Besides, this was getting them nowhere. "Tell me about Douglas Kilroy."

"What about him?" Arthur sneered back at her.

"How is he related to the family?"

"Just 'cause he killed your daddy, don't mean—"

"How did you know that?" Autumn interrupted when she saw Winter go pale. "How did you know he killed Bill?"

"Didn' you see them papers downstairs? It was in them, big news for a while. But this is family news." The old man stressed the word "family" as though it should frighten her. "Your daddy thought he was too good for this family, that don' change the fact that he *was* family. We all knew. We knew when it happened, and we knew when Doug was kilt too. Family is family."

Winter gasped and the gun rose in her hand.

"Did you say anything? Go to the police?" Autumn asked, trying to ignore the way Winter was gaping at the old man, a look of betrayal and hurt on her face.

"O' course not. It's a family affair, no business of theirs."

"My parents were murdered. My brother was kidnapped!" Winter surged forward, only just stopping short of putting her hands on the old man. Autumn tensed, ready to interfere. The last thing they needed was an assault charge.

"And now you want revenge. Is that it? Doug's dead. You want vengeance on the family? Then shoot me. I'm just an old man, no one will know or even care that I'm dead. No one but the family. The family will know I'm dead and who kilt me."

"Will they care?" Autumn asked.

Arthur shot her a look as though remembering for the first time she was there. "Nope. Not a damn one of them. Didn't care when Bill and his wife died neither. That's your family, Agent Black. That's the legacy you come from. Happy?" He looked mean enough to spit as he stumped over to a straight-backed chair and sat heavily. The wood creaked in protest, wobbling precariously. "You can leave any time."

Autumn put her hand on Winter's arm. The rage and hate that came from that contact was almost too much for her to bear, but she shoved that aside and applied gentle pressure on Winter's arm. "Please," she whispered. "He's right. It's time to go. You got what you came for."

Winter's jaw tightened and a vein stood out on her forehead. "Just tell me this." Her voice was calm, reasonable, though the emotions she gave off were anything but. "Did the *family*," she put a great deal of sarcasm in that word, "know *before* he killed my parents that he was about to?"

"Don't think so. I didn't." Arthur sighed, leaning forward so that his arms took the weight of his upper body. "Look, you going to leave or not?"

"But you knew after. You could have saved years of pointless investigation and all that pain. Kilroy could have been behind bars and my brother safe." Her nostrils flared. "Did you know that bastard took my brother?"

Arthur stayed silent, but his glare matched Winter's. They were locked in a silent struggle of hate and bitterness. Autumn grasped her friend's arm. It was getting harder to keep pushing aside the feeling that came with touching this hurting woman.

The gun wavered in Winter's hand. "Who was Kilroy to your precious 'family?'"

Arthur stared at the unsteady barrel and seemed to reach a decision. "My cousin. Doug was an only child, and his father was my uncle. He was a dick. Called himself 'Preacher.' Tried to make his son into one by beating him until he could give a sermon in his sleep. But Doug's father, he had brothers and sisters, most of them died fairly young, it was a rough life during the depression and lots of young people never got old. About half got old enough to squeeze out their own kids. My daddy was one of those. Too bad too. He should have died when he was a baby."

"Then you would never have been born," Autumn said in the silence that followed.

"Win-win, ain't it?" Arthur grinned, yellow and brown teeth showing age and neglect. "Hell, there's a few people that wouldn't mind that, if I ain't never been born."

"I bet." Winter bit off the words through a clenched jaw.

"We're family," Arthur said and shook his head sadly. "Biology or no, you're just like your daddy, too good for the likes of us. Maybe won't no one care about one old man, more or less, but family won't be ignored. Like me or no, there's a price to pay. You hurt the family, the family will take its due."

"Like the 'family' took its due with my little brother?"

"That was Doug's idea." Arthur met her gaze squarely. "You wanted to know why nobody told the cops? Because Bill, he rejected us all. He held himself and his precious bride and her get above us. The family wrote him off. Doug was family. Bill weren't. Not no more."

"Why wasn't I taken?"

Arthur regarded her for a moment. "You wasn't never part of the family. You were hers, not his. She was fat with you when they met up. Don't matter what some piece o' paper says, you ain't blood." He grinned a little. "You ain't under the protection of the family neither. That badge might help a bit, but you're as easy to dispose of as anyone else." He nodded to Autumn. "Just like her. Now, I'd take it kindly if you'd get the hell out of my house and leave an old man alone with what time he has left. I've had about enough of *family* for one day."

24

Noah stood in the cemetery as the backhoe moved into place. Two men in yellow reflective vests watched as the driver of the equipment maneuvered the heavy machinery around tombstones, leaving deep tread marks in the sod. There was no way to get the big thing into the cemetery without driving it over the top of some of the graves, and the thought of that made Noah wince more than a little. Someone somewhere was going to take offense at the callous disregard this particular operation required.

It wasn't superstition, or how the dead would take to be being driven over. This was a matter of respect not only for the dead, but for the living. For the survivors who still looked to their departed with love and memories of their time on this earth, these tracks would be an abomination. To come and see the final resting place of a parent—or worse, a child—and find large tread marks ground into the grave site seemed to be a terrible thing for someone already mourning.

Yet, there was no other practical way to do it. The two men in the yellow vests leaned heavily on their shovels. Noah wished something so simple as gravediggers might have been an option, but it was December, and the ground was frozen. It would take the power of a diesel engine to break through the hard surface and tear up the earth over The Preacher's grave.

Noah had a single superstitious moment, however, as the thought that maybe Kilroy wasn't in the grave after all and was still at large, his death being faked. It was a foolish fear, and not founded in reality.

But then this was The Preacher. They were digging up the boogeyman. A serial killer was the stuff of nightmares.

To think that after all this time, to exhume his body and find the box he was buried in empty was too creepy and too much like a Hollywood version of The Preacher's life to not consider it.

Noah shuddered and crawled deeper into his coat, hands buried in the pockets, the lapels turned up to block the wind from his neck. Bree stood next to him, but her attention was fixed on the digging in front of them. The shovel of the backhoe skidded on the top of the grave, the ground refusing to give way under the teeth of the machine.

"It's worse than I thought." Marcus Finch, the general manager of the cemetery looked at Noah from under a knit hat with a big red poofy ball on the top. His round, florid face was bright red with the bite of the wind, but the bright bulbous nose spoke more of a heavy drinker than frostbite. "It's going to take a little time to pull him out of there."

Noah nodded absently.

"Why don't we wait in my office?" He gestured with his head toward the small building at the center of the cemetery, the little puff ball on his cap bouncing wildly.

"We're required to be here to witness the exhumation," Bree said. Noah could see the haze of her breath as she spoke. His own breath came out in little plumes of steam.

For some perverse reason, the order from the judge for

the exhumation of one Douglas Kilroy had been delayed long enough for a cold front to roll down from Canada and freeze the city. Of course, it would be the same day that he had to stand outside for an hour or more while a grave was being desecrated.

With a partial match from Winter, it was now all but certain that it was Justin's DNA that was left at the scene of the Ulbrich murders. Justin's claim that Kilroy was his "grandfather" was unsubstantiated, and since there was no DNA report filed in the server, this was the only way to be sure. To be brutally honest, finding out if there was a connection between Justin and Kilroy wasn't going to be much help in locating Winter's brother, but to establish a blood-relationship might be helpful in other ways. At least that's what he told himself.

Lately, he'd been telling himself a lot of things. Starting with the idea that when Justin was caught, there was bound to be a lengthy trial and one that would be under close scrutiny. Of course, he wasn't so naïve to think the boy would be taken alive, but for Winter's sake, he liked to make the leap of faith.

Carrying through that particular fantasy, he had to think about whether there was a chance of not convicting him. If there was any doubt in a jury's mind that Justin wasn't the killer that the Bureau knew him to be, then a preponderance of evidence might just be enough to bring them around to his eventual conviction.

On the other hand, a genetic relationship to someone who was clearly insane might be what a good defense attorney might need to plead insanity and get Justin life instead of the death penalty. In most cases, it wouldn't have mattered that much if the suspect had gotten either sentence. Either way, the killer would be off the streets for the remainder of his life. But for Winter's sake, Noah wanted

Justin put away nice and safely, preferably in a way that kept him alive and well. It was tough enough on her for her brother to be a hunted man. Putting him on death row for the next decade would be brutal.

"Really?" the manager was conversing with Bree, asking her exactly how this was supposed to work. Noah supposed this kind of thing didn't come up often, then almost laughed on the unintended joke. He wasn't sure anyone would appreciate the darkness of the humor. The manager shook his head to whatever she'd replied. "Why do you need to watch? They're not opening the casket here, are they?"

"No," Noah answered for her. "They'll take him back to the coroner's office and then bring him back and rebury him later. The testing will need to be done there."

"Then why freeze your ass off out here?" The rotund man rubbed his thick mittens over his face.

"Just need to be sure that all the procedures are followed," Bree answered. She ducked her chin back into the thick rolls of her scarf and pulled her heavy coat up a bit farther. She had a hood lined with some kind of fake fur that looked toasty as well as fashionable. Her face was framed in a gray fox faux fur that somehow made her smile seem brighter, like a burst of sun in the clouds.

Of course, what he'd given was the diplomatic answer. The truth was that they had to watch to be sure no one swapped bodies during the process. It had been known to happen. There had also been instances where the person to be dug up had already been removed from the ground. Grave robbing still happened even in modern society.

Noah stamped his feet and shifted, trying to find a way to warm himself. The men with the shovels seemed to be just as cold, but as the backhoe was able to break through the frozen level of the ground, they jumped in to continue the work. Dig too deep with the machine and the coffin would be compromised, so they had to do the fine-tuning work to dig out the box without shattering it.

"Call me if you need anything." The manager waved a thick mitten and turned on his heels, heading for the warmth of his office and the coffee he'd offered them when they'd arrived. Apparently, he'd decided there was no particular reason for *him* to wait.

"I almost envy him," Bree said through chattering teeth.

"Being able to get to a warm place?"

"No." Bree shook her head and flashed him a mischievous grin. "I was referring to the extra weight he carries. I could use a little of that insulation right now."

Noah barked a laugh. "It's not that cold." He regretted the words the moment he'd said them as the wind picked up and the chill it carried grew worse. He glared at the sky, wondering what he'd ever done to Mother Nature.

"You had to say that." Bree dug deeper into the warmth of her jacket.

"I have an idea." Noah turned toward her. "One of us has to be here to oversee this. But only one."

"You're my partner." Bree shook her head in immediate protest. "You freeze to death, so do I. That's how it works."

"What I'm suggesting is that we take turns. Go inside for twenty minutes, warm up and get some coffee in you. Then come back out and spell me while I go do the same for twenty."

Bree looked at him for a long moment before grinning. "Okay. That actually sounds reasonable." She turned and half ran to the building the manager had entered only moments before. Noah grimaced against the wind. He would have smiled but his face would probably crack under the strain. He pulled the collar of his coat more snugly about his face and resolutely stared at the activity in front of him.

The two men with shovels, at least, had their physical

labor to warm themselves. For a moment, the wild thought of grabbing a third shovel and helping out just to keep from freezing played in his head, but there were rules against that. It was his job to stand and try not to lose body parts to frostbite.

The driver of the earthmover was cocooned in the cab of the machine, the heat from the engine keeping him warm enough that the windows on the cab steamed up. Periodically, Noah could see a bright red cloth wiping at the glass from the inside. It took a few close observations to realize that the driver was using a scarf to remove the condensation.

He pulled the collar higher and ducked his head to try and get his ears covered. *Lucky bastard.* He needed to get a scarf. Maybe a hood like Bree had. Maybe just a backhoe where he could sit in the warmth all day no matter where he went. It would make parking a bother, though. At least it would for other people. He wondered at how hard it would be to shift a Prius with that bucket on the front.

Noah smiled at the little fantasy, stamped his feet and began walking in circles to keep the circulation going and warm himself as best he could.

At least it's too cold for the press. There was that dubious benefit to the biting wind chill. The judge's order to dig up Kilroy was public record, so there had to be someone at city hall who monitored the paperwork and reported it to the press. Police news almost always made it to the papers. It seemed odd that, so far, the frenzy he'd expected at the grave site hadn't materialized.

That didn't mean it wouldn't. It was likely that the morning papers would be filled with half-truths and suggestions, which just meant that the eye-witness reporting would be done from the comfort of a warm office somewhere by reporters who didn't want to risk frostbite.

Noah stopped and stared. They were almost done. It had

taken a lot less time than he'd thought it would. They were bringing thick, heavy straps to the site, which were being lowered from the shovel of the backhoe down into the open grave. A few minutes later, the two workers guided the machine and brought the straps back up, presumably having wrapped the casket.

As he watched, Bree reappeared beside him. "Your turn." She looked at the grave site and shook her head. "Sorry I took so long."

"It's okay." Noah said, never taking his eyes off the activity in front of him. "I really didn't want to listen to that manager anyway."

"I can understand that." Bree snorted in amusement. They both fell silent as the two workers scrambled out of the grave and gave the thumbs-up to the backhoe driver. The shovel lifted and Kilroy's casket dangled from the end of it, swaddled in two straps.

The backhoe swung gently and lowered the remains on a wheeled platform, guided by the two workers who unstrapped the coffin and slid it into a waiting hearse.

"You know," Bree said as the rear door of the hearse closed on its cargo, "we could have used one of those core sample drills and gotten DNA from that. So much easier."

"Procedures." Noah chuckled at the thought. He turned and headed to the car. Now that the show was over, he was anxious for the warmth and wanted to get out of the wind. "Always procedures. And red tape. The right way is always the one that costs the most."

Bree followed and climbed gratefully into the car. The engine had cooled, and it would be a while before the heater would blow anything but ice, but it was good to be out of the wind. They tucked in behind the hearse and began following it back to the coroner's office.

"At least we don't have to be there for the opening," Bree pointed out.

"If it's going to be this cold," he said under his breath, "at least it should snow. The city looks so much better under a blanket of snow."

They followed the hearse in companionable silence until they reached the medical examiner's office. There, they signed over the body to the coroner so he could do his gruesome work.

Within minutes, they were free to go.

To wait.

To learn if Justin Black, in addition to being Winter's half-brother, might also be the spawn of a devil.

25

I t was me. My picture. My image. Me. On television, large as life. My name. My face. Everything. I couldn't believe it.

I'd been so careful. I thought I'd been completely draped in shadows. I thought I was hidden in the darkness, but they'd somehow shone a light on me, brought me out into view, and there I was for all the world to see.

They knew my name. They knew me. Jaime Peterson. They called me Justin too, but that was no longer the real me. I hadn't heard that name for a long time. Grandpa would get mad if I used that name. I once had a friend named Justin at one of my schools, but I had to stop being his friend because Grandpa refused to let me even say his name.

If I ever forgot…I shuddered at the memories of Grandpa having to teach me a lesson. The pain. The terror of not knowing when it would end or how bad it would get.

The humiliation, followed by the love Grandpa showed me when it was all over.

Grandpa loved me. He told me so, and he told me that

making me feel good even when I'd been bad was how he showed that love.

I closed my eyes, trying to shut away the thoughts. Or was I trying to savor them? I couldn't always be sure.

It was so confusing. The Bible said that a man should only be with a woman, but Grandpa said that didn't count with us. Because we were special. I was special, and he needed to show me his love.

Opening my eyes, I immediately wished I hadn't because my face was on the television screen again.

They were saying bad things about me.

They said bad things about Grandpa too. He never minded that. Grandpa said that no one understood his mission. "No prophet is accepted in his own country." It was a verse he quoted from the book of Luke. He never cared what people said about him. He didn't care what people said about me. "Turn the other cheek, forgive seventy times seven."

But my name. That mattered. That mattered a lot. No one could know that other name, that old name, that boy I used to be. That bad boy who thought he was better, that weak boy who moaned and cried and wet himself.

I wasn't him. Not for a long time. I was Jaime Peterson, and now everyone knew. Everyone. Everyone knew I was the disgrace, the spoiled boy, that...*Justin.*

This was bad. Lots of people watched television. Lots of people. My neighbors watched TV. I could see the glow flicker in their windows. They lived in RVs, they lived in trailers, they lived in tiny little places with large televisions that glowed all night long.

The TVs were bigger than their bedrooms, bigger than the RVs they lived in because the television was more important, more consuming than their lives. Each of them saw my face. They knew me too. They knew where I lived.

And they were connecting the dots right now, even as I sat there, trying to think of what to do.

I had to stop thinking and start acting. I needed to move.

Right now, I could imagine each of them picking up their phones and calling the police to tell them that they knew where I lived. They knew the kind of truck I drove too. Hell, most of them probably knew what I'd had for breakfast that morning. Nosy bastards.

They'd be wanting that reward too. Two hundred thousand dollars for my head, dead or alive.

The Judases. Every last one of them.

All this because I left a message for my half-sister, because I just had to set the record straight. I told her the truth just the way Grandpa told me, and this was because I told her that she wasn't my father's daughter. In so doing, I'd failed. I was about to be caught. I was about to fail to carry out Grandpa's mission because of my own arrogance and stupidity.

I hated myself.

I couldn't breathe. The air left my lungs in a single whoosh, and I couldn't breathe anymore. I was about to be caught. I was going to jail and there was nothing I could do about it.

They were talking about me on the television. Reporters crawled over each other to shout questions about me, about Grandpa, about the mall. I couldn't move. The lack of air in the RV made me unable to move, the questions they asked, the warnings that people shouldn't approach me. That I was dangerous, that I was deadly and needed to be put down like a rabid dog kept me from leaving. Kept me from running.

Running?

That single word brought me back to reality.

Why would I run? Why should I?

I needed to be smart, yes, but it wasn't running. It was planning. Following the path.

I wasn't the one in the wrong, after all. I was doing something important. No, more than important. Something *worthy*. Something that Grandpa had started and would have finished if not for my si...my half-sister. She was the one who had gotten in the way. She was the one who defied the natural order, the way things should have been. She was the one who caused all of this, the one who had gotten Grandpa killed. She was the one who needed to pay for her crimes. Not me.

Suddenly, I could breathe again. I could stand, I could scream, I could swear, and I could fight back. I reached for the gun, for Grandpa's pistol.

I watched them clustered around microphones, smug and full of sin and themselves. A woman was in the back behind them, answering questions as if she had a right to tell anyone anything about me. The bottom of the television said "Agent Bree Stafford." Who cared what her name was?

I'd lost Winter's redheaded friend. She'd out-drove me. The shame and anger from that made me shake. I hated her. I hated the woman on the television, the one who told the group of salivating, slathering reporters who I was—my other name, the bad boy name, the name no one was supposed to know—and all because I had to tell the truth to that bitch of a half-sister. The half-sister who'd simply slept while I'd been taken away.

I didn't remember pulling the trigger, but the gun went off. The television exploded as the bullet slammed into the Bree woman's head. That silenced her. Somewhere, a dog started barking, but it was hushed quickly. Someone didn't want attention from the killer next door with the bad name.

I grabbed the keys and a box of bullets and ran for the truck, then stopped. I needed to think. After I calmed down, I knew I needed to play this smart. I needed to move or else I was a dead man. I was about to be captured, betrayed, because I'd been stupid, stupid, stupid. I should have just killed Winter and let her die instead of trying to make her fear me.

Ignorant. Foolish. Stupid. I shouldn't have sent the video. Shouldn't have told. Shouldn't have, shouldn't have...

After hooking the RV up to the truck, the tires squealed as I pulled out of the complex. They all knew my truck. It was Grandpa's truck, and when he saw the dashboard, he'd kill me. Except he was dead. I reminded myself of that. He was *dead*.

Only death didn't matter. He'd still be mad. Mad from beyond the grave. I had to hide it. I was driving fast, looking for somewhere to get rid of the truck. They knew the truck. They *all* knew the truck. It was Grandpa's truck, and they would find it. I had very little doubt of that.

Simple enough to solve. I needed to replace it. If Grandpa saw the damage to the dashboard, he'd kill me, leave me hanging off the bed with blood pooling under my head. He'd done it before. He would again.

I needed a truck with a good dash. Something without holes. If Grandpa didn't see the holes, he wouldn't be angry, and he wouldn't slit my throat and watch me as I bled out. He'd liked watching that.

He tried to save the soul, but he still liked to watch the body die. "If by the Spirit you put to death the deeds of the body, you will live." He said those words a lot. Grandpa liked that verse.

I needed to find a new place to park the RV, and I had to find a new dashboard. I threw the gun into the passenger side seat and hit the gas, careening around the corners and through the streets. The police were everywhere. Everywhere. They would have already gone through my trailer, seen the bullet hole in the television, and they would know that I had killed the Bree woman.

There was nothing left for me now but a single thing, one thing I could do and no more, no less. Something I had to do before Grandpa killed me. I had to make things right with my half-sister. I had to make it right.

It had been a private message, after all. I told *her* that she wasn't any part of my father, that she wasn't part of the family. She took that and spread it all over the television and spread the old name, the bad name and now everyone knew that name, the bad boy name, and it was all her fault.

I had to take my gun and set things right with her. I had to put a bullet in her head like I killed the Bree woman. All that was left was Winter Black. She had to die. All of this was her fault. She killed Grandpa, she betrayed me, she made my message public and *she...*

She gave my bad name to the world. And now the secret was out, the terrible secret Grandpa would beat into me at night, the horrible, awful lie about who I was.

Everyone knew the horrible secret. Grandpa wouldn't hurt me if she was dead.

But I had to be careful. If I was dead, if I was caught, I wouldn't be able to finish Grandpa's destiny.

Stop. Don't worry about that now. I had to do this much. I had to end Winter Black.

Then I wouldn't be that other boy. She wouldn't be related to me anymore, and I could be a part of the family. It was her that kept me from my family name.

I would find another dashboard. I would take one from the street, the gun would help me. All I needed was to put a bullet in the driver, and I would have a clean dashboard and Grandpa would never know.

Then I would put a bullet into my half-sister.

Freedom. I would be free then. I would finally be part of the family.

Taking in a calming breath, I let my mission settle into my bones.

It was the right path. The good path.

I would end Winter. End her. End her. End her.

Smiling now, I realized I felt better than I had in weeks.

Grandpa would be so proud.

26

The weeds were overgrown. They covered the ground and shot through the boards on the stairs. They had shriveled in the cold, becoming nothing more than emaciated tendrils of brittle, brown grass. White paint peeled off the building like birch bark. The arctic air that whipped through the empty field around the building shook loose an old flashing on the roof that spun to the ground below. Winter watched it fall, all reflection and blinding light under the cold, gray sun.

There were windows...several windows that lined the side of the building. Stained glass, heavy panels of it, surrounded by thick trim boards that framed them like works of art in a gallery. Bright red tiles on the roof gave way to the occasional bare spot where dark oil paper shone through where the tiles had fallen. They had slid in a small cascade down the roof to crumble on the ground by the downspout.

Three steps led up to a wooden door with a cross carved into the surface. Just to the left of that, a large rectangular addition jutted from the edge of the building and rose above the roof to a belfry. A second cross stood atop that, defying the water-color wash of gray and orange skies while reflecting the dirty white of clouds that raced their shadows over the ground.

The belfry was long muted. If it'd ever had a bell, it had fallen or been taken and melted down for scrap. One of the stained-glass windows was broken, a jagged hole beside a surprised looking rendition of a saint. Sharp pieces of glass jutted from the lead traces that separated one illustration from another, and bright slivers of glass scattered on the floor.

Inside the church, pews lined up reverently, facing a small raised area, though the pulpit had tumbled and lay over the steps between the parishioners' seats and the nave. A great tapestry hanging behind where the preacher was to have stood was tattered and rent, not from vandalism, but from age, rot, and neglect.

Whatever image might have once been in the weft of the great cloth was now buried in dirt and disuse. Leaves scattered and chittered across the floor like flat vermin as the wind found the small hole in the window and played with the trash and leaves and dust, flinging them in all directions. The wind shifted direction again and the detritus stayed locked away in the church.

A handful of refuse chased from one corner to another, depending on the whims of the winds that breached the hole in the glass. Inside too, there were signs that the weeds were coming in through the walls and the floors, and perhaps the floorboards were no longer the most dependable. Dry rot had its fingers in the grain and was sapping the strength from the boards.

"Oubliette." Winter whispered the word, letting it fall before her in the cold air. "A place of forgetting." Historically, the word referred to a place where prisoners would be thrown and then ignored, left to starve or die of thirst. In such places, even their bones were left undisturbed, forgotten, and abandoned. Left to rot.

Winter stood facing the defiled pulpit, leaves dancing over her boots and beating against her ankles. The boards under her feet felt like sponges, and she felt them give and flex with every step.

The floor was beginning to collapse as muted sunlight filtered *and focused through the bright lens of the windows. Light heated the wood in the day and then left at night so the floor could cool again. The expansion and contraction from the temperature change gave the appearance that the old place was taking long, slow breaths. Inhale under the sun. Exhale under the stars.*

Cold air seared Winter's lungs, and her breath plumed in front of her as she turned around. The door behind her, the wooden double door with the cross deeply inscribed, swung open and the angry winds burst into the room, gathering up the dead and brittle leaves and cleansing the moldy space. It pressed the leaves into flight, and they ran up the sides of the pews and slammed into the old pulpit. They chittered to each other in dry tones of old parchment or small, sharp claws trying to gain purchase on hardwood floors.

She began to move without moving. Her feet stayed still, her body erect and tall, but she slid along with the leaves and the trash as the wind blew her out of the building.

The doors slammed shut the second she was tossed onto the grass, and she turned to watch the church close itself up even as it spat her out. As the sound still echoed through the trees, Winter knew that the church had locked itself. It would have bolted the doors closed if it could.

She could sense rather than see the hole in the window plugged, the doors and windows reinforced against her reentry. The church did not want her to return.

Even as she stared at the building, she felt something else. Something bad. Something cold, like a knife in her side that pressed against her flesh and dug in harder, deeper, forcing into her skin until it tore at her flesh. She would have cried out if she could. Instead, she was forced to suffer in silence as the blade ripped into her, parting muscle and shattering bone, driving deeper and deeper.

She looked up at Justin. He was smiling at her as the knife tore through her heart.

Winter jerked awake, her hands reaching to grab the

dashboard and the door handle.

Dashboard.

As her fingers dug into the hard material, her heart raced. Her breathing was shallow, causing pain with each inhalation. Autumn was watching her, a look of pure concern on her face as she held a tissue under Winter's nose. With shaky fingers, she took hold of the tissue herself, giving her friend the best smile she could muster.

I'm in a car. Autumn's car.

She swallowed and willed her erratic pulse to slow. Her breath caught, and she found her hand reaching for her side where the knife had pierced her so deeply, but the skin was whole. Unharmed.

"Another vision?" Autumn's expression ranged from concern to curiosity and something more...fear. Fear for her friend. She knew about Winter and her visions, but this one was different somehow. It was one thing to be told that someone experienced visions, another to witness the person have one.

Winter couldn't speak. There were no words yet for the place where she'd been. Winter couldn't remember diving this far into a vision, to get lost in it so deeply she'd forgotten where she left her body. Coming back from this one was going to take a lot longer than most. It was so *vivid*, so real that she might as well have been transported to that old church.

That old church. I know that church. I know that place.

Winter nodded, though she was still as much in the church as she was in Autumn's car. "Yeah, it was a deep one." She checked the tissue and realized the bleeding had stopped, then looked owlishly through the windshield. Several cars were parked at a curb with a small building in front of them. "Where are we?" Her voice sounded rusty from disuse.

"It's okay," Autumn assured her, pulling out additional

tissues along with a bottled water and a small container of hand sanitizer. "We're at a rest stop. I pulled over when I saw that you had...fallen asleep. What did you see?"

Winter flipped down the visor and cleaned herself up before looking over at her friend. "A church."

"A church?" Autumn was clearly trying to understand what Winter was saying, and more importantly, what she wasn't. "What church?" Her demeaner changed with each question.

Despite still being a worried friend, she slipped into the professional Autumn, the woman who was an expert at analysis and ferreting out the truth. Winter might have found that to be comforting were she not so rattled. At least one of them had to be handling this like a professional.

"The old church..." Winter pressed her fingers to her temples. She tried again. "The old church outside of McCook. The one that gave The Preacher his nickname."

Autumn gasped. "Oh." Her fingers beat a restless tattoo against the steering wheel. "But that's been abandoned for a long time. And the local police have been keeping an eye on it since Kilroy was killed. If anyone had been there since, they would know about it. Wouldn't they?"

Winter had her doubts. It was off the track, and the local constabulary would have to make a special trip to check on it. In those rural areas, an approaching car could be seen for miles.

Winter took a deep breath. She knew she'd sound crazy but...why not tell Autumn the rest? Of everyone she knew, Autumn was the one who would understand more than anybody else. If she couldn't trust her, who could she trust?

"I saw Justin."

"Wait...in the church?" Autumn twisted to look at her, her expression fierce. What followed was a series of questions, meant to clarify, winnowing out every last detail right down to the way the weeds grew up through the steps. This was Autumn doing what she did best, what she was trained for—examining the witness to glean as much information as possible.

In some ways it was helpful. On the other hand, whatever comfort Winter had taken from her attitude evaporated in the frustration of trying to remember every last excruciating detail from the vision. No matter how many answers she came up with, Autumn pressed her for more. The fact that it was as irritating as fingernails on a chalkboard to someone still trying to come back from a vision didn't matter. This was necessary. Winter knew this and tried to answer Autumn's questions as fully as possible.

In the end, there was little left to say. She went through the whole thing again in detail, ending with Justin's part in it. "Well, no. He wasn't exactly inside the building. It was after that, I felt this presence."

"But you're sure the presence was him?"

"Yes," Winter insisted, wondering just how many times she was going to be asked the same question. "I saw his face."

"Wait a minute. I thought you said you felt him. You *saw* him there?"

"Yes, I mean…" Winter held up a hand for Autumn to give her a minute. She'd forgotten this particular detail until this very second, proving Autumn's battering at her had a point, after all. "At first, I only felt him, but then…later, I saw his face."

Autumn seemed to consider this a moment. "Where was he?"

"I think…maybe just outside…I'm not sure." Winter tried to place Justin in the vision.

"So, Justin wasn't *in* the church?" Autumn asked, her expression intent.

"No." Winter wracked her brain to get the memory of the

vision clear. "No, I was already ejected by the time I saw him."

"Ejected?"

Okay, maybe she hadn't been explaining things well. Winter went back over the feel of the place, the idea that the church was alive, the feeling of being unwelcome. When Autumn fell silent, Winter thought she'd run out of questions, that maybe they could leave now, but Autumn still had not moved the car.

"What was Justin doing?" Autumn asked again.

"Pushing a knife into my side," Winter said ruefully, "very, very slowly. He cut into my heart." She gripped the place to show her where and almost winced, expecting to feel pain. The memory of that was so clear, it still came as a surprise to find herself uninjured.

She pulled up the edge of her shirt. Her mind and memory told her that there was a large gash in her side, between two ribs, but the flesh was uncut. She remembered the sensation, though, the feel of the blade as it cut through her.

"Where are we?" Winter repeated. She had her mind firmly rooted in the here and now, and "rest stop" wasn't the answer she was looking for.

Autumn seemed to understand. "We're about an hour outside of Richmond."

"Autumn..." Winter looked at her hands in her lap, being the one to look away so Autumn wouldn't have to. "I can't... it's not fair to ask, but—"

Autumn held up a gloved hand, a small smile playing on her lips. "Do you know how to get there from here?"

"Thank you," Winter whispered and sat back in her seat.

It seemed imperative now that she go there. The church would welcome her or not. Either way, it was where she needed to be.

27

Bree's hand on his upper arm startled him awake. It showed the concern she had for him that she woke him so gently. There were others in the department that would just as soon blow an air horn behind his head. Not for the first time, Noah was thankful to her as a partner.

Now, if she would only go the hell away and let him sleep.

"Noah." She spoke each word gently but clearly, almost like she was soothing a small child. "Go home. Take a nap. You know the DNA won't be back for a while, and you don't need to babysit putting Kilroy back into the ground. You only needed to be there for digging him up. Get some rest while you can."

He considered the possibility for a long moment. Laying down on something that was long enough for his frame was tempting, to say the least. The couch he'd been catching naps on wasn't all that comfortable. Either the arm dug under his ankles, or he had to fold himself into the confines of the seats, meaning he wasn't able to sleep on his back or stretch out. The idea of being in a real bed, if only for a few hours, held a certain appeal.

Bree had an excellent point too. The test results wouldn't be back anytime soon. They'd only delivered Kilroy that morning, and it wasn't yet three-thirty. Even with a rush, it could take up to twenty-four hours to hear anything. There were no new leads, and going through the old Preacher case files *again* was wholly unappealing. Noah nodded and carefully set the reports of the Ulbrich murders on his desk and reached for his coat.

The shower earlier had done wonders for his mood and he was probably a lot more acceptable to those around him. An early night of it would likely sharpen his mind and let him see something...anything in those damn papers that might lend a clue to Jaime Peterson's whereabouts.

"Yeah." Noah nodded slowly. "Maybe I will." His thoughts, though, were with Winter.

He imagined her look of surprise when he came home. Maybe they could have an early dinner, then they could lay in each other's arms for a long sleep afterwards. She needed rest as much as he did, and they needed some cuddle time together. In his mind, he wanted to take her thoughts off Justin for a short time, and if cuddle time led to something more sexual, he wouldn't turn it down.

It wasn't even the sex. Just being together was important, reconnecting to each other, not letting the pressures and strains of the investigation get the better of their relationship. It was already strained, but it was strong. They just needed to be reminded of that, both of them.

He looked at the couch and had a sudden urge to spit at it, and even cleared his throat to start a good old loogie. He turned the noise into a deep-throated chuckle and shook his head.

"What?" Bree smiled, wanting in on the joke.

"Nothing." Noah wasn't sure he could explain it. Sleeping at the office had become a symbol, a marker for the entire process of hunting down Winter's brother, and he was anxious to be done with it, even if only for an hour or two. "But if I'm going to have to take care of myself, then you do too. You're working as hard and as long hours as I am."

Bree looked up through long lashes at her partner. "The difference is, I make this look good." She laughed at her own joke, but that didn't make her any less right. Still freshly pressed, not a hair out of place, clean clothes, she looked like she'd stepped out of a spa and was ready to take on the world. As long as she'd been his partner, he could never figure out how she pulled that off.

He shot her a quelling look.

"All right!" Bree laughed, her hands in the air to signal her surrender. "I could use a good long soak in a tub. I'll see you back here in, what…?"

"Let's call it a night," Noah said suddenly. The urge for a normal life was overwhelming, and Winter needed him to be there for her, something he'd not been able to do for a while.

Bree looked at him for a long moment and then smiled. For the first time, he realized just how much she probably needed this too. "Good idea. See you in the morning."

"Good night." Noah draped his coat over his arm and threaded his way through the maze of desks and workers on the phone or tapping away at their computers.

Daylight almost came as a surprise. He'd seen so little of it lately, especially when it was also connected to going home. Being out in the open, despite the nasty chill in the air, was energizing all by itself.

The drive to the apartment was un-notable for a city commute. It consisted of the usual close calls and idiots who wove in and out of traffic to get three feet farther ahead at the next light. There was an old pickup that tailed him for a while, but as soon as there was an opening in the next lane, the truck sped by him and flashed him a finger for his troubles.

"Go ahead," Noah grumbled to the driver as the truck accelerated out of sight. "I'm armed, try me." He half-heartedly waved the kid off and headed for his exit.

He pulled into the parking lot next to the apartment building. The bright overhead lights were just turning on in the gathering twilight, but they covered the parking area well enough. Not that it mattered, usually. The building was in a good neighborhood and there hadn't been any incidents reported in the area since long before he'd lived there.

It was easy to let your guard down. Even professionally trained agents relaxed when they got home. He parked, got out, and headed for the front entrance. Only something felt wrong. Off.

Noah stopped halfway there. There was a distinct feeling in the air, a sense that things had changed, shifted subtly. Just then, he wished Autumn and her sixth sense was there, just to get her feeling on the parking area. Something was just *wrong* somehow.

His hand slipped inside his coat, and he half pulled the pistol from the shoulder holster before thinking better of it. There was nothing there, no threat, certainly not enough to justify a shooting and all the paperwork that would go with it. He was being paranoid, having spent too long studying boogeymen. He was starting to see things that went bump in the night. Hell, even late afternoon.

He stuffed the gun back into place. The echoes of traffic and the occasional finger of wind that found its way between the buildings to stir the paper cups and scraps of paper on the ground bounced off the walls and back to him, but that was all he heard.

There was no breathing, no footsteps, no indication that

anyone was near him. In the end he shook off the feeling and resumed walking.

And stopped.

Damn it, there it was again, that feeling.

Noah spun, gun in hand, pointing it in the direction he'd come from.

Nothing. There was no one there, just rows of cars stretching away behind him, one after another.

I'm jumpy. I really do need some sleep.

The gun went back into the holster, and Noah berated himself for being so easily spooked.

A front door opened, drawing his attention. An elderly woman carrying a cane nodded to him as she stepped onto the sidewalk and headed down the line of cars. He smiled and nodded in return before jogging to his door.

Paranoia.

It wasn't paranoia if it was true.

As he reached his apartment, it occurred to him that he hadn't called Winter first to let her know he was coming. She was probably poring over her papers. Walking in on that would be breach of the unspoken agreement. Not that it could be helped, he was already there, and he wasn't about to turn around now.

He slid his key into the lock and twisted the knob with a little extra rattle, not wanting to startle her.

"Winter?" He waited in the doorway for her to answer, wanting to give her extra time to put her papers away.

He heard nothing. No rattle of papers, no shifting of folders. When he looked around the corner, the boxes she presumably kept her research in were still neatly stacked under the end table. The living room was in pristine condition. He'd been gone for hours, yet nothing had changed.

"Winter?" He called her name a little louder, wondering if maybe she was sleeping. Maybe she'd felt the fatigue of the day the way he had and was taking a nap. But the apartment *felt* empty. He knew that she wasn't home without having to go through and look.

He pulled his cell from the inner pocket and pressed the speed dial for Winter.

"Hi, this is Winter, I'm not around right now, leave a message." The phone beeped, followed by the long, expectant silence of a machine waiting for the human to do what they were supposed to. He hung up and scrolled to Autumn's number, but the result was the same. Neither of them were answering their phones.

He didn't like it.

After leaving messages for them both, he placed the phone in his inner pocket next to the gun. He blew out a breath, looking around the apartment, going from room to room and ending in the bedroom. His gaze fell on the bed. A king-sized bed with lots of room. It was all very appealing, but without Winter, he was looking at just another nap.

Dammit all to hell.

No longer tired and more than a little miffed, he took another shower, unsure of when he'd next get that chance. After changing into a fresh suit, he went to the kitchen and opened the fridge. He threw together a ham and swiss on wheat and grabbed a can of soda. He didn't wait around to eat it, wrapping the sandwich to eat in the car. Within moments, he was out of there, carefully locking the door and testing it before heading back to his truck.

As he walked, that feeling returned, and the hair stood up on the back of his neck. He turned in a full circle, examining every space and shadow.

Nothing.

"Stop being stupid," he told himself. Maybe he just needed to turn his ass around and go to bed.

Better yet, he'd go back to the office and find this motherfucker.

The sooner this investigation was over, the better. Maybe they'd all get back to normal again? Maybe he wouldn't be jumping at shadows like some pussy on crack.

With nothing else to do, he headed back for the Bureau. There was work to be done, and he was willing to bet Bree hadn't left, nor had she ever had any intent to do so. When it came down to it, she was every bit as bad as he was.

He maneuvered the truck down the row and back out to the street.

It'll be over soon.

He clung to that thought all the way there.

28

Aiden sat upright as Noah Dalton passed the open door to his office. "I thought you were taking the rest of the day off," he called.

Noah swerved, changing direction to come back and lean on the open door. "I did."

Aiden grinned and relaxed back in his chair until it creaked. "Power nap? Took you all of five minutes?" He gestured to Noah's clothing. "At least you look better."

"Couldn't rest. Winter wasn't there. I have no idea where she's gone."

"Are you worried about her?" Aiden tried to keep the question casual, but what he really wanted to know was whether or not *he* should be worried about her. Going missing without mentioning plans to Noah was unusual. Despite the fact that he'd asked Autumn to keep an eye on Winter, he'd heard nothing from her since they'd met in his office.

As if he'd read Aiden's mind, Noah said, "Not really. She's spending the day with Autumn. Winter is a smart woman and a good agent; she won't get in over her head. And even if she does, Autumn will help keep her grounded. After all, it's not Autumn's little brother in question."

"There is that." Aiden would have felt a lot better if Autumn would have just sent a text, some update on Winter to let him know how she was doing. Then he might have been able to have something to reassure Noah too. As it was, the news he *did* have wouldn't be reassuring anyone.

He sighed. Might as well spit it out.

"I just found out that Winter went to interview Cameron Arkwell."

Noah cursed. In a flash of movement, the big agent no longer lazed against the door and was halfway into his office before he realized he'd even moved. "What the hell for?"

Well, at any rate, Noah had lost the tired, hangdog look. Hell, it had woken *him* up as well when he'd heard it.

"I don't know. I wasn't there. The guard that took her to him didn't hear everything clearly. Whatever he said, it got a rise out of her. Apparently, Winter left in a hurry and Cameron giggled all the way back to his cell. He kept saying something about 'baby Preacher,' whatever that means."

"Baby Preacher?" Noah echoed. "Jaime Peterson? I suppose it makes a kind of sense; I just hope the media doesn't pick up on it. With a name like that, the press will have another darling and the world will form up into fan clubs for yet another serial killer. That's the one thing we don't need."

"No, we don't." Aiden studied him intently, not liking the dark shadows under Noah's eyes. "Why did you come back here, Dalton? You should be pounding your pillow."

Noah shook his head, stepping back to close the door. "I wouldn't have been able to sleep. I think it's this case, but I felt like I was being followed."

"You had a tail?"

"No." The answer was automatic, but something about

the day had clearly left him unsettled. Noah shrugged. "Maybe. I don't know. There was this kid in a truck that flipped me off, but other than that, things were fine until I got to the parking lot. Then, something just felt..." He shook his head, as if hoping to rattle the correct word into his mouth.

"Off?" Aiden offered.

Noah met his gaze. "Yeah. Off. I was most likely letting this investigation get to me."

"You hesitated with your answer. You're a good agent, Dalton. I trust your instincts, maybe more than you do. Why don't you get with the Richmond PD, have them send a car into that parking lot and have them take a look? Couldn't hurt."

Noah nodded, but Aiden could see that Noah didn't think much of the idea. He wasn't sure why. After all, having a patrol car swing by a parking lot wasn't a great imposition, and if there was a legitimate reason for Noah's discomfort, they might be able to scare it away. Which could be good or bad. The fact that it was so close to the place where Winter lived was unnerving.

We're all going to sleep better once her brother is safely behind bars.

A knock on the office door caused Noah to jump. Aiden noticed the jolt with interest. So, it wasn't a feeling easily dismissed after all. To his credit, Noah recovered quickly, and Aiden pretended not to notice. Aiden edged past him and opened the door to a messenger, who handed him a large manilla envelope, an interdepartmental memo of some sort.

Aiden closed the door again and sat back down in his chair, already opening the envelope as he sat. He read the note, skipped to the summery, and handed the entire thing to Noah.

"What's this?" Noah took the papers and began paging through them.

"The report we've been waiting on. I managed to get it on the highest priority. Apparently, yes, Kilroy has a direct relationship to Justin Black, but none to Winter. It's not as direct a bloodline as a grandfather," he reached out to tap the area where that was stated on the bottom of the report, "but it's close enough to be, say, an uncle or grand-uncle."

"So, he really was Justin's long-lost relative." Noah shuffled through the papers. "Does that explain why Kilroy took him?"

"What do you mean?"

Noah closed the report and slipped it back into the envelope. "I mean if Justin was his nephew or grand-nephew, considering what sort of man Kilroy was, and considering the sort of man Winter remembers of her father, it's logical to think they had a falling out."

"You're stretching that one, you know. Girls always remember their fathers with a certain amount of hero worship. And that presumes that Bill Black knew about Kilroy's ideology before Kilroy began killing."

"So far as we know," Noah countered. "But that would explain a great deal about why Justin was abducted."

"Explain." Aiden wasn't following the logic. "What's your reasoning?"

"I'm not sure." Noah handed the envelope back to Aiden. "I'm just thinking that..." he dropped into the chair across from Aiden, seemingly thinking out loud, "if there was a falling out in the extended family, Winter's father seemed to be a decent sort, regardless of Winter's rose-colored glasses. So, if he broke off ties with a family member who was a psychopathic killer, then someone of Kilroy's mental illness might want to reclaim his extended family."

"All right, it's thin, but I'll buy it for now. It's not something that would hold up, but if it helps…" Aiden folded his hands on his desk. "What else you got going on in that head of yours?"

"Well, if he's stylized himself as Jaime's grandfather, or even guardian, then we need to start thinking about where he would have taken the boy. He can't have kept him in a cell all these years. Justin might be more than a little twisted, but he's no shrinking violet either. He was running with Kent Strickland and Tyler Haldane. He had to have been wandering around like any kid, only under the name Jaime Peterson. I would think that calling himself Justin Black would have been problematic, and he apparently didn't want there to be a problem."

"Where are you heading with this?" Aiden didn't want to make Noah lose his train of thought, but so far none of this was anything they didn't already know, even if none of the details had come together quite this clearly before.

"Not sure." Noah exhaled noisily. "Maybe I'm just letting things gel a bit, but Justin sent that video. I'm still wondering about that. That was a stupid move. We weren't even sure it was him before that. He basically stood up and confessed in front of a camera. Why? All just to tell Winter she wasn't related to Bill Black? Why was it so important to him that she know that?"

"Maybe he's cutting ties with her."

Noah's face grew pale. "Like her father cut ties with Justin's…" he threw up his hands, "whoever in the hell it was. Grandfather? Grand-uncle?" Aiden watched as Noah's face showed understanding and then fear. "That has to be it. Think about it, what if Bill cut ties with Kilroy. Kilroy reclaimed his extended family and killed Bill. Now, Justin cut ties with his half-sister, officially taking her out of the family tree."

"You think Winter is his next target?" Aiden bolted upright in his chair, a feeling of horror washing over him.

"We haven't heard anything out of Justin for days. What if he's *not* keeping a low profile? What if he's trying to find the right opportunity to strike? Winter hasn't left the apartment except with Autumn, and then they've gone to very public places."

"After that feeling you had in the parking lot?" Aiden reminded him.

Noah sprang to his feet and headed toward the door. "I'll have a patrol car head over immediately. They can get there a lot faster than I can. At the very least, they can do a well-check at the apartment in case she's back."

"I'll arrange for the local cops," Aiden said, already picking up his phone. "You head home. And Dalton..." he waited until Noah turned to face him, "watch your back and trust your instincts."

Noah nodded and headed out of the office while Aiden dialed the non-emergency number for local law enforcement. Picking his cell phone up in his other hand, he considered who else to call. He hated to call Bree back in. She'd only just left, but for this...he called and left a message when she didn't answer the phone.

The office phone continued to ring in his hand. Finally, someone answered, but he was quickly put on hold.

He tried Autumn's number next. It went straight to voicemail.

Damn it! Autumn, where are you?

"Call me!" he barked into Autumn's phone, and hung up.

"Excuse me?"

For a moment, Aiden had forgotten about the office phone in his hand, and quickly turned his attention to it. "This is SSA Aiden Parrish with the Federal Bureau of Investigation. I need a patrol car to do a thorough sweep of a parking lot, fast."

"What's the address?"

He rattled it off. "One of my agents is on the way there," Aiden informed the dispatcher. "I want him to have back up when he gets there."

There would be interdepartmental hell to pay for this, but Noah's life and Winter's life might be in the balance. If Winter was still with Autumn, that added another vulnerable point. He'd call in every favor he'd accumulated over the years to make sure the three of them were safe.

Life was filled with irony.

They'd been looking for Justin, but Justin might have just found them.

29

Figured. Of course. Winter was just like the rest of them. Whore.

I didn't know who the big guy was. Not that it mattered. He had a key to her apartment. He was probably one of a dozen, maybe more than a hundred who traipsed in and out of her place, a line of men all wanting to use her. Or more accurately, waiting to be used by her. The way all women used men.

As I watched, though, he came and went from Winter's apartment fairly quickly. Which was strange.

But even stranger was the way in which the guy acted. He seemed paranoid. No, more than that. He seemed to know.

Know that I was watching. Waiting. Even though I knew he couldn't see me. The dude had even drawn a gun once, turning and pointing it in my direction.

Very strange.

Had he been able to feel me watching him? Did he have some unholy devil whispering in his ear, telling on me? Or maybe he was one of those psychics who fed on the evil of the world?

I almost left then, worried about the man's ability to sense me being so close. But I wasn't a coward. Grandpa didn't raise a weakling, and I feared his wrath more than I feared being seen.

So, I waited. I didn't want to know what he was doing in there, what *she* was doing in there with a man who had a key to her apartment.

I knew she wasn't married. She still used Bill's last name —Black. She had no right to it, and she hadn't changed it, so she wasn't married. She was just a whore.

I'd settled back into my hiding place, expecting a long wait, but the man had left after only ten minutes or so, dressed in a different suit than he'd worn when he got there. His hair had been wet too.

Something was wrong. He didn't stay long enough for… anything. At least I didn't think so.

I took the paper I printed out from the library, the one that had her address and a little biography about Winter. It was a lookup feature on a website that cost me fifty dollars. It had been worth it. Federal Bureau of Investigation. I knew that. She was the reason Grandpa died. She was the reason Tyler died. She had a lot of blood on her hands, and she got away with it because she had a badge.

And she let men into her apartment.

I had waited until the man's car drove off, and her caller left unsatisfied. Maybe he'd walked in on her and she was with a different man. Maybe there were a string of men waiting up there. It didn't matter. I had six bullets in the gun and a box more in my jacket. I'd shoot all of them if I needed to.

Being very careful not to be observed, I headed for the stairs. The blood pounding in my ears was deafening, and I found my hands twitching. That surprised me. Why should *I* be nervous? My mission was holy and just; she was the one that should have been nervous. Still, my hands didn't know that, and they trembled.

I knocked on the door. Hard. I was just another one of the men lined up for her, just another faceless stranger waiting for her to open the door so that I could...

Gritting my teeth, I knocked again, louder. No one came to the door. Maybe he left because she wasn't there.

I pulled the knife out of the sheath attached to the belt on my side. It was an excellent knife, wide and thick, hard steel a good foot long with a reinforced tip. I slid the blade under the trim around the door and set it angled against the latch. The trim gave way under the blade and separated from the frame, the paint pulling off in jagged strips.

I found the bolt on the lock and tipped the blade to one side so it would catch and popped the pommel with my hand. The door sprang open like it was on a spring. Sloppy. Here she was some big deal agent, and she had a cheap lock on her door that could let anyone in. Maybe that was the point. I walked in and closed the door behind me. The damage done to the frame wouldn't be visible unless someone was right there, facing it. Looking for it.

If anyone noticed something wrong and came to investigate, I'd put the blade through them. I didn't mind.

The apartment was neat. Spotless. I hadn't expected that. A woman as loose as her, a woman that would give keys to men she wasn't married to, should live in squalor. They should stay in a hovel as befitted their status of harlot. I looked around in surprise. I supposed that my half-sister was a very accomplished harlot, if she could pay for an apartment this nice.

I walked around a little, touching everything. Large screen TV, teacups in the sink, milk in the fridge. I went through the drawers in her bedroom and found a surprise. One of the drawers contained men's underwear. There were men's suits in the closet, men's shoes under the bed. So, she was living in sin with that man. There wasn't a long line as I thought. There was just one man who was being corrupted by her.

That didn't make her any more virtuous. She was still a whore, but at least her evil had only poisoned one lost soul, and she wasn't taking a bunch of others with her to hell. On the floor of the closet was a dark suit. His, I assumed. It was crumpled and stank like old sweat. On the other side of the closet, there were smaller suits. Women's this time. Some of them had skirts, but most had slacks.

The pants didn't surprise me, the skirts did. It was a little late to pretend to be a proper lady when you were shacked up with some guy. I pulled a few out of the closet to look at. Those I threw onto the floor and stepped on as I went into the bathroom.

Men's shaving cream and razors, women's hair care products, birth control pills. If there was even a hint of doubt about her propriety, this killed it. She was as my grandpa said she was, just a cheap whore like the rest of them. My resolution to kill her took on a new fevered pitch; I needed to do it for her sake as well as mine. This wasn't just about revenge anymore. I needed to cleanse her from being a blight on humanity. The fact that she was my half-sister meant nothing to me. She was nothing more than an obstacle.

I found a tube of lipstick. Grandpa said that the purpose of lipstick was to make a woman's lips look swollen and larger, like when the blood goes to their sex when they're in season. I opened the top and extended the red stick as far as it would go. It was shaped like a phallus, one she rubbed on her lips.

She had to die. There were so many reasons now. I set the lipstick down, but only after I wrote her a message on the bathroom mirror. This time, she couldn't steal my face and spread it over the television. This time, it was the message that mattered, not the video, not the shades and shadows that betrayed me. This time, it was all about the message.

I walked into the kitchen and opened the fridge. It was well stocked. Winter certainly didn't go hungry. That pissed me off too. What did she know of hunger? What did she know about your stomach being so empty it felt like it stuck to your spine? The people who lived here had never experienced real hunger pains, hadn't known deprivation.

Grandpa said that, "Through the fire are we forged," and that, "Hunger pain brings us closer to God and the holy mission." He was probably right. He usually was, but it pissed me off to see the wicked prosper. Sinners, heathens, and yet, they had the nice suits, the stocked fridge, the waste. Judging by the number of Styrofoam containers, they ate out a lot. All that food and it still wasn't enough.

I added gluttony to the list. A good and godly man like Grandpa had to tighten his belt, and that was an old battered belt at that.

I found some Chinese food in a container and dumped it into a bowl and microwaved it. I walked through the house as I waited for the oven to finish.

There were boxes under a table in the living room. They looked so out of place in the tidy apartment. I pulled one out and set it on the table and opened it as the oven dinged. I ate chow main while shuffling through the papers.

The box was full of old records, all cross folded and stacked as if they'd been placed there as a system. I couldn't make head nor tails out of most of the records, but there were birth certificates from nearly a hundred years ago and death certificates and papers chronicling marriages and divorces.

There were some handwritten pages too. That was the key. Names I knew or had heard of and arrows and relationships that all pointed to Grandpa. So, the little whore was trying to be part of the family after all?

I finished the Chinese food and carefully set the bowl on the chair next to me. I then upended the box of papers and dumped them on the floor. She wanted to claim she was part of the family, did she? Well, she wasn't, no matter how she twisted the past, no matter how she perverted the records, she was no part of the family, of Grandpa, of Bill.

I waded through the papers like I was walking through the surf, kicking up waves as they settled at my feet. It became a game, making the pages fly. I got one to land on top of a lamp, another slid under a cupboard. I thought of *Singin' in the Rain*, the way that handsome fellow kicked up the water while dancing, but Grandpa said dancing was for men without balls, so I just ground the papers in harder, hearing them catch and tear under my feet.

I took the empty bowl to the kitchen and washed it along with the fork I used. I found a pen and grabbed one of the pages from the floor and wrote a note that I left under the clean bowl before taking my leave. I was just about to leave the sinful apartment when I saw the flashing lights.

They must have found my new truck with its shiny clean dashboard. I bit back the stream of swear words I wanted to say because Grandpa didn't like it when I used some of those words. It wasn't fair. I liked my new truck. It was a shame to lose it like that.

It was okay. There were others. Hell, this was a big city, with dashboards all over the place. As I slipped along the shadows of the big apartment building and into the trees in the back, I reminded myself that I'd find another. I just needed to choose the one I wanted.

Simple.

30

The headlights shone on a dilapidated pile of wood doing an imitation of a church. To Winter's eyes, it looked as if they'd just arrived to see the entire thing lean over and collapse under its own weight. Not that anyone would mourn the demise if it did.

Some of the boards on the side of the church were sprung, like the heaviness of the passing years had squeezed them free of the nails that once held them in place. She wasn't sure, but it looked like something ran past the door, frightened by the glare of the headlights.

Autumn halted the vehicle as close as she dared without inflicting damage on the car itself from the loose debris scattered over what used to be the parking lot. "Okay. We've seen it. Let's go back."

Winter shook her head. "There has to be a reason that this came up in my vision. We drove a long way to get here. We're not just leaving." She reached for her cell phone and turned on the flashlight app. She looked at the screen for a moment. "I have zero signal."

"Me too." Autumn showed Winter her phone.

Indeed, instead of any bars at all, Autumn's phone also showed a circle with a line through it, indicating there was no service. It was unusual to not catch even the most remote signal from some random tower somewhere. Winter supposed this far out in the country, there was no populace large enough for a cell service to care.

"Well, let's check the place out and get out of here. I'll get you dinner at the first sign of a decent place to eat."

"I don't think we'll find much around here except maybe the roadkill of the day. Served on a hubcap with WD-40 sauce," Autumn muttered, clearly not liking the look of the place.

Winter laughed. "You're in a mood."

"Yeah." Autumn nodded vehemently. "I am. That mood is called 'scared.' You have no idea the feelings I'm getting off that place."

"You mean that the building is alive, and it doesn't want us here? That feeling?"

"All right." Autumn's eyes widened in surprise. "Maybe you do have an idea. I thought I was nuts and imagining it."

"No." Winter opened her door, suppressing a shudder that had nothing to do with the blast of cold air infiltrating the car. "You may be nuts, but you're not imagining it. This place doesn't like us."

"And why are we willingly going in there? I think I just saw a rat. A *giant* rat." Autumn pointed behind her.

Winter turned to look, but whatever Autumn had seen was gone again. Figured. "Because," Winter told her, "this place showed up in my vision. There has to be a reason for it."

"A warning, perhaps, a command to stay away? Hell, I'll buy dinner, let's go." Autumn crossed her arms, ready to stare down the church itself if need be. Winter laughed and got out of the car. Autumn sat still a moment and then seemed to realize that Winter seriously intended to leave her alone. Not that Autumn really was scared. Much. She definitely had a weird look on her face as she joined her.

Autumn's expression was somewhere between a frown and a scowl. "I'm not kidding, Winter. The feelings I'm getting off his place." She shuddered. "It's not just the Addams Family paint job or the charming mold smell. This place really freaks me out."

"Duly noted." Winter took a deep breath, trying not to show that she was becoming just as rattled as Autumn, if not more so. After all, it was her vision that had placed her here. That the place looked so exactly like she'd envisioned was jarring, to say the least. The blatant malevolent feel emanating off the building itself was just the icing on the cake.

She stepped up to the double door and pushed. To her surprise, the wood refused to give. She tried the old brass push handle on the front, but the tab wouldn't depress. She shone her phone light on a piece of paper that was tacked to the door. It was yellowed with age and impossible to read since the print had faded in the sun. She bent closer to get a good look at it.

"What does it say?" Autumn asked.

The wind was cutting through the layers of clothing, chilling her to the bone. Winter shivered. "Condemned." She frowned and squinted at the faded print. "This place was condemned and scheduled for demolition," she tilted her phone, trying to get more light on the faded words, "almost a year ago."

"I wonder what's taking them so long?"

Honestly, Winter would have preferred that the destruction of the place had happened a year ago. The place was a deathtrap. "It was probably lost in red tape," Winter murmured, tilting her head back to look up at the steeple.

"Wow." Autumn activated the flashlight app on her phone. "How insignificant do you have to be when no one can even remember to come put you out of your misery?"

Winter turned to Autumn, her eyes widening as a single word sang through her mind. "Oubliette."

"Come again?"

"It was a form of torture," Winter explained. "It means a 'place of forgetting.'" The prisoner was left to die, just ignored to death. That was running through my head, that word. During the vision, I mean. I thought that meant that this place was a place of forgetting, that someone or something here had been abandoned, but it was the *church*. It was the building itself that was left and abandoned. This place isn't the oubliette, it was left *in* an oubliette, this field, this dying town. We all ignored it, forgot about it. This is the very place where a serial killer spent his formative years, and we've shunned the building as though it's to blame somehow."

Winter stood at the butt between the two great doors. In an explosive burst of energy that left Autumn screaming in surprise and backpedaling away from her, Winter dealt a strong blow in the crack between the doors. They flew open, the right one slamming on the door jamb as they shook and lay bare the contents of the room.

"This is what I saw," Winter said under her breath.

Autumn let out a shriek and stamped her right foot.

"What?" Winter shot her an impatient look.

"Something ran over the top of my shoe," Autumn said, her foot raised as she looked around for either a safe place to set the foot down or a target for her heel. Not that it mattered which. Either one would suffice in Winter's opinion. Normally, neither one of them was so easily creeped out, but this place was seriously doing a number on them.

Winter entered the building. She could feel Autumn hesitating behind her. Winter paused, trying to figure out just what made the place so foreboding. Maybe it was because it was so blessedly *dark*.

Even with the car lights on bright and shining directly into the church, the light didn't penetrate into the gloom. She shone her light overhead, visions of a wall of spiders ready to descend worrying through her brain, but there was nothing above her except wood.

"Let's split up,"

Autumn protested immediately. "No. Absolutely not."

Winter kicked at a rotted floor mat just inside the door, sending up a cloud of dust. "We can cover more ground. It's obvious no one is here…"

"No."

"…and we'll be sure that we get everything."

"No!"

"Autumn, you don't understand." Winter held her hands together in a pleading gesture. "I know about this. We're not going back, not now."

"All right, all right." Autumn turned toward the black pit of the chapel, her expression grim. "But we are *not* splitting up. I am not walking in there on my own."

Or on your own.

She didn't have to say it. Since this whole thing began, Winter had noticed how protective Autumn had gotten. It was sweet in a way. And…truth be told…it was kind of nice to be fussed over a little.

Winter grinned. "Deal." Her light caught on one of the stained-glass windows. The image looked familiar. She caught her breath, stepping carefully to get a closer look.

"What?" Autumn asked from behind her.

"I saw that hole in the window," Winter whispered. "Next to the saint. The pulpit should be laying on the floor just up…" She shone the light ahead of them but cried out as her foot went through a floorboard and she tumbled forward.

Autumn caught her at the expense of dropping her phone. The two women were plunged into darkness as they scrambled to extricate Winter and then find their phones again. Thankfully, the brightly lit screens made at least this part of the task easy enough. Given how the floor creaked dangerously, Winter was more worried about them both falling through into whatever lay below.

What did lay below?

Winter shone her light into the hole she'd just made. "Look. There's a basement down there."

Autumn circled the room with her light. "Great. The only thing creepier than a church building that hates us, is a church *basement* that hates us."

"Come on." Winter ducked her head lower, trying to see into the space below. "It'll be fun." She grinned at the look Autumn gave her.

Autumn sighed. "All right, Ethel. Lead the way," she said, referencing the old TV show they both sometimes watched together. "I don't recall signing up for urban exploration."

"I think…" Winter pointed her light to a door to the left of the nave. "There. Watch your step. This floor is rotted through as well."

"I noticed." Autumn was already putting down each foot with infinite care. Winter watched her and tried to imitate the careful actions, trying not to put too much weight on any one place. Maybe it was a good thing that she'd lost a few pounds recently.

"And if anyone's Ethel, it's you," Winter murmured as they traversed the floor to the doorway. "I'm clearly Lucy in this."

Autumn pointed to her red hair. "I'm Lucy."

"This is my adventure; you're just along for the ride."

"Shit." Autumn shot her a glare. "I hate to admit it, but you're Lucy." She rolled her bottom lip out. "I don't want to be Ethel."

Winter stifled a laugh, grateful to her friend for purposefully lightening the mood with humor. "I'll be Ethel next time."

"Deal."

The steps going into the basement were also made of wood, but they had metal strips meant to reinforce them from the bottom. In two places, the wood was gone, but the strips remained intact, and they held up under the weight of two light women treading very carefully.

There was a great deal of testing of each step before Winter committed to standing on any of them. It was hard to be so cautious when she couldn't escape the feeling that there was something down there she needed to find. She wanted to just bolt down the stairs and be done with it.

In the basement, an old desk and chair marked what might have been a church office of sorts, though a basement office didn't allow for light or fresh air. The benefit to them was that the contents of the office had taken less exposure to the elements and therefore sustained less damage over time. Not that there was much there. An old desk. A couple filing cabinets tilted to one side and clearly empty if the gaping drawers were anything to go by.

Winter pulled the drawer on the desk. The drawer front fell off in her grip. Okay, well, so much for escaping undamaged.

At first glance, it seemed empty inside. On a hunch, she wrenched out the remains of the drawer and looked all the way back. Nothing.

She was about to lose hope that they'd locate anything worth finding when she pulled out the third drawer from the other side of the desk. In the very back was a small bundle of several papers. Winter's cheer of celebration abruptly turned into a startled yelp as a mouse ran over her open hand.

Autumn screamed as the rodent scurried in her direction

but quickly caught herself, clamping her hands over her mouth. She blushed furiously as Winter gave her a shaky grin before reaching in to grab the pages.

Just as her hand closed over the documents, the doors of the church slammed shut hard enough to rattle their teeth. This time, when Autumn screamed, Winter almost joined her. The hate she felt coming from the building ratcheted up several notches. All Winter wanted was to get in the car and leave. Immediately.

Autumn was clearly of the same mind. "Let's get out of here!" Before the words were fully out, she bolted for the steps, Winter right behind her.

They threw themselves between the pews that seemed to have shifted since they'd gone downstairs. Everything sat at an angle now, as if to watch them run. The floor cracked and splintered under their footfalls, but neither of them stopped.

For a wild moment, Winter feared that something waited for them on the other side of the door, but it was still better than what waited for them from every darkened corner. Evil lurked in those rafters. Something as old as time itself.

"Come on, Lucy!" Autumn yelled as she attempted to wrench the front doors open. For one terrible moment, Winter believed they were sealed shut, much like the doors of a mausoleum.

This church would become their grave.

Burying them with the demons that still roamed the patch of Earth on which it set.

With one final mighty pull, the door slammed inward, crashing into the wall with a bang. The women raced out of the church, Winter holding the documents against her chest, protecting them from whatever was intent on her never reading them.

Autumn's car sat where they'd left it, the engine running and the headlights on. It was a beacon of sanity in chaos.

Autumn pelted for the driver's side, Winter nearly over-taking her on her way to the passenger's door.

They piled into the car, and Autumn threw it into reverse, sans seatbelt. She pulled out through the dirt and scrub and whipped the wheel around, spinning the car and throwing it into drive.

Turning around in her seat, Winter watched the old church grow smaller. For a moment, she thought she saw something move.

"Stop," she yelled at Autumn, who slammed on the brakes with a yelp.

"What?"

Winter said nothing, just opened her door to get a better look. Autumn got out on the other side.

They both watched as the church groaned mightily, the creak echoing in the frigid air. With a great shuddering cry, the old house of worship fell over. The roof collapsed in, the steeple teetering and falling last, taking the rest of the tower down with it. Dust and filth erupted into the night air.

They waited, Winter holding her breath as the church creaked again, the entire pile of wood and nails and tiles collapsing still further. She guessed the floorboards must have given way as the entire church fell into the basement with a crash hard enough to shake the ground under their feet.

The waves of hate she'd felt gave way to bitter resent-ment. The church was sullen, sulky, dying. Winter's heart was pumping hard enough to make her chest hurt. Autumn had her hand over her mouth as she watched the old church die at long last.

Autumn moved slowly back into the car, sitting heavily in the driver's seat and closing the door with infinite gentle-ness, as though to do otherwise would somehow disturb the dead. She buckled in as Winter joined her. For extra measure, she locked the doors as soon as Winter was in place. What might have been coming at them now was anyone's guess, but at least it made them both feel somewhat better.

"What are those?" Autumn's voice seemed unnaturally calm. She pointed to the papers still clutched in Winter's hand. Winter looked down at them as if she'd forgotten they existed.

"Deeds. I think. They all looked the same when I grabbed them. This one was the deed to that place." She pointed a thumb at the rubble behind them. "There are three others." She shuffled through them. "Huh. All churches."

"How could that get past Kilroy's investigation? Any property he owned would have been red-flagged." Autumn was looking at the papers but checking her phone too.

"Because," Winter pointed to the name on each one, "these aren't Douglas Kilroy's property. These are all under his father's name. That wouldn't have come up on a records search since his father's been deceased for years."

Autumn tossed her phone into a cup holder. "I still don't have a signal."

Winter nodded, still feeling shaky and maybe a little shockish. "Let's find a diner or gas station or something. I'd like to wash up and call this in." She waved the pages in the air. "Get some coffee. Lots of sugar."

"Good idea." Autumn put the car into gear and got back on the road.

It took a long time before they found enough civilization to feel normal again. By the time they found a diner, texts and voicemails were blowing up both their phones.

As Winter listened to the various notification rings, she closed her eyes.

Would this nightmare ever end?

31

"I'm getting a lot of messages." Autumn listened to her phone buzz over and over again. She tapped the screen once the car was in park, the glow of the diner's OPEN sign reflecting off the windshield, and whistled. "Lots of calls and texts. Aiden and Noah and a couple from...Max?" She showed her phone to Winter, but her friend was still looking at the papers in her fist. "Did you get these too?" Autumn pointed to her phone again.

"Look at this." Winter showed her the pages. She flattened them out on the dashboard, reaching up to turn on the light in the car so Autumn could see more clearly.

"Did you say they were for churches? Sorry." Autumn glanced at the papers, but her attention was on the phone that still dinged with annoying regularity. The phone carrier had been saving her messages until she was back where a signal could reach her. Some of the texts were marked URGENT. Those were from Noah.

"Proof of ownership of at least three different churches in the area. All of them in the name of Reverend Melvin Kilroy." Winter met Autumn's eyes. "Douglas Kilroy's father."

"Any chance *those* are still standing?" Autumn was thinking of the church that had fallen as they came running out. Her phone had settled down, but there were a dozen messages and several texts she should probably be reading. The texts she looked at all said the same thing in different ways: *CALL IN NOW.*

"Winter…" Autumn shoved the phone in her face, "look."

Winter glanced over at her phone and did a double take. She pulled her own phone from her jacket pocket. That one seemed like it had even more missed calls than Autumn's. Her stomach growling, she gazed through the windshield at the twenty-four-hour diner they'd just pulled into and sighed. "So much for dinner."

Autumn's battery was nearly dead, but Winter still had a decent charge. "Why don't you call in? I'll go next door to that station and see if they have a charge cable. I left mine at home again."

Winter nodded and called Noah on the speaker of her phone. Autumn hesitated, then decided to wait, as her phone was full of messages too. Very likely whatever was going on involved her.

The relief in Noah's voice was thick when he answered. He obviously had been beside himself but was trying not to show it. The forced casualness was sweet. For a moment, Autumn felt a pang of jealousy. It must be nice to have someone care about you as much as Noah cared for Winter.

Maybe I should give them some privacy.

She was about to get out of the car when Noah interrupted Winter's explanation about what they'd been doing with a question. "Are you all right?"

"Yeah, I'm fine. I'm out with Autumn, we ran a little late." Winter grinned up at her friend and rolled her eyes.

Autumn shook her head at her friend. His voice was

strained and sounded like he was upset. All those messages. Something was up.

"Aiden and I have been calling you both. Where were you?"

"There was no cell reception." Winter leaned her head back on the headrest, closing her eyes. "I called as soon as I saw you'd been trying to get hold of me. It was a very weird night."

Autumn snorted. Talk about an understatement.

"Winter, Justin was *here*."

Winter's face drained of all color, and Autumn froze with her hand on the door latch. A cold chill crawled up her spine, though the engine was running and the car was toasty warm.

"Where?" Autumn asked when it looked like Winter was too deep in shock to do it. "He was where?"

"Here," Noah said, his voice becoming more strained, more hoarse. He was definitely worried. Very worried. "In the apartment. *Our* apartment. He broke in."

"H-h-how…?" Winter swallowed and started over. "How do you know it was him?"

"He left a note on the bathroom mirror. It says, 'I won't miss you,' and it's signed 'J.' It's either him or the Joker."

"Is…" Winter glanced at Autumn, clearly having trouble putting her thoughts into words.

"Is anything missing?" Autumn finished for her.

Winter nodded vigorously.

"Not that I can tell. You remember the chow mein you couldn't finish the other night?"

"Yes?" Winter frowned at the change of topic.

"Well, that's gone, but the container is in the trash and there's a bowl and a fork that was recently washed sitting on the kitchen counter. There's a note stuck under the bowl."

"He ate my *leftovers*?" Winter shuddered. Autumn reached out to take her hand, wanting to comfort her, trying to ignore how the waves of fear and anger warring with the love Winter had for her little brother intensified through her own body. "Another note? What does that one say?"

Winter's brow creased as she strained to listen, though Noah's voice was coming through clearly.

"Please get chopsticks for next time."

A joke. Only Noah wasn't laughing. God, it was chilling, suggesting that Justin was convinced that this was not the last time he would be visiting Winter's apartment.

"And Winter..." Noah blew out a very long breath. "Your papers. The ones in the boxes. They've been scattered across the floor. They're everywhere, and we have several distinctive boot prints on most of them. In fact, the note about the chopsticks was written on a copy of a death certificate."

"Whose?" Winter asked, her voice barely audible.

"The local police took all that for evidence. I only got a glimpse when they showed me the note on the back. It was a Lynn someone."

Winter's hand went to her throat as if someone was strangling her.

"There's more," Noah said softly. "I know this is already a lot to take in, but the local police found a truck in the parking lot of our building. It was stolen, a carjacking. The owner was slashed with a large knife and left to bleed to death in a parking lot of a hotel."

"Oh my god." Winter choked, moving her hand up to cover her mouth.

Autumn tried desperately to think of a way to distract her. Or comfort her. Or something useful. She grabbed the papers off the dashboard and began paging through them. *Concentrate on something you* can *do, something you do* have *control over.*

"Noah?" Winter's voice was nearly an octave higher than normal. She cleared her throat before continuing. "Noah, we found something. That old church Kilroy had...we went there."

"What?" Noah nearly exploded through the phone. "Without backup? Justin could have been waiting there for you. He knows that we know about that place."

"No." Winter swallowed hard, her hand moving to her stomach. "I was with Autumn. We were fine. If I had stayed home," she pointed out, "I wouldn't have been safe."

Noah said nothing. It was hard to argue with that logic.

Winter pressed on. "Anyway, that church is gone now, it...collapsed. But we found something in it before it went down. Some deeds."

"You went into a collapsed building?" Noah sounded incredulous.

"Um..." Winter looked absolutely exhausted. "It was only half collapsed until we got ready to leave."

"Do you know how dangerous that is? Without backup? I could have lost you. How did you get into a building that was collapsed anyway?"

"Noah! Listen to me, please! The important thing here is that there are deeds to other properties."

"The important thing is your safety," Noah fired back.

"Please, Noah..." Winter waited until he was calmer.

It took nearly a minute for that to happen. "Why wasn't that found before?" he asked, sounding much more calm.

Winter leaned her cheek against the coolness of the window. "Maybe no one thought to look in the basement."

"You went into the basement?"

"Just listen!" she snapped, and Autumn smiled. They sounded like an old married couple. "I found some deeds. It seems that Melvin Kilroy was not only a circuit preacher, but he owned four churches, lock, stock and barrel."

"Four?"

"Right." Winter started shifting pages.

"The one we knew about, that one is destroyed," Autumn said to fill in the silence, "but Justin might very well go to one of the other three, especially if he thinks he's been exposed."

Noah was silent again for a moment. "Give me the addresses. I can have teams to each one in a couple of hours. I can't move faster than that. Besides, it might take some time for him to go to ground from Richmond. I would like to get him *after* he holes up for the night."

Winter read the addresses of the three off to Noah.

"All right. Come home, both of you, and stay together. I'll call you as soon as I know anything."

"All right." Winter didn't sound happy, but she did agree to stand down. She was officially off-duty, and it was up to Noah, Aiden, and Bree to handle it from there.

Winter hung up the phone and clutched it to her chest. She sat back and closed her eyes for a moment. When they opened again, she seemed alert and in control. Autumn didn't need to touch her to know that she was pushing down her fears and trying to pretend that she wasn't afraid for Noah as well as for Justin.

"I imagined being with my brother again for many, many years," Winter said to the dashboard. "Even when I thought he was dead, I had a fantasy that we would be reunited somehow." She turned to Autumn, her eyes belying the calm that surrounded her. "But I never once thought that when we were reconciled that Justin would try to kill me."

"Let's go home," Autumn said softly.

Winter nodded but opened her door. "Let's get you that charger cable," she said, lifting her chin toward the convenience store behind the gas pumps. "I need a good, strong cup of coffee after that..." She pointed her thumb behind her.

Autumn understood she was talking about the church and nodded in agreement. "Yeah, I think I need the restroom."

"I nearly didn't!" Winter laughed. The sound was hollow. Maybe it was a little forced, but at least it seemed like a genuine laugh.

Autumn grinned at her and clasped her arm. Winter was worried, but she was exhausted too. She was worried not so much about Noah, who was trained and had backup, but for Justin, who was crazy enough to not be taken alive. This was the Winter she knew and loved. *Atta girl.*

They walked close together, mutely sharing the night.

Autumn felt a new sensation from Winter and looked at her in surprise. Winter was basking in their friendship, feeling the comfort of a best friend for life. Autumn reached out and squeezed her hand. It was good to have a best friend, and even better to *be* someone's best friend.

It was one of the few times she actually welcomed her ability to read another person.

32

Noah spun the wheel and the car skidded over gravel and loose dirt. For a moment, it drifted, and Bree clutched the door to keep from sliding into him. She didn't say anything to criticize his driving, though she had every right to. Since leaving the apartment, he'd been driving like a madman.

The headlights cut through the moonless night. Flashing red and blue lights ahead showed that the closer FBI teams had already arrived on the scene. The Stony Creek church was in surprisingly good condition and seemed to be well-maintained.

Local law enforcement walked the perimeter of the building and had their lights trained on the old church by the time Noah and Bree pulled up, gravel skidding under their tires. Noah was out of the car almost before it stopped. He held up his badge high. "FBI, who's in charge here?"

"That would be me." A young man with a badge hooked to his belt jogged from his car to Noah's. "We secured the perimeter first. Agent Thompson. Nice to meet you." The young man reached out a hand for Noah to shake. "No one has been in or out since we arrived. Once the building was secured, we waited for your arrival."

"Thank you." Noah nodded to the man. "Do we know if anyone is in there?"

"We were ready to search but waited for you."

"Good." Noah reached into his jacket and pulled the Glock from the holster. He checked with Bree, who nodded, her gun pointing at the ground. The young agent and his partner, a man he identified as Carl Travers, went to the backside of the building while he and Bree headed to the front.

Bree flattened out against one side of the wall to the right of the door. Noah took the other side. He tried the doorknob, which turned easily in his hand. That sent up warning flags, a building like this unlocked? That was unusual. His heart pounding, he nodded once to Bree and flung the door open, stepping back in case anyone inside tried for a lucky shot.

There was a deep silence beyond the door opening. Noah hesitated and spun around, his gun pointed into the church. Bree stood behind him, her weapon covering his left.

Still, there was no resistance. Noah stepped in, half crouching behind the last pews, his gun pointed in the direction of the over-sized pulpit. Bree took the other side as they cleared the building.

Moments passed as doors were kicked open and "clear" calls rang out. Then it was over.

Thompson and Travers entered the sanctuary, looking as disappointed and frustrated as he felt.

Noah exhaled and holstered his weapon. Bree did the same.

"No one home." Bree sounded disappointed too.

"No," Agent Thompson admitted. "But there is someone here I think you should meet." He gestured to a frazzled and frail-looking older man who was nervously shuffling behind one of the cars.

"Who's that?" Bree was already busy taking notes.

"He's Mark Gustof." The agent handed her a driver's license. She started jotting down his information. "He says that this is his church."

Noah examined the card after taking it from Bree. She looked as confused as he felt. They followed the policeman to the nervous older man and Noah handed him back his license. "Mr. Gustof?" Noah offered his hand to shake. "Agent Dalton, this is Agent Stafford." He nodded to Bree.

"Reverend Gustof."

Noah realized that the older man wasn't nervous. He was cold. Wearing only a plaid shirt, jeans, and tennis shoes, the wind must have frozen the man from the bones out.

"*Reverend* Gustof," Noah corrected himself. "Why don't we sit in my car where we can talk out of the wind?" He gestured to the back door of the car and Thompson opened the door for them. The reverend looked askance at that. Noah smiled. "No one is being arrested, I promise you that. I just want to get out of the cold."

Gustof nodded once and climbed in. Noah followed, and Bree climbed in on the other side.

"You own this church?" Noah asked him as soon as the doors were shut.

"Yes, sir. Well, not legally, but we been havin' service in here for nigh on twenty years now. The owner, he gave it to us, rent free, and we kind a called it 'home.' He don't want no rent. We do all the fixing up that needs to be done. It's ours as much as his, I reckon by now."

"Who was it that gave you this place?" When the old man couldn't meet Noah's eyes, he knew. "Was it Douglas Kilroy?"

"Now, I know what he'd done." Gustof rubbed his hands together, trying to get them warm. "I reckon everybody knowed what he done, but we ain't part of that. Ain't none of us even seen the man for more than a decade. If you're coming to confiscate the place, I think we got squatter's rights to it by now. We jus' put a new roof on the place come last March, and that was a pretty penny as you can imagine."

Noah sighed and pulled a picture from his pocket. It was of Justin, taken from the video. "Have you seen this man?"

Gustof took the picture and held it nearly at arm's length. Noah realized his sight wasn't the best either. "Yessir."

Bree leaned over, her face betraying her excitement. "Where? When?"

"Just the other day." Gustof handed the picture back to Noah. "On the television."

"Have you seen him in person?" Bree asked. Noah could see she was trying not to smile as the situation quickly became more and more surreal.

"Nope, can't say that I ever have. Say, are you trying to repossess a church?"

"Mist...*Reverend* Gustof," Noah corrected himself, "have you seen anyone unusual coming around the church lately?"

"No!" The reverend seemed indignant. "That's what I been telling the cops. It's an empty building at this time of night. No one comes here except for services. Services are Wednesday and Sundays. Bible study on Saturday nights whenever Mrs. Wellington feels up to it."

Noah rubbed his face. A dead end.

"If you all decide to look around, best be careful around the old cemetery. Some o' them graves is awful old, the ground gives way under foot sometimes. The dead don't much care for bein' intruded on." He looked directly at Noah. "Might wanna send someone expendable, just in case."

"Expendable?" Bree echoed. She looked at Gustof from under her brows. He was looking directly at Noah.

"Yessir." Gustoff smiled. It wasn't a warm smile. It was

more like showing his teeth.

AIDEN PULLED up to a line of cars. The agents he'd called in were all still in their cars. The two who had followed Aiden to the location pulled in behind him. From what he could tell, the whole crew had gathered around a large empty lot. Aiden climbed out, hooking his badge to his belt.

The others got out of their cars and gathered around him.

"Gentlemen," Aiden said with a nod. There were six of them besides himself, and they all looked cold and miserable. "We're after a killer. This is a very dangerous man, so all precautions should be observed. Stick with your partners and don't venture out on your own."

He waited to make sure he had everyone's attention before continuing.

"The goal is a church less than a mile away. I asked to meet here because we're going in together. I don't want any heroics, is that clear?" Every man and woman there nodded, listening raptly to him. One young woman was looking slightly confused and looked to the road, but she seemed to be paying attention, so Aiden let it go.

"When we get there, I want everyone to be ready to be fired upon, just in case. We're going to assume that the area is hostile." He looked for questions, but no one had any. Even the woman that had looked confused when Aiden mentioned the church said nothing.

"Suit up," Aiden told the agents in front of him. He wanted to keep Miguel separate. As the ranking agent under Aiden, Miguel had to be his right-hand man and take charge. "Get your gear together, tactical vests, the works. We're going in. Miguel, when we get there, cover the door while we get set."

The agents ran to their cars and opened the trunks. Jackets came off and Kevlar vests were put on. In just a few minutes, everyone was armed to the teeth.

"Let's go!" He windmilled his arm and headed for his car. He pulled back into the road and followed his GPS to the address Winter had found. There was a long dirt driveway, a rusted mailbox with the numbers still on it, but no church. Only a large cement slab, nothing else.

Aiden got out of the car, the others joining him.

"This can't be right," Aiden said, looking at the slab, thoroughly pissed.

"Excuse me, sir?" The female agent who'd reacted to his announcement of a church less than a mile away broke into his thoughts. "I used to live near here. There hasn't been a church on this lot for seven or eight years. We had a tornado a while back." She shrugged. "The church here was already old and dilapidated, so I guess the wind just took it down."

Aiden took a step closer to the slab and then stopped. "Why didn't you mention this at the briefing, Agent..."

"Martella, sir. Janice Martella. Sir, I thought maybe there had been a different church built in the area since I'd been here. It's been a few years."

"What's that?" Aiden pointed to something metallic behind the trees. "Looks like an old Airstream."

Agent Martella shrugged her heavy coat, catching the collar in her shoulder-length black hair and pushed up her glasses. "There's lots of trailer parks around here."

Aiden looked past the trailer, and true enough, there were more RVs and trailers past that one. There was also a fence. "Yeah, but, "he pointed to the one that'd caught his attention, "that one is on the church property. There's a line separating them."

The agents turned as one to look. It was difficult to see in the darkness. Had they arrived during the day, it would have been more obvious.

Miguel came up behind Aiden. "Think he's in there?"

Aiden shook his head but never broke his eyes from the trailer, just in case he was wrong. "No, we didn't even see the thing until we were all gathered. The fact that no one got hurt suggests that our boy wasn't home when we arrived."

The agents lined up on either side of the door. They crouched down against the aluminum walls of the RV, scant protection against a bullet, but anyone shooting from inside would be shooting blind. The real danger would come when they forced the door open and exposed themselves to fire without any cover at all.

Aiden found himself holding his breath as one of the men reached out slowly and tested the latch on the door. It popped gently open, and the agent who had tested the catch crouched again. Aiden could imagine him taking a deep breath. He wore his Kevlar vest, but that did nothing to safe-guard against a head shot. Even with a helmet, it took a moment to gather oneself to jump into a situation like that.

The man opened the door and lay so that the upper part of his body could slip around in the trailer doorway and cover both ends. He was lost out of sight of the watching men for a moment but must have risen as another agent came up directly behind him, his gun drawn. There was a great deal of shouting, but no shots.

One by one, the agents filed out again.

Aiden and Miguel walked up to where an older man, Agent Richards, was waiting for them. "It's empty," Richards reported, not quite winded but obviously coming down from an adrenaline rush. "No one here, but they were recently."

Aiden clasped the man's shoulder. The team had been doing a great job of it. It wasn't their fault that the suspect wasn't home. Aiden stepped up into the RV.

There was a flat-screen TV mounted to the side of the trailer. It was shattered. A bullet hole had pierced the middle section of the screen. Old pizza boxes and dirty dishes lined the little kitchenette. The place reeked of old dirt and neglect. The bed was made, however, and the tiny room looked as if it hadn't been lived in for quite a while.

There was a pull-out couch that was filthy and looked like it was primarily a bed, not a couch. In one corner, there was a stack of pictures. Aiden knew he should wait for tech to process the scene, but he also needed to see what they were dealing with.

Taking a wooden stick from a clean evidence kit, he used it as a pen to push the pictures aside, one at a time to get a feel for what he was looking at, trying to keep any prints intact. They were all of Winter. All of them recent. All of them candid. They were taken at her apartment, on the street, at the store, and even in front of the Bureau.

There were several of Autumn too, mostly in her car. He frowned at the pile.

"Well?" the older agent asked when Aiden stepped out of the trailer. "Was this his? Your killer?"

"Yeah." Aiden straightened as he left the doorway. "This was our guy. Order a forensics team down here to sweep the place for as much evidence as we can get. I need you to set someone here in the meantime to watch and make sure no one disturbs the site." He looked at the man with a hard glare. "And remember who we're dealing with. Don't treat this like a false alarm, all right?"

The agent nodded and headed off for his car. Aiden strode from the trailer, Miguel so close on his heels that he nearly bumped into Aiden as they left the protection of the trees. Aiden barely even noticed. He was staring at the distance, his attention fixated on a distant light.

33

I t was late. Really late, and I was tired all the way to the marrow. All I wanted was to get some sleep and forget that this damn day had ever happened.

I was bitterly disappointed. At Winter. At myself. Mostly at myself.

Grandpa would be furious.

When I didn't find Winter at her place, I'd let my rage and bitterness take over. Instead of leaving things well enough alone, I'd gone and written notes and torn up things, letting her know I was pursuing her. Warning her.

Which was stupid.

I was so stupid.

On one hand, I left enough clues for her to know it was me and hopefully scare her enough to shit her pants. That would make the next time sweeter, if she knew with absolute certainty that it was me. Then she could be left in her fear for a long time. She could anticipate me and my next arrival.

On the other hand, her guard would be up, and she would be anticipating me even more right now. Worse, she'd probably go tell all the assholes at the FBI, and they would probably increase my bounty to half a million, or even a million damn dollars if I scared them enough.

A part of me wanted to be the one to get the highest reward ever. The smarter part of me knew that was a bad idea. It was enough to have every law enforcement official looking for my ass. I didn't need every greedy bastard in the country looking for me too, hoping to make a buck by taking me down.

That couldn't happen.

She wanted to expose me? She wanted the world to know my name? Well, I got my revenge, even though my gestures were now leaving me with some remorse. I wasn't able to exterminate her from existence. Not yet. But that time would come, and she wouldn't be able to stop me. Instead, I would be the one to stop her. I had to. For the purpose. The mission. For Grandpa.

The car I'd found was small and quick, even though it had seen better days. It handled well, but the blood stains on the upholstery were incredibly difficult to get out with just the fast-food napkins I found in the glove box. I'd never seen anyone so stubbornly hang on to a car before. People were strange. They didn't seem to realize it wasn't worth their life.

All in all, it had been a frustrating day. I'd ended up with a car instead of a truck, and then Winter had slipped through my fingers. If I had known that she was shacking up with some guy, then I would have killed him while he was in my sights in the parking lot.

Opportunity lost, eh, Grandpa?

He would be so furious at me.

I tightened my hands on the steering wheel as a shudder ran through me at the thought. "I won't fail you." I told the ghost in the passenger seat. "I won't. I promise I won't."

The ghost looked on, clearly not convinced. But it was also not screaming at me. Hitting me. Hurting me.

Which I took as a sign. Maybe I hadn't screwed up too badly.

Okay, so I hadn't killed her yet. Until I did, I couldn't carry on his original mission. I couldn't do *anything*. Every time I thought that I had her or one of her minions in my sights, they got away.

Focus, boy. Focus on the mission.

"I will, Grandpa." And I would, but I had to find Winter before I could fulfill that mission. Didn't he understand?

I turned on a state road that ran past farms and silos with very little in between. It was a peaceful drive in its way, especially in the darkness like this. One nice thing about living in the country was meeting nice folk, like the woman who owned the car I was now driving. She'd seemed nice. Good-looking too, with long legs. She shouldn't have held on to the car for as long as she did. I really was in a hurry. I even said I was sorry, but she was pretty far gone by then.

The car drove well, though. It handled the potholes and ruts better than Grandpa's old pickup ever did.

I found myself smiling as I got closer to my destination. There were shadows and some lights all gathered up in the trailer park again. It looked like someone's party spilled out into the woods.

The smile faded as I realized there were cops hanging around. Nothing I needed to worry about, I told myself. Trailer parks were often crime infested, and this one was probably no different. Cops would be normal in a place like this.

As added insurance, I'd moved the RV to a new location after my bitch of a sister broadcasted my face for all to see. No one in this new park knew me. They hadn't even seen me.

But still...

I turned right down a dirt road before the driveway to the

trailer park and slowed the car even more. The flashing lights, the shadows of people walking, they were closer than usual. They were...

I got to the old church driveway and stopped, staring in horror. The shadows and flashlights weren't in the trailer park. They were all gathered around *Grandpa's* RV.

The door was open, the lights blazing, and they were going in and out of it like ants running from a hole in the ground. My hands shook. My mind couldn't understand what I was seeing.

How could this be happening?

Heart pounding in my temples, I threw the car into reverse. Before I did, I spotted a few guys in suits running to where their cars were parked.

I couldn't breathe. I couldn't think, and I couldn't...

Go, boy. Go!

At the sound of Grandpa's command, I slammed it into drive and pressed the gas pedal to the floor. The little car fishtailed and tried to come off the road. But it didn't.

It wouldn't.

Because God would protect me now. He had to. I had a mission to fulfill.

BEHIND MIGUEL, Aiden stared at the distant road, watching a pair of headlights heading toward them. The car started to pull into the long drive that led to the remnants of the church and then came to a dead stop.

It's him.

Aiden knew it with a certainty he didn't question.

He was running before he knew he'd moved, heading straight for his car. His eyes were trained on the headlights. If ever a pair of lights could look panicked, it was those.

The little car reversed and headed down the same road it had come in on. Why was no one else noticing what he was?

"Miguel, there he is!" Aiden screamed, his right arm windmilling in the direction of the road. "Stop that car!"

He dove into his vehicle and savagely turned the key, seeing from the corner of his eye that Miguel was doing the same with a car a bit farther down the lane.

He threw the gearshift into reverse and pulled a circle in the driveway, gunning the engine as fast as he dared. He was working on instinct and putting a great deal of trust into the chase. But he was absolutely certain now. The car he was chasing contained Justin Black.

Behind him, other law enforcement vehicles were gathering and heading out for the chase, but they were too far back to be of any help. The suspect was driving a small car that seemed to have trouble handling the dirt roads. It fishtailed when Aiden spotted it and then again when it hit the state road, and the driver lost the turn, the tires screaming as they slid along the blacktop.

He was pushing the little car hard, but it wasn't gripping the road at all well. Bald tires? God, Aiden hoped so. They could use a vehicle mishap just about now.

The perp finally got it steady as he hit a straight run on the state road and kicked up a line of smoke as his wheels tore up a half-mile of asphalt.

Aiden followed suit, punching the accelerator, praying that his instincts were valid and that he wasn't chasing down some old woman who'd had a panic attack. No, it was him. It was *Justin* in that car. He knew it with every fiber and ounce of his being that he was following the right person.

Aiden's car belonged to the Bureau. It got poor gas mileage and looked like something a Soviet official might drive in an old movie. It also had a large engine block and could outrun most police cruisers. The car he was pursuing was a four-cylinder model built for improved gas mileage and to lessen the environmental impact.

That he was going to catch the small car was never in doubt, but the question was whether he could stop it before he reached a populated area, making pursuit that much more difficult.

He saw the headlights of Miguel's car shrinking behind him. His car wasn't up to the task. Aiden was it or nothing. He realized suddenly he'd not put on his seatbelt. He checked the speedometer. They were doing eighty-five. The state road was paved, which probably saved both of them, but at that speed on a back road, Aiden didn't dare take the time to belt in.

Aiden growled. Damn kid. Why didn't he stop?

But Aiden already knew the answer to that question.

The kid had a purpose. A mission.

And just like his "grandpa," he'd rather die than fail.

Aiden pressed his foot harder on the gas. His relationship with Winter would be at an end if he killed her little brother, but that was a chance he had to take.

He needed to take Justin Black down.

Now.

34

Winter still couldn't believe it.

When she'd cautiously opened the door of her apartment a few hours ago, she'd hoped that what Noah had told her hadn't been the truth. Instead, it had been worse.

The damage to the door trim was like a scar, a reminder of the knife she had felt slicing into her side. She'd forced herself to breathe through the phantom pain, reminding herself forcefully that that part of the vision had never, at least, come to fruition.

Autumn had watched from the doorway and gasped as she witnessed the mess inside.

Noah had warned her, but the damage had still been a shock. The Bureau had been there, and they'd swept for evidence, fingerprints, DNA traces, and all the rest. With so much traffic, the apartment no longer felt like home. Worse, the fact that Justin had broken in when they weren't home, had left Winter feeling violated and vulnerable. Walking into the apartment felt unnerving.

The papers were still everywhere. The boxes had been emptied out, like Noah had said, and some of the pages were likely down at evidence with Justin's fingerprints, boot prints and who knew what all else being held in storage. What hadn't been deemed important had been left for her to sort, like so much fallen snow awaiting a shovel.

"Oh my god, Winter." Autumn pulled papers from under a cabinet, revealing a copy of some unknown person's birth certificate. "I am so sorry." She smoothed it out and set it on top of the box that now sat on the table.

The bowl and fork had been bagged and tagged, though to her way of thinking, they weren't worth checking. After all, they had been washed. Neither was there any sign of the note requesting chopsticks for the next time he came over. She took a shaky breath and left the kitchen, heading for the bedroom, noting two of her suits were currently on the bed waiting to go to the cleaners along with Noah's suit that she had given him such a hard time over.

Had Noah left them out, or Justin? Suddenly, she wasn't sure. She desperately needed the time alone, but having Autumn at her back was reassuring.

The bathroom mirror still held the message. She imagined they'd photographed it from every angle. It was a wonder some enterprising tech hadn't felt the need to take the mirror itself in for evidence.

She backed away, not wanting to see how pale she was. Not wanting to see fractured slices of her face between the words scrawled in her own lipstick.

It felt like a stranger's house, like she was the invader. It was a strange place, as if her and Noah's claim had been dissipated like so much smoke.

She held herself tightly and wondered if she should have taken Autumn up on her offer of staying with her for a while. She should have thanked her friend, hugged her, and sent her on her way despite Autumn's protests. That she was still here with Winter just felt like giving in to Justin and his cruelty. If

Winter was going to reclaim the apartment, then she had to...what...clean up the mess and move on? Suddenly, it all seemed overwhelming.

The phone rang, the sound making her jump. She caught herself and mentally whispered a harsh reminder that she was a federal agent and needed to be able to face things like killers and madmen. She stormed into the bedroom, grabbing her phone from her purse.

It was Noah.

"Hey."

"Hey, honey. You okay?" Noah sounded excited, his voice higher pitched, his words tumbling over each other in his haste to speak.

She sat heavily on the bed. "Yeah. I'm good. You sound happy."

"Not happy, but cautiously optimistic."

His words made her smile. "What's going on?"

"They may have found Justin's RV."

Winter was on her feet in an instant. "Really?" She said the word so loud that Autumn rushed to the door, concern on her pretty features.

"Remember the word 'may,' but it's looking good."

"Where?" Noah hesitated, and Winter repeated the question, her voice more demanding. "Where?!"

"No, Winter. You're not going. I'm on my way there now."

She was already grabbing her purse and heading for the door. She glanced back and watched Autumn grab hers as well. It was good to have friends.

"Winter...?" Noah said as she locked the door. "I can hear your footsteps."

She made her shoes click harder. "Glad to know your hearing is so good."

Noah sighed. "Look, I called to let you know what was

going on because I love you and knew you'd want to know. You need to stay right—"

"I'll never sleep with you again if you don't tell me where you're heading."

Another long silence, and despite the current situation, it made her smile.

"Winter, that's not fair."

Winter went to the driver's side of Autumn's car, holding her hand up for the keys. With no hesitation, Autumn tossed them to her. Within seconds, they'd piled in and Winter had the car in drive and was roaring out of the parking lot.

"All's fair in love and war, baby," she said once her Bluetooth picked up, and she was talking over Autumn's speakers. "Now, you can tell me where to go, or I'll call someone else who will tell me and you'll have to deal with blue balls for the rest of your life."

Beside her, Autumn placed her hands over her mouth to stifle a laugh.

"Shit."

"Listen, Noah, I already know that he could be at only one of three places. The churches I gave you." She shot an apologetic look at Autumn as she ripped around a corner. She'd make sure she was given credit for the find later. "You can either…"

Winter's vision went dark, but only for a second. Actually, it must have been a little longer because, by the time her gaze was on the road again, Autumn had taken the wheel.

"She's having a vision," Autumn yelled. "Tell her where we need to go so she can drive!"

Pain ripped through Winter's head, and the warmth of blood trickled from her nose. She needed to pull over, but she also needed to find Justin…before he was killed.

"Tell me," she screamed, though the sound was more like

a roar. She took her foot off the accelerator while she fumbled for a tissue to stanch the flow.

"Let me drive," Autumn said, her hand still on the wheel. "Pull over and—"

She was interrupted by Noah, who was spitting the address out at them, like each syllable was a bullet from between his teeth. Autumn let go of the wheel and typed the address into her GPS.

The vision cleared, and Winter felt more normal now that her brain wasn't trying to feed her the information. She hit the gas. "Thank you, Noah. You can hate me later."

"I could never hate you."

Winter smiled, feeling the warmth of love rush through her. He did love her, and she loved him. She had a good job, good friends, a generous lover. Her life was complete, and she'd soon have fulfilled her mission of finding Justin again.

Alive. Please let it be alive.

"In a quarter of a mile, turn left on Gallagher Way."

Winter was eating up that quarter of a mile at breakneck speed when she heard someone speaking on Noah's radio.

"What's that?" she yelled, taking a curve too quickly and slamming Autumn against the door. "Put your seatbelt on."

"I already did," Autumn mumbled.

"Aiden's on his six. They're going to get him, Winter. Stand down."

"Like hell," she murmured and glanced at Autumn. "Call Aiden...now!"

Autumn did as she was asked, and soon, she heard Aiden's voice on the cell phone speaker. "Do you have Winter?"

"Yes," Winter shouted. "She's got me, and we're heading in your direction. Where are you exactly?"

"Dammit to hell," she heard Noah say over the car's speakers.

"We've got this, Winter," Aiden said. "I'm in pursuit and

don't have time for a lively conversation, but I need you and Autumn to stay put. We've got this. Do you understand?"

Winter pressed the accelerator harder. "I'm coming your way. If you're behind him, I can cut him off from the front."

"What?" Autumn and Noah said in unison.

"No, too dangerous," Aiden added.

Winter gritted her teeth. "I'm a highly trained federal agent, in case you've forgotten. I can do this. I'm not that little girl anymore."

She held her breath, praying he'd make the right decision.

"Okay." He gave her the name of the road and the mile marker he was on. "Justin is a few hundred yards in front of me, but I'm gaining."

They were close.

"I can let you out," Winter told her friend, who was holding on to the "oh shit" handle with all of her might.

"No!" Autumn shouted unnecessarily loud in the car. "Let's get him."

Winter smiled. "I was wrong. You're not Ethel. You're Thelma and I'm Louise."

Autumn laughed, but the sound was shaky. "Just don't drive off a cliff. Please."

"Which one was doing the driving?" Winter asked, calmed by this nonsense conversation. "Thelma or Louise?"

Another shaky laugh. "I have no idea."

Just then, bright lights appeared in the distance. Those were followed by another pair, then more.

Winter blew out a breath. "Guess we don't have time to Google it and find out."

Autumn grabbed the handle tighter. "Nope."

"Don't do this," Noah was saying, but Winter couldn't listen to him right then.

"I love you, Noah," she said as they shot down the highway, taking up the center lane, "but you can't put Baby in a corner."

Autumn laughed, though the sound was more hysterical now. "Wrong movie."

"Whatever."

The entire world narrowed down to just this road in Winter's mind. As Justin's headlights grew brighter, she grew calmer. More steady.

"There you are," she whispered.

She'd been searching for her baby brother for forever, and he was now, very literally, in her sights. Her headlights beamed off his car.

Chicken.

She and Justin used to play that game as a child. They'd belt pillows around themselves so that, if they crashed into each other, it wouldn't hurt too much.

Justin always won.

Being so much older and taller and stronger, Winter hadn't had the heart to hurt her little brother.

Until now.

She had to have the heart now.

"Ohhhh…" Autumn moaned as the distance closed with surprising speed.

Winter stayed in the middle. So did Justin.

"Godddddd…"

With a clarity she'd never known, Winter tightened her hands on the wheel, loosening her body for the impact she knew was coming.

I'm so sorry, Justin, she thought, *but I have to do this. I have to stop you from hurting anyone else. I'll be the last.*

She would turn the car at the last instant, taking the impact on her side of the vehicle in the hopes of saving her friend.

Winter wanted to tell Noah that she loved him one more time, but time was no longer her companion.

Blinded by the oncoming light, Winter forced her eyes to stay open.

Waiting...

Waiting...

Justin turned first. The scream of his tires echoed through her mind as he began to spin, out of control. She slammed on her brakes, a sob spilling from her lips.

In the rearview mirror, she watched in horror as the second car tried to stop. It was Aiden. At that speed, he wouldn't be able to stop in time, and before she could even scream, his car t-boned into Justin's. Metal screamed as the cars twisted together.

The moment Autumn's car came to a halt, Winter had her door open and was running toward the wreckage.

She pressed her face against Aiden's cracked window. He didn't move. She tried to open his door, but it was crumbled shut.

As she screamed his name, he lifted his head from the white of the air bag. Blinking rapidly, he lifted a hand to his nose and winced. Winter banged on the window as other agents and emergency personnel ran up beside her, some pulling her away.

She covered her mouth with both hands, letting out a cry of relief when Aiden held up his thumb. He was okay. Relief made her body weak, but...

What about her brother?

Aiden's car had hit the rear driver's side panel of Justin's car, not the driver's door as she'd feared. On legs that didn't feel like they would carry her another step, she walked to the front of the little car.

Please be dead.

Please be alive.

The two thoughts warred in her mind as she tried to see her brother through the broken glass. Just a glimpse.

A paramedic was entering the passenger side of the car. He was feeling her brother's neck. Putting a brace around it too. Another joined him, and they worked to find the source of the blood that had stained the airbag red.

He still didn't move.

An arm came around her. It was Autumn, her friend. Winter leaned heavily against her, grateful for her support.

"He's alive," Autumn whispered.

Winter didn't know if she needed to laugh or cry. The words ran through her like an electrical charge, after all the effort and fear and confusion. How could it be over? She looked around at the wreckage and couldn't comprehend the fact that it was over.

Or was it?

She swallowed hard, sinking to the pavement when her legs refused to hold her up, Autumn following her down. She suddenly needed to know more, a lot more. "And Aiden...?"

"He got banged up a little, but it's all superficial. He'll be fine."

Federal agents shouldn't cry, but Winter no longer cared. The sudden relief of tension and knowing that Justin was captured after all they'd been through made something in her rip apart.

She choked on a sob, the kind that started so far inside that the entire body shook with the effort to get them free. Once started, there was no stopping. She cried for her parents. For her brother. For herself.

She cried for the people who had been harmed in such terrible ways.

Autumn simply held her, holding her as she cried. Then, there was another set of arms around her. Big arms. Familiar arms.

Noah.

And as he pressed his lips to her hair, she knew everything would be okay, no matter what happened next.

"YOU HAVE MATCHING NOSES," Noah said.

Aiden good-naturedly flipped him off.

Both federal agent and suspect bore a white stripe of bandage across their noses, coincidentally being the only real damage either of them had taken from the accident. Justin's arm wasn't broken. In fact, the doctors gave him a full workup and found only bruising, nothing broken but the nose. They were calling it a Christmas miracle.

Aiden had a thorough inspection as well, same Emergency Room, same hour. He likewise was found to have no injury other than the air bag exploding into his face. The attending doctor pointed out that, without the airbag, it would have been a lot worse.

"The car is totaled," Aiden said with a grimace. "Frame damage. I'm feeling much the same way."

"Bet Max loved that. He hates paperwork that involves high-speed chases."

"We…discussed it…" Aiden said dryly, "at length. You'd be surprised though at how much you can get away with if you catch a crazed killer now and then."

"I'll keep that in mind if I need a day off."

It felt good to joke. After what they'd been through, maybe they all needed the release.

Noah watched Justin through the one-way glass. Winter's brother was still rocking back and forth in his chair, his lips moving. Noah didn't bother turning on the sound again. He already knew what Justin was saying. He'd been saying it for several minutes.

"Where do we start?" As Noah watched, Justin turned toward him. The one-way mirror between them never fooled anyone. Justin was no different. He knew what the mirror was really there for and seemed to like playing to the crowd. At least he couldn't see who was behind it.

So far, he seemed to enjoy talking to the mirror, saying "Winter" as though he suspected that she was behind the mirror, not two agents he didn't know. Then he would revert to the same singsong nonsense he'd been muttering since he'd woken up.

At least he couldn't get free to make good on any of his threats. He was shackled, wrists and ankles, and they were, in turn, chained to an eyebolt in the table. The room was unadorned cinderblock and doors that were half-inch steel. There were no chances taken with this prisoner. His ubiquitous guard wasn't in the room this time. They were letting Justin stew for a little while before beginning. Now, the question was, which question to start with first.

"Has he lawyered up yet?" Aiden asked.

"He refused. Said that lawyers were corrupt devils."

Aiden shook his head and took a breath. Whatever he was about to say vanished as Bree opened the door behind them and Winter followed her into the observation room. Autumn closed the door behind them. Aiden and Noah both scrambled to make room for Winter to approach the mirror and really look at her little brother in person for the first time since they were children.

Autumn's hand on her back fell away as Winter reached out to hold on to Noah's arm. Justin looked so young, so fragile and so angry. Noah tried to see him the way Winter would, but he knew that Winter's reaction was too far removed from his experiences to fully understand.

"Are you going to talk to him?" Noah asked her.

Aiden jolted upright, a move that had to hurt given how

many bruises he sported. He was probably thinking of the ramifications of the question and wondering just how messy this was going to get. Winter wasn't just family, she was an agent too. That made things complicated. Even so, Noah didn't rescind the offer, and to his surprise, Aiden said nothing.

"No," Winter said softly after thinking this over for a long moment. "Not yet. I'm not ready."

Aiden visibly relaxed at her response. While it was only fair for her to talk to Justin, it would have made Aiden's job, even the job of the prosecutor's office, a lot harder. She cleared her throat, struggling to speak in a calm and professional tone. "Where is his lawyer? Shouldn't his legal counsel be here for questioning?"

"He refused counsel," Aiden said. He too was watching Justin, though the boy hadn't moved.

Winter blinked. "Are you kidding?" She shook her head. "We're getting him a lawyer. I don't want anything left to chance." Winter squeezed Noah's arm tightly and leaned against him. "Is that a conflict of interest?" she asked Aiden, turning her head to include him in the conversation.

"Probably," Aiden said. "But he's refusing one and that's his right."

"Is he saying something?" Autumn poked her head around Winter to see into the room. She looked between Aiden and Noah. "I also have to ask about conflict of interest, but at the moment, I'm slated to give him a psychological eval. It's easier for me if I can observe him for a while."

"He's saying the same things he's been saying," Aiden said, speaking up before Noah could. "Then he started rocking back and forth in his chair, repeating the same thing over and over again."

He reached over and flipped the intercom setting on the voice monitor.

Justin's voice filled the observation room. "Winnnttt-terrr...come out to play! Winnntttterrr ...come out to play!" He laughed a little and fell silent for a moment before starting up again with a harsh laugh as he looked straight at them. "Winnntttterrr...come out to play!"

35

W inter stood still, watching the interrogation through the one-way mirror. Autumn had offered her a chair, Bree had gone to get one, but sitting would have blocked her view. She couldn't leave Justin alone, not again. At the same time, she couldn't face him either. Not yet. Too soon.

She pictured herself going in there, talking to him, seeing him without a pane of protective glass between them. Every time she tried, she felt the incredible sadness well up in her, the hate for Kilroy, even some residual anger at her parents for dying and letting Justin disappear, forcing Winter to go live with her grandparents.

The emotions were too raw. The atrocities Justin had committed in order to have been placed here like this...it all mixed together like a witch's brew of emotion. Right now, she wasn't strong enough to see him. She knew that from her bones out.

She turned the audio down a little, Noah and Aiden had been asking him questions for some time. The court-appointed lawyer sat in the room, saying nothing. Winter had been serious about paying for a lawyer in order to get a good one, but none of the attorneys they'd contacted would take the case. More than a few had jokingly expressed interest in being with the DA for this particular case, but the FBI had done its usual thorough job and no one believed that Justin had a leg to stand on.

Still, the judge assigned to the case had serious doubts about Justin being competent to decide if he should have an attorney or not, so within hours of the initial interview, he had one.

This young man from the public defender's office spent more of his time watching Justin than watching the men who questioned his client. He did manage to speak up once in a while, but that was only when he felt Noah or Aiden were making progress in their questioning. As soon as one of them asked a leading question, or Justin was about to blow up and say more than he wanted, his lawyer burst in, advising Justin not to say anything else and advising the FBI to rephrase or ask something else.

He was doing his job and doing it very well, and the part of Winter that was an FBI agent hated the man for it. The part of her that was Justin's sister was delighted that someone was finally looking out for her little brother. Correction, someone was *properly* looking out for her little brother.

At either rate, whatever emotion she felt, she kept it off her face. Her posture was rigid, her jaw was clenched, but she couldn't take her eyes off her brother. That was Justin. For so many years, she'd thought he was dead. She'd mourned him but had never been able to let him go. Now he was there, sitting right in front of her.

Yet, even as she watched, he was being taken from her again. Whatever the young lawyer might be thinking, the FBI had this case well in hand, the I's were dotted, the T's were crossed, and the buildup of the case was airtight. They leapt to the lawyer's demands, treated Justin with all the respect and special treatment his attorney wanted because… it didn't matter. Surely to god, it didn't matter.

They had him. Even Justin knew the Bureau had him, and there would be no sneaking out of this one.

At least, that was the way it was supposed to be.

Winter wasn't so sure.

Her baby brother was smart, and she didn't think the justice system would soon see the end of him. No, she was afraid this was only the beginning of his manipulations.

"WHAT CAR WERE you driving when you had your accident?"

"A red one." I looked up into The Sinner's face, a small smile playing on my lips. The car had been red. It had ultimately been a piece of garbage. I could have outrun that futzy old agent if I'd had my truck. But no, they had my truck now. I only took that car because it blended in. My mistake. I should have taken a car with some guts to it.

"You trying to be funny?" the broken-nosed man asked me.

"Agent Parrish, I might point out my client did answer your question. It's not everyone that knows about cars and auto manufacturers." The mouthpiece spoke up. They forced him to be here. He didn't want to be here, I didn't want him here, but they forced it. Just like everything else, they forced their will on others.

I tolerated the lawyer's presence because he was turning into a pain in the butt for the cops. It was fun to see them spun up. Nothing could piss off a cop faster than a lawyer.

I stared at The Sinner, the same exact man I'd seen going into my half-sister's apartment. I hated him. I should have killed him when I had the chance. I'd kill him now if given the chance.

The Sinner shot my attorney a look before returning his attention back to me. "Where did you get it?"

"Get what?" I asked, just to be a pain.

"Where did you get the car?"

"Oh that." I grinned. "I plucked it off a tree. It was ripe, and I needed a ride."

The Sinner pulled a picture from his jacket. It was a woman, late thirties, kind of pretty, long black hair fanned out from her face and stuck in the pool of blood under her.

I gasped and tried to reach for it, but my hands were cuffed. "Very pretty."

"Funny guy," Broken Nose growled at me.

I was surprised. I wasn't being funny. She was pretty. She reminded me of my mo...of someone I knew once. I turned to The Sinner. "You fuck my sister." I stated it calmly, coolly. I thought that might open a dialog with him. I wondered if I would be able to warn him about women, about my *half-*sister in particular. He needed to be warned. They were living together. They weren't married, which meant they were going to hell forever. Their mutual damnation was her fault, and he needed to know.

I was shocked when he got angry. He slammed the table in front of me like Grandpa used to before he punished me, and I jumped. Only the chains, they didn't jump with me, but pulled my hands down as I tried to leap to my feet. It *hurt.* The pain that laced through my arms was incredible.

"Agent Dalton." My lawyer raised a hand. "Is this true?"

"Of course it's true!" I shot back, but the lawyer kept his hand raised as he shot me a look that told me to be quiet.

He clearly didn't want to hear me, he wanted to hear what The Sinner had to say. "Agent Dalton, this is a clear conflict of interest. If you're involved in a relationship with my client's sister, I—"

"Half-sister!" The Sinner snapped.

I didn't really care what the two of them talked about, it gave me a moment where the questions weren't directed at me, and I could breathe again. In those moments I could tell myself that Grandpa was dead and that he could never punish me again. I had to force down his voice sometimes. I had to force the fear deep inside of me.

"Then this is only half illegal." I looked at my attorney to see if he got the joke, but he didn't. He was a lawyer, and Grandpa said that all lawyers were minor devils who worked for Satan. I believed it. This one had no sense of humor, despite the fact that he wore a stupid-looking mustache. A man who looked like a joke should have a great sense of humor.

"Does that tickle your wife?" I stroked my upper lip and pointed to him, because I really wanted to know. It seemed like it would. I kept clean-shaven because Grandpa insisted, back when that first hair appeared on my chin, that I had to keep my face clean and my hair short.

"Are you trying to get off on a mental?" Broken Nose asked me. "You might want to work on your acting if you are."

I touched the bandage on my nose. I had no idea where I got it from. It was just there. I think it came with the prison clothes, like it was some strange part of the orange jumpsuit. Except my nose hurt when I touched it. It hurt a lot.

This guy had a broken nose, and he wore a bandage over his like I did. I thought maybe he knew why I had one, but when I had asked, he got mad. I'd stopped asking. That was before the lawyer got there. Back when the conversation was friendlier. Once the lawyer got there, that was when they started getting nasty. I didn't like the lawyer.

"What happened to the Ulbrichs?" The Sinner asked me.

"Agent Dalton." The attorney sounded angry. Everyone sounded so angry all the time. "You must be excused from questioning. If you are in a relationship with my client's sister, you…"

"HALF-SISTER!" I screamed at him. For Pete's sake, he just didn't listen.

"…should not be in this room. You should not have been the agent in charge, for that matter. It's a mistake that could be costly for your cause."

Broken Nose grabbed The Sinner and whispered something in The Sinner's ear. The Sinner's hands rose like they were going to embrace, and I stared at the pair. Were they like Sodom? Grandpa used to talk about Sodom a lot, but mostly how we were different from the Biblical story.

My mind spun back in time, flittering through my past as The Sinner and attorney argued about things I simply didn't care about.

I cared only about one thing. Winter.

No one seemed to realize I was waiting for her. If they wanted me to answer any questions, then those questions needed to come from her mouth. Only then would I speak to these bastards.

Why hadn't she come to see me?

Was she sleeping again?

She'd just stood there while they'd taken me away, just as she'd laid on the floor when Grandpa had taken me away.

Didn't she care?

I made a sound that came out very much like a childish giggle, and the three sets of eyes turned on me. I made the sound again, only louder this time.

They thought I was crazy? I'd show them crazy.

When The Sinner stood up and slammed out of the room, I waved my fingers in a childish goodbye, then stuck my thumb in my mouth. It felt good. Right. Grandpa used to yell at me when I sucked anything but his…

I closed my eyes and began to rock, humming the song he used to play on the radio when he "loved me in our special way."

Come, and partake the gospel feast
Be saved from sin; in Jesus rest
O taste the goodness of your God
And eat His flesh and drink His blood!

Grandpa liked when I drank his blood, except his blood wasn't red. He said his blood was special and only for me.

Because I was special.

Special.

So very special.

And now I'd failed.

I'd failed to fulfill the mission. I'd failed to bring about Winter's end. I'd failed it all.

Broken Nose was talking to me. I could hear his voice and I could even hear the words, but they didn't make sense. Would anything ever make sense again?

I wasn't sure.

Because I'd failed.

Failed.

Failed.

In the end, I shut down as Broken Nose tried to get me to answer questions, and my attorney tried to get me to not talk, and I wondered why Winter didn't come to see me. She'd left me again.

It was too bad really. I had a surprise I was saving just for her. Something she wasn't going to like, but then Harlots never did like the truth, did they?

Maybe soon.

Soon.

36

Winter sat in the passenger seat of Noah's truck while he drove. She was watching the sidewalk slide past as the streetlights flashed over the windshield. She could feel Noah's concern for her, and though it was sweet, she didn't really want to talk just then. The two or three times he'd tried to pry her from her shell, she'd answered with single syllables and kept her face resolutely pointed toward the passenger window, staring at closed shops and the fading lights of the city as they headed home.

Home.

It had become an interesting concept. She'd scrubbed the mirror clean, the last message she'd gotten from Justin was gone, but her memory placed it there every time she stepped into the bathroom. She'd taken a shower after cleaning the apartment, and the steam from the hot water had fogged up the mirror but didn't cling to the letters she'd scrubbed for so long.

Justin's threat had reappeared, written in steam. She guessed it would take time for the oils to wear off the mirror. It would take much longer for the oils to wear off her.

The papers she and Autumn had so carefully gathered had been shoved back in the box, in no particular order and without regard to their condition. The more she'd found about Bill's family, the less she wanted to be a part of it.

Bill Black had been a good man. She had to remind herself of that now. He'd been kind and gentle. She was still proud to call him "Daddy," and there were probably others like him somewhere in that family tree, but she had no more interest in finding any of them.

Arthur was just as bad as Kilroy, though if Arthur had killed anyone, he'd gotten away with it. She flashed on Arthur's wife, Lynn. Even if he hadn't killed her with a blow, the abuse Winter had seen in her vision lay the poor woman's death directly at his feet.

That box Arthur kept with Lynn's picture in it was so typical for a bully or a sociopath it was almost cliché. That he loved Lynn was as obvious as the fact that he had driven her to an early death.

Kilroy was from that family. The Preacher. The mass murderer who killed people for being immoral, as if killing wasn't the ultimate in immorality.

Then there was Justin. True, Kilroy had mistreated Justin, it probably wasn't a genetic predisposition to violence, but by all accounts, Kilroy's father had been a right bastard to his son too. If anything, their bloodline carried a legacy, if not a genetic one. Winter was well rid of the chains of that part of the family. Even though their blood wasn't hers, it was a little too close for her comfort.

She sighed and looked at the clock. It was too late at night to call her grandparents. She made a mental note to call them in the morning and thank them for raising her.

Noah pulled silently into the parking lot next to their building. She shook herself to get her mind back on the business of getting out of the truck and back into her life. The dumpsters the tenants used were just behind the corner, out of view. At least one of them contained a printer box full of copies of old family records.

Everything that hadn't been taken for evidence but had looked like Justin might have used it or pawed at it had been tossed or taken to the cleaners with specific orders to remove any smells or dirt that might or might not be in the fabric. She had cleaned him out of her life as much as she could and still felt like it wasn't enough.

They walked to their apartment in silence, the way they'd ridden in the car. The broken trim around the door still looked ugly, but the deadbolt had already been replaced. The building manager had promised he would fix and repaint the frame within the next day or two.

Winter wished that everything broken could so easily be fixed.

"Wow." Noah whistled appreciatively as he walked in the door. "This looks amazing. You cleaned this place down to the shine."

"It helped," Winter confessed as she stripped off her jacket. "I had a lot of nervous energy I needed to burn off."

Noah walked up behind her and placed his hands on her hips. He was being so careful with her, and she leaned back into his chest. It almost felt like her home again. Almost.

"Noah..." Her gaze was on the big window that faced the stars and a velvet sky. Their reflection in the glass was faint, ghosts against the starry night. "Can we get a tree?"

"A tree? Maple?"

Winter laughed, the picture of a maple tree in their apartment striking her as funny. "A Christmas tree, dufus. It's nearly Christmas, you know?"

His arms wrapped around her from behind, and he set his chin on her head. He hummed a little in his throat and kissed her hair. "Of course. We'll pick one out tomorrow. How about that?"

"I'd like that." Winter closed her eyes. "I couldn't do it, you know?"

Noah froze a little, but he didn't stop holding her. Waiting her out.

She studied their reflection, glad she couldn't make out his eyes. "I couldn't talk to him. Not yet. It's been...too rough, too emotional. I needed...I need time, time to adjust, to be able to talk to him as a sister and not an agent."

"That makes sense," Noah murmured into her hair, "and you're tired. You're exhausted." As if to prove his point, his mouth opened with a jaw-cracking yawn.

Winter laughed at him, but found yawning to be contagious. "Now you've got me doing it." She smacked his arm playfully as she broke free of his grasp. "Get to bed, you."

"Me?" Noah brought a hand to his chest in surprise. "I was saying *you're* the one who needs the rest."

Winter hopped from one foot to the other. That nervous energy was back. "I don't know if I *could* sleep right now. My mind is going in a hundred different directions at once."

"Because you didn't talk to Justin?" Noah asked, his face serious now.

"No. I mean, yes, but no." Winter shook her head and rubbed at her eyes, hating the tired burn when she had so much energy. "I didn't talk to him because I'm too tired to face him the way I want to. It's just...with all the crap that we all went through because of him, because of the investigation, the collapsing church, the strain it had on you, on Bree, on Autumn..." She stopped and shook her head. To her ears it all sounded crazy. Like too much. "The toll it had on me physically and emotionally is intense. I'm too tired to sleep."

He bobbed his eyebrows. "I could suggest a way to burn off some energy."

She bobbed her eyebrows in return. "I like the way you think, then I'll take a Benadryl to make sure I stay conked out. My thoughts are racing, but I know I'm tired." She put her hand on his arm. "I'll be in in a bit," she told him and headed for the bathroom.

"Wait...collapsing church? You mean literally collapsed? I thought it had already fallen when you went in. Do you mean it fell while you were inside?"

"I'll tell you later!" she called over her shoulder as she closed the door. She stood in the bathroom staring at her reflection warily. The words on the mirror danced through her memory.

She stripped, took a quick shower, brushed her teeth, and got ready for bed. Normal things. At least they felt normal, natural. She hadn't felt that way for days. She swallowed a Benadryl and walked into the bedroom where Noah was waiting under the covers for her.

She climbed in, and Noah immediately reached for her, wrapping his arms around her, spooning her naturally. She snuggled into his embrace. Without a word, they made love with an urgency that appeared to surprise them both.

They both needed it. Needed each other. Needed to remember that nothing else mattered when it was just the two of them like this, this close.

"Tell me more about this collapsing church," Noah said after the sweat had dried on their bodies and their breathing had grown even again.

Winter grinned, rolling over to face him. "You really don't want to know..."

"Try me. I think I do."

In the end, she told him about her adventure and how she came by the deeds in an old desk in the basement. Noah snorted in amusement at her and Autumn, interrupting her narration to agree with Autumn's assessment. "No, you're *definitely* Lucy in this case." He lifted up on one elbow when she told him about the church falling in on itself.

"Next haunted church," he said harshly, his eyes dark with concern, "you wait for backup."

"Deal." Winter laughed. Noah settled and held her tightly. It felt good. They hadn't been able to be like this in weeks. She missed the closeness, but as soothing as his arms were, her mind was still too active to sleep. "Noah." She whispered his name, not wanting to wake him if he was asleep.

Noah grunted, but the inflection went up at the end, like a question.

"Is it my fault? Justin being like he is? Should I have... could I have done something different that night when my parents were killed? I've thought about it a lot over the years. I snuck out that night and was in the middle of sneaking back in while they were being killed. If I'd stayed home, then maybe I could have done something to save them. Save him."

He held her more tightly. "Or you would most likely be dead. You were only thirteen years old, sweetheart. You might be a badass now, but I'd suspect you weren't very badass back then."

She smiled, thinking about how she looked at that age, all elbows and knees, and not an extra ounce of fat on her skinny body.

She grew serious again. "I can't help but think that Justin is messed up because of me."

"That's because kids take on all the guilt of their families."

Winter snuggled into his chest, remembering how this big strong man had taken on the guilt of his failed family too. It was under very different circumstances, but guilt was guilt all the same.

Noah raised himself up again, but somehow managed to hold her tighter. "You've seen a lot of traumatized kids in this job, we both have. I defy you to take the memory of any one of those children and tell that hurting boy or girl that it was their fault. That's just cruel."

Winter nodded and felt a tear run down her nose. She wiped it away angrily.

He kissed the next one away. "Tell me what you remember about Justin *before* that night."

"He was a hellion." Winter laughed a little, knowing he was trying to distract her, and letting him. "He was always the troublemaker. He got into absolutely everything. Did you know he had this stuffed giraffe that he carried with him everywhere? Its neck was broken and its head flopped every which way."

Winter yawned as she spoke. Surprisingly, the tension in her body eased, both from the strong arms around her and from the Benadryl beginning to take effect. Somewhere in the night, between stories of a small boy she once knew, sleep crept in and claimed her. Noah still holding her was the last thing she remembered till morning.

37

"All rise!" With that formal command and everyone in the courtroom coming to their feet, the arraignment of one Justin Black began.

Aiden, sitting in the front row of the spectator's box, stood, and the entire press corps stood up behind him with the sound of a small avalanche. The only one in the court not standing was Justin himself. He was locked into a chair at the side of the courtroom.

The prosecuting attorney looked smug. Thanks to the feds, he had a relatively simple job. Justin's fingerprints and DNA were everywhere at the crime scenes, his RV had yielded an expensive necklace that could be traced back to Sandy Ulbrich, and his video was practically a confession. Aiden didn't even figure this to go to trial.

He hoped, even as his gut churned in warning that this wasn't going to be as clean-cut as it appeared.

After the arraignment, the defense would probably try to bargain for life in prison and avoid the death penalty. If it were anyone else, Aiden would have welcomed such a verdict for someone who had done the things Justin had done, but what that would do to Winter made him willing to take a plea deal.

The judge entered and pounded the gavel, signaling the court could sit again.

"Before we begin," he shot a hard look at the observation area, "I want to caution the ladies and gentlemen of the press. I have you here under some misgivings, and in order for this court to indulge the members of the fourth estate, I will insist on decorum. I will have no outbursts or shouted questions, upon penalty of each and every one of you being evicted from this room or held in contempt. Is that quite clear to you all?"

He waited until the heads behind Aiden began nodding. It was like watching a schoolteacher scold three-year-olds, and Aiden felt a little better already. Maybe this wouldn't become a media circus after all.

"This is the arraignment of," the judge picked up some papers and began reading, "Justin Black, also known as Jaime Peterson. The charges against the defendant are six counts of murder, four counts attempted murder, grand theft auto, kidnapping…"

Aiden wondered about that one. Then he remembered the woman Justin had killed to get her car. She'd fought him, and he'd pushed her into the vehicle and taken off with her. He'd gone a half mile before tossing her dead body from the car.

"…armed robbery, assault with a deadly weapon, breaking and entering, aggravated assault…"

The number of charges were astonishing. By the time the judge finished, there was murmuring in the press behind him. The judge shot them a warning glance and hit the gavel once, and they subsided.

"Counsel for the defense," the judge peered over his glasses at the attorney, "how do you plead?"

Aiden exhaled a breath that had grown stale in his lungs. Finally, the horror of The Preacher was done. A guilty plea, a negotiation and it would be over.

"Not guilty by reason of insanity, Your Honor."

The press exploded behind him, questions and opinions and shock registering at full volume. Even the gavel couldn't quell the commotion that simple response created. The judge glared them down, and when they wouldn't hush, he ordered the courtroom cleared. The bailiffs had their hands full of yelling reporters. The families of Justin's victims were, if anything, louder and less inclined to be escorted out.

The prisoner was hauled to his feet, penguin-walking in the chains that bound him. They would keep him in the courthouse jail until the judge resumed the hearing after the chaos was over.

In the middle of the confusion, Justin caught Aiden's eye and smiled.

And Aiden had a terrible, terrible feeling. The little bastard was going to get away with it.

AUTUMN WAS WAITING in Aiden's office when he returned. She'd helped herself to some of the Bureau's coffee and spent her time paging through a file. It was a very poor breach in protocol to occupy the man's office when he was out, but she was a well-known fixture at the Bureau by now, and given her closeness to Winter, they were likely granting some leniency.

She wondered how that looked to his colleagues. A woman waiting in Aiden's office might seem a little...familiar. Maybe even a little proprietary. She glanced up from the file and looked at his empty chair. She could do worse than a man like him. Aiden was a handsome man, smart, capable.

There was a history there, but if the past few days had taught her anything, it was that clinging to the past was a fool's game. She smiled at the empty chair and thought about the man who sat there. The question was, what did she want? She was only just starting to figure it out. He might fit nicely into her future. It might be worth it to find out for sure.

The past was past.

She went back to the file, flipping through it when she heard a minor commotion from the main area where frazzled agents and support staff fielded phone calls and cursed the endless stream of paperwork that comprised the FBI. It was like a moving disturbance in the ordered chaos of the place.

Aiden was back, and as he walked into the area, men and women called to him, stood to fist-bump or high-five. Aiden was a sort of celebrity, and the men and women were all smiles as he passed. He was the hero of the day, the man who'd caught Jaime Peterson.

Aiden's expression was anything but heroic. He took their accolades in good stride, but his face had a very set expression. He was frustrated. Autumn could feel it coming off him in waves. She rose and waited for him to arrive, frowning in concern.

He brightened considerably when he saw her standing there and slowed as he entered the office. "Well, hello." He slipped off his coat and hung it up.

"Happy holidays and all," Autumn said, her smile widening as the tension eased out of his shoulders when he saw her. He was instantly more relaxed. It felt good to brighten someone's day just by being there. It also felt good to have someone be that happy to see her.

"To you too. I see you've found the eggnog." He pointed to the coffee cup in her hand.

She laughed at his joke and set the cup on his desk. "You seem to be in a mood."

He waved it off and came to sit next to her instead of behind his desk. "I got thrown out of the courtroom. Did you hear about Justin's arraignment?"

"Yes, insanity. I'm not so sure it's not a legitimate argument. At any rate, I'm about to find out. I've asked the DA and they're finding no conflict of interest being Winter's friend, so I've been assigned to analyze Justin's mental health." She held up the file she was carrying, which was filled with Justin's medical records and assessment so far.

"Lucky you. Do you think he's crazy?"

Autumn winced a little at the word. "We try to avoid that word in the professional circles," she reminded him and shrugged. "I won't know that until I talk to him."

"Just be careful. He's dangerous, whatever he is."

Autumn couldn't argue with that. "What do you mean you got 'thrown out' of court? What did you do?"

"Nothing!" Aiden's frustration ramped up again, but he was able to let it go, at least mostly. There was still a line of tension at the corners of his mouth. "When the plea came in, the press went wild and the judge ordered them evicted and—"

Autumn laughed. "And the bailiffs thought that you were with the press?" She saw the expression on his face and just about rolled in her chair. Eventually, the absurdity of the situation caught up to Aiden too, and he began to smile. A chuckle soon followed.

"They refused to look at the badge. When the judge orders everyone out, they throw out *everyone*. I decided the easier solution was to come back to the office."

In a moment, they were both letting off some needed steam through laughter.

A girl could do worse.

38

Winter swallowed again. The only thing harder than seeing Justin would have been not seeing him. This was something she had to do.

The jail doors rattled as a guard opened them from the inside. She was escorted into a small conference room. The sound of her shoes on the tile echoed in the sterile hallway as she was shown to a door that was closed and locked. Her escort looked in through a window and nodded before shoving a key into the lock. The great tumblers fell with an audible click and the door opened.

Winter walked into the room to find Justin already seated. He was wearing the same sort of chains that Arkwell had, wrists chained to the table, ankles to the chair and another chain that ran between them.

As she walked in, Justin looked up, and for a moment, there was confusion in his face, as if he didn't recognize her. A look of recognition and surprise lit his face and his smile got bigger. This was a real smile. Even the look in his eyes softened as his entire face relaxed. He was genuinely happy to see her.

"There she is," Justin said slowly, as if in wonder at some miraculous event. "My dear half-sister. I was wondering if you were going to come and say hello."

"Hello, Justin." Her voice went high, like a little girl's, and didn't sound like her at all. She cleared her throat and perched on the edge of the chair facing him.

"Miss me?" Justin tilted his head as he asked the question, as though the answer meant a great deal to him.

"For a very long time," Winter said quietly, struggling to swallow down the emotion that left her throat thick with unshed tears. "More than you know."

"Well, I'm here now. How about we go get a drink and catch up on old times?"

Winter caught her breath and looked down at the hands entwined in her lap, fighting not to cry. God, how he hated her. "I thought you were killed that night."

"I was." When Winter looked up, Justin's smile was gone. His face seemed blank. Empty. Like he wasn't even home. "Justin died that night. Jaime Peterson was born. It was the first time I became someone else. Grandpa taught me how."

"He wasn't your Grandpa," Winter shot back more vehemently than she'd intended.

"You're not my sister," Justin countered. His smile was back, but now it was mocking, snide, cruel. His eyes had narrowed and grown cold. "If you can call yourself my sister, then I can call Grandpa my grandfather."

"Why did you do…?" Winter tried to find a way to ask him about the killings, the things he'd done.

"I think I'm supposed to have my lawyer present, *Agent* Black." He shook his head, clucking as though he were a parent chiding a child. "You kept that name, even when you knew the truth?"

"You refused a lawyer," Winter reminded him. "The state

forced one on you because the judge didn't think you were mentally stable enough to defend yourself."

"I find that I like having a go-between with the feds. He really pisses you people off. I can see that. It's fun to watch, really."

"Of course I kept the name," Winter said, referring to his previous question. "It's my name. Bill gave it to me when he kept me as his own."

"Black is not your name. You're not part of this, and you're not part of the family either." Justin was sitting upright as far as the chains would let him, so vehement in his words that spittle formed at the corner of his mouth. He bit the words off savagely. "He wasn't your father! He only married your whore mother. He *lied* about you to legitimize you."

"She was your mother too," Winter said through clenched teeth. "I remember when she was carrying you, when her belly swelled with you inside of it. I was so excited to have a baby brother or sister."

"She was. So what? You're my half-sister, after all. Congratulations, come give me a hug." His hands opened up as far as the chains would allow. "Let's be friends, we can... listen to records, order a pizza, maybe...what...draw pictures of teachers we don't like?" He yanked hard on the chains on his wrists, but they refused to move under his efforts.

Despite her experience with prisoners, Winter pulled back a little at the force of the movement.

"Justin, I—"

"I'm Jaime!" he screamed, and this time, Winter was able to keep her composure. She didn't even flinch.

"Jaime, I—"

"How many years did you spend doing that?" he asked, his voice turning into a little boy's. "How many friends, how many boys did you while away the hours with on your *bed* playing with...records? Me?" He leaned forward so he could thump his fist into his chest. "I hunted. I crawled through mud and barbed wire like a special forces marine! That was my childhood fun." He lifted his head and faced her with a certain pride. "I shot rifles and learned how to handle a knife. Now, you're the FBI agent. Who have you shot? I mean, besides old men like Grandpa? Him you murdered in cold blood."

"I didn't kill him." The words were out of her mouth before she could take them back. "I wanted to be the one who pulled the trigger, but it wasn't me."

She didn't know why it was important for him to know that.

Winter fought the memories, not wanting to relive that day with Douglas Kilroy and his ominous pronouncement that Justin was still alive. Justin's version of events was deeply flawed and wrong, but Winter was suddenly tired. It seemed that her little brother had died all those years ago, after all. This person across the table from her wasn't Justin. This was Jaime. He only *looked* like Justin.

She stood up, ready to go.

Justin winced as though he'd been hit. He lowered his head, dropping his face into his hands, moaning.

"What's wrong?" Winter asked but made no move to get closer. Justin or Jaime, he was still a violent person. He only moaned harder, his hands gripping his forehead, knuckles turning white with the strain.

His hands dropped to the table and Justin stared at the chain. He pulled it once, twice, very gently. He seemed surprised to see his hands caught like that. He looked around the room in a complete panic. Then his eyes settled on her. They were larger, softer. They looked fearful and confused.

"Winter?" His voice had changed too. It was quieter, pitched differently so that he sounded younger. It was the voice of a child. "Winter?" He pulled the chain again, harder, his face a mask of horror. "What...why are my hands chained? Why am I in here?"

Winter sat down heavily, her body refusing to move. "I don't—"

"Where is Raff?" Justin wailed. "I want Raff!" He pulled the chains rapidly. The clanking of the metal as it ran through the eyebolt was deafening.

"Justin!" Winter yelled, rising from the chair.

Justin stopped, and the look he gave her was pure hurt and sadness. "Winter? Will Grandpa be mad?"

"What do you mean?"

"Grandpa gets mad when someone calls me 'Justin.' He says my name is 'Jaime' now. When he gets mad, he...he hurts me. Sometimes he hurts others because of me, and he makes me watch. If my hands are tied, I can't put them over my head, and those are the hits that hurt the worstest."

Winter stared at her baby brother. Was this an act? Or real? She just didn't know.

"No one is going to hurt you, not anymore." Winter sank back into her seat, confused. She found herself desperate to console him. A moment ago, she'd never wanted to see him again.

"Do you promise?" Justin asked her in such a child-like way it broke her heart.

"Absolutely. Kil...that man you called Grandpa, he's dead. He can't hurt you ever again."

"Promise?" Justin asked again, a single tear sliding down his face.

"Promise," Winter said gently.

"Hope to die?" Justin asked. With the last word, his smile grew and widened on his face. This time, it didn't reach his eyes. It was predatory, cold, cruel. "Do you, dear sister? Do you hope to die?" His voice had transformed into something hard, harsh, and growling.

"No," Winter said, stumbling upright and taking a step backward. "No."

"Too bad." Justin looked down at his chains. "Just as well, though, not much I can do about it in here." He cocked his head to one side. "Being Jaime Peterson was the first person I had to become. It wasn't the last. Sometimes, I had to be many people. Sometimes, I had to be a girl. Grandpa did a lot to me, Winter. He hurt me in ways I can't even remember. I survived, though. By god, I survived."

"Justin..." Winter couldn't think of a thing to say after that. The transformation was so startling and so abrupt. "I'm...sorry."

Her mind raced, wanting to say more, do more, *fix* him somehow, but Cameron Arkwell's voice telling her that there was unfinished business that "Baby Preacher" was trying to finish ran through her head. What was it he'd said? That Kilroy must have loved Justin to take him away like that? Winter wanted to help Justin, wanted to have her little brother back, but she couldn't help but wonder if this was all play-acting.

"Me too," Justin said, staring at his wrists. "Me too." He looked up at her again, his head tilted and his eyes bright and distant, as though he was looking at something far away. "Ever wonder what would have been different if you hadn't..." he exploded in fury and hate, his chains straining as he tried to get up, "if you hadn't taken a nap in the hallway?!"

The guards had had enough. They stepped in and pulled Justin back down to a seating position.

"Miss, you need to come with me." A third guard touched her arm in concern, drawing her away. He escorted her out even as Justin screamed and fought the guards who were trying to calm him down.

The door closed behind her, muffling the sounds of struggle.

Winter stood in the hallway, shaking. She felt clammy and cold, as though she'd absorbed the prison itself in the last hour and carried the bars, the desperation within her. The raw feeling of being caged clawed at her stomach, making her sick. For a moment, she debated on finding a bathroom to throw up in, or to fight the urge until she got out of the prison walls.

The nearest bathroom won.

39

"Parrish!" Noah shouted and barreled toward Aiden's office.

Aiden saw him coming and stepped aside with a magnanimous gesture to precede him into the room.

"Did you hear?" Noah accosted him without preamble.

"Hear what?" Aiden asked, taking a moment to shut the door after giving Noah a quizzical look.

Noah took a breath and smelled a trace of perfume in the air. He stopped mid-sentence and turned toward Aiden. Noah didn't think the man would wear a lavender scent. Interesting. "I'm not interrupting anything important, am I?"

"No. I just got back a few minutes ago. Have a seat." Aiden gestured to the chairs in front of the desk before taking his own, leaning back to regard Noah somewhat uneasily.

Noah sat, but the scent was stronger here. It suddenly clicked why the aroma seemed so familiar. "Was Autumn just in here?"

"Yeah." Was it his imagination or did Aiden hesitate a little before answering? "She came to see me because she's been assigned to assess Justin."

Noah's leg jumped, moving up and down with restless energy as he leaned forward to speak, trying to pull himself under control and failing greatly. "He's going the insanity route. Just like you thought." He hated when Parrish was right.

Aiden held up a hand. "I know, Noah." He looked weary to the core. "I was there."

"At the arraignment?"

"Yeah. I was in the courtroom when the plea came in."

Noah didn't tell Aiden why he hadn't also attended. He'd been sitting on Winter, trying to keep her away.

"Did they set a trial date?"

"I don't know yet," Aiden confessed. "I'm waiting to hear. They cleared the court and hauled the little shit away before additional business could be done."

Noah pinched the skin between his eyes. "Don't let Winter hear you call him that."

It had been a slip of the tongue, which wasn't like the behavioral analysis leader. Normally, he held a tight filter on his thoughts.

Aiden nodded. "I'll be more careful. I'm just worried."

"About what? About Justin being found insane?"

"Yes." Aiden leaned forward to place his hands on his desk, the chair snapping back upright with a creak. "He's playing the system. He's hoping for a lighter sentence in a clean, quiet hospital somewhere so he can play the system even more and be released before he's thirty."

Noah sat upright, his jittery leg stilling. "The scary thing is, that's a possibility. He's a killer. There's enough DNA and other evidence that this should be an open and shut case, but it won't be. Will it?"

"I don't think so." Aiden shook his head. "And with a judge already having to force an attorney on him, he's already laid the groundwork for mental incompetence."

Noah groaned, covering his face with his hands, giving it a hard scrub. "You're right. He's playing us, and worse, there's not a damn thing we can do about it."

"And just our luck, most legal aid types are the overworked recent grads who are trying to get some experience before moving on to better things, but this one…" Aiden waved his hand in a helpless gesture.

"This one figured out he was in a losing position and decided to make the most of it. He's just making a name for himself, using Justin as a launching pad," Noah groused. He hung his head and smelled Autumn's perfume again. "Autumn is on it?"

Was he seeing things or did the magnanimous Aiden Parrish just blush? "She's on the case, if that's what you mean."

Interesting. "What else would I mean?" Noah teased. He simply couldn't let this chance pass by. It was kind of nice to see Aiden flustered, even though that wasn't what Noah had meant. Aiden taking it in a different direction showed what he was thinking, more than answering Noah would have. It appeared that Aiden misunderstood his smile too.

Aiden shot him a look. "We talked about the case. She was just here to talk about Justin. That's all." When Noah just blinked at him, he scowled. "What? So, she waited in my office for me. It's not like I have a big waiting room out there like a doctor's office. She had to sit somewhere."

"I imagine she did." Noah kept his face carefully neutral.

"Don't start on me." Aiden pointed a warning finger at Noah.

Noah raised his hands in surrender. "All I said was 'Autumn is on it,' meaning she's giving the assessment to Justin. That was all I meant."

Aiden narrowed his eyes. "If you say so."

Noah dropped the joking and went back to the subject at

hand. "No chance of her being accused of anything because of her friendship with Winter?"

"No. She'll just be one of the several who'll do evaluations, and Justin's lawyer had no problem with her doing the assessment."

"Good." Noah sat back and linked his hands behind his head.

"Good." Aiden said the word a bit more forcefully than needed, giving an emphasis where none was required. After a pause, he sighed. "If anyone can get to the heart of this, it's Autumn."

"She's good," Noah agreed. "Smart. Very smart."

Aiden nodded, sitting back in the chair again until it was leaning against the wall behind him. "I'm sure she'll get to the heart of Justin's plea, then we'll see if he's sane enough to stand trial."

"I'll let you get back to work." Noah stood and walked out without looking back at Aiden, slowing as he quietly pulled the door to behind him. "We might have one bad guy off the streets, but we have dozens more to find."

"There will always be bad guys," Aiden said as the door clicked shut between them.

He was right.

That part of life would never end.

40

Winter sat cross-legged with a fresh cup of tea. She was taking a few more days before she returned to work, time to decompress and reclaim her life. The interview with Justin still stayed with her, though it was two days ago already.

The boxes with all the papers were gone. The obsession with finding everything she could about Kilroy's relationship to her, and more importantly, to Justin was gone. She took a sip of her tea, looking at the lights flashing on the Christmas tree. They'd settled for a fake tree. It was too late in the season to find a really good live one. The lots had already been picked clean.

It was silly to buy one since they were seldom home anyway. To have a tree in the middle of the living room with miles of lights and tawdry, shiny decorations seemed ridiculous. It was also pretty and comforting in a way that made her think of childhood and home. The good parts of those memories.

If it were later in the day, she'd curl up with a hot chocolate and be in her pajamas. She made a mental note to do that later. She wondered if she would be able to talk Noah into joining her.

With Justin safely put away, safe for him as well as for others, she could finally think about other things. Yet, it was Justin who kept creeping into her thoughts. Justin wouldn't let her concentrate even now for more than a moment on anything else. She took another sip of tea.

The evidence against him was overwhelming. The video he'd sent her was condemning enough, there was no way out for him but a lengthy sentence. It should have bothered her more than it did, and she wondered for a long time if she had been an agent for so long that she couldn't be a sister anymore, or a lover for Noah, or a...a person. Was she an agent and no longer capable of being anything more?

Justin's attitude toward her, the way he'd behaved when she saw him was disturbing. How much of that was acting? How much of that was really the way his mind was broken, and how much was just a ploy to get away with murder? She didn't want to think that of him, but even without the theatrics, the fact was...the man she'd talked to wasn't her brother.

But if not him, then who?

Could you break someone so thoroughly that they became a monster? Whatever she'd been talking to was *not* her brother. He was a twisted version of him, a version created by Kilroy.

Winter stared at the Christmas tree until everything blurred into a multicolored kaleidoscope of flickering lights. She was mourning Justin again, as though he'd died rather than having been taken away to jail.

A knock on the door interrupted her reverie. Glad to have the break from sitting alone with her thoughts, she went to answer it, delighted to find Autumn waiting outside.

"Hi!" She stood aside and let her friend enter. "I just had the pot on, want some tea?"

"Yeah." Autumn nodded, already shrugging out of her coat. "I would like that very much, thank you." Autumn set a leather bag down on the couch and followed Winter to the kitchen, taking down a cup while Winter turned the heat on under the kettle. "I mostly stopped by to say hello and see how you are doing."

Winter leaned against the counter and took a sip of her own rapidly cooling tea while trying to figure out how to answer that. "I'm doing...okay. I saw Justin the other day."

"I heard." Autumn chose a tea bag and dropped it into her cup. The water was already warm, so the kettle began whistling almost immediately.

"I told Noah about being in a collapsing church."

Autumn shuddered at the memory, nearly causing the scalding liquid to miss the cup as she poured. "What did he say to that?"

"That I wasn't allowed to go into basements of falling buildings anymore."

Autumn laughed. "Good advice."

They carried their tea to the living room and Winter pointed to the satchel. "What's this?"

Autumn lifted the tooled leather and showed it to her. "My brand-new briefcase. I saw this beauty on sale yesterday and fell in love with it." She handed the satchel to Winter, who looked at the bag appreciatively. She didn't open the flap; the contents were none of her business.

"I heard about your visit with Justin," Autumn said, opening the bag. "That's another reason I'm here." She pulled out a report folder and showed Winter the front. The name on the label read "Justin Black." "I've been assigned to do his assessment."

"You?"

Autumn nodded. "Will that be a problem for you?"

"Me?" Winter looked surprised at the question. "No. I can't think of anyone I would trust more."

"Thank you." Autumn took a breath and looked uncertain, uncomfortable. "Can I ask…how it went with Justin?"

Winter sighed and looked to the flashing lights of the tree. "Rough. There was a lot of rage and bitterness at first. Well, at *first*, he seemed happy to see me, then he became bitter and angry. Then…I don't know, he acted like he had a great migraine, and suddenly, he's four years old again and screaming for Raff."

"'Raff?'" Autumn asked, eyebrows raising.

"That was the stuffed giraffe he had as a boy, dragged it with him everywhere. He was acting like a frightened little boy and was telling me how mean Kilroy was to him and all the bad things Kilroy had done to him. It was creepy as hell." Winter couldn't repress a shudder that ran through her. The hair on her arms stood upright at the memory.

"Have you ever heard the term D.I.D.?" Autumn asked her.

"Did?"

"Dissociative Identity Disorder. It used to be called Multiple Personality Disorder. It's where the victim creates new personalities to 'share the burden' as it were. If it's not the victim getting beaten, then it's someone else. This other identity can take the pain and humiliation so the victim doesn't have to."

Winter thought about this a moment. "How does that make the pain any less?"

"It doesn't, not really. But it helps the victim to compartmentalize the experience. The personality that needs to exist to take the abuse, the one that needs to exist to overcome that pain and still be able to perform at school or in public, what have you. D.I.D. is a response to severe and continuous abuse at a young age. It's a coping mechanism."

"That's why he killed those people?"

"No." Autumn shook her head. "Motive is something I can't assess until I talk to him. The problem with D.I.D. is that women who have it can often hide it successfully, even from themselves. They become victims again, in abusive marriages, unable to hold down jobs because sometimes one personality doesn't know how to do the job they've done for years. Men with D.I.D. are usually violent, passive aggressive. They're easy to anger. The next moment, they're calm and don't understand why people are afraid of them."

"So, people with D.I.D. lose time? Like blackouts?"

"Not always, no. They retain memories, or think they do, so that there is no gap in their day."

"Then is...does Justin have D.I.D.?" Winter wasn't sure which answer she wanted to hear.

"I don't know. I have an interview set up with him tomorrow. I'll have a better idea then. Until then, I was hoping you could tell me what you talked about and how he reacted." She opened the folder and turned to a blank page and produced a pen. "You said he was calling for his stuffed toy. What was the name?"

"Raff," Winter said. "He couldn't say 'giraffe' at that age, and Raff was as close as he could get. It was his constant companion. I remember that mother used to despair at how dirty that thing got, but he wouldn't let it go long enough to put it in the washer."

Autumn made a note and Winter saw the compassion there, but Autumn was a professional, and a good one. Along with compassion, there was determination. Autumn would do her job and do it well. "Tell me what you remember about Justin from before the night your parents were killed."

Winter did a double take. Autumn's request was almost

word for word of what Noah had asked her the other night. "I…ah…I remember he was mischievous. He was always getting into things, always leaving little sticky fingerprints on everything. He liked to take things apart but didn't have much interest in putting them back together again." Winter took another sip. She shrugged. "I don't know. He was only six. I sometimes think that he was taken before he had been there long enough for me to get to know him."

Autumn made another note. Winter stared at the pad of paper in Autumn's hands and wondered what she was writing down. "There's no conflict of interest like there was for Noah?" she asked, frowning.

"No." Autumn finished the note she was writing and looked up. "No, I've been cleared by the judge and by Justin's lawyer."

"And by Aiden?" Winter asked over her cup. She could swear Autumn was blushing.

"Aiden? What about him?"

Winter hid her smile in taking another drink. She'd hit a sensitive spot. "Just asking if the Bureau had a problem with you taking on this case."

"No," Autumn answered a little too quickly. "No, he didn't have a problem with me."

"He?" Winter asked.

Autumn put the pad away and lay the folder on the coffee table. "All right, I've been thinking lately that—"

"He's a good man, Autumn."

Autumn bit her lower lip and grinned. "Yeah. He is."

"Cute too." Winter couldn't resist digging in a little.

"Yeah, I suppose he is. I hadn't noticed." She pressed her lips together, but the blush gave away her feelings. "It's a professional relationship. It didn't occur to me to notice one way or the other."

Winter grinned and held her cup out. With a wink, Autumn clinked their teacups together.

Winter's smile faded away. "On another, less handsome subject, I want to thank you for hanging with me while we were trying to catch him."

Autumn smiled and covered Winter's hand with her own. She felt a rush of love seep from her friend's skin and into her own. "Can I be Lucy next time?"

Winter laughed. "Of course you can. You can be Lucy or Ethel or Thelma or Louise. Your choice as long as you never stop being my friend."

To Winter's surprise, tears glimmered in Autumn's eyes. "Friends to the end."

The hair raised on the back of Winter's neck, but she managed to keep her smile firmly in place. "There are no ends. With friends...or family. Only beginnings."

Autumn lifted her cup. "To beginnings."

The sound of the clinking cups was sweet. "Beginnings."

As they sipped, the door opened and Noah stepped in. He was carrying a pile of gayly wrapped presents, a big smile on his handsome face.

Winter's heart squeezed with love. Love for him. Love for her friend. Love for the life she'd made for herself.

She didn't know what else was to come for them all, but she was looking forward to figuring it out.

With them.

41

"Thank you for seeing me today," Autumn said softly.

Justin rattled the chain through the eyebolt and grinned at her. "Not a lot of choice, really. I'm glad now that I did."

"Really? Why is that?"

"Because you're really pretty." Justin's smile grew wider even as his eyes grew colder. "You don't need to be afraid. I'm chained up here pretty well. I can't hurt you."

Autumn took a steadying breath. "Is that what you want? To hurt me?"

"You drive pretty well for a girl," Justin said. When Autumn frowned in confusion, Justin laughed. "When you lost me at that furniture store, driving between those posts. That was a thing of beauty."

The memory of that night came back to her. It had been him. It was a good thing she hadn't known that for certain in the moment, or else she would have been terrified.

"That was you?" she asked casually, refusing to be pulled into his games.

"Yeah." Justin's smile faded. "You didn't know? People

usually try to follow you like that in the middle of the night? It happens so often that you're just used to it?" He ran his gaze over her face and down to her neck, then lower. "How did you up and vanish on me anyway?"

"We're here to talk about you." Autumn opened the folder she'd brought with her. "You were born Justin Black and—"

"No!" Justin slammed his hands down on the table. "No." This time the word came out more quietly. "You tell me how you got away or this interview is over."

"This isn't an interview," Autumn reminded him. "This is an assessment to determine if you are capable of standing trial. This is a court-ordered assessment. This isn't a choice."

Justin set his jaw and stared at her.

Autumn sighed and relented. Give him something, and maybe he'd give her something in return. "Drive-through liquor store." She tapped her pen against the folder. "I sat in the back of the building and waited for you to blow by."

Justin's face cracked a smile, and he threw his head back with a raucous laugh. "That's a good one. I never heard of that before. Drive-through liquor saved my life!" He cupped his hand and punctuated each word with a gesture as though he was reading a marquee and laughed again. "You're smart. And good-looking. Let me tell you, if my hands weren't cuffed, I'd…" The laughter died as quickly as it had come.

"What?" Autumn prompted. "What would you do?"

Justin licked his lips and laughed once more, but the sound felt forced this time. "Trust me, you'd enjoy it."

"Tell me about your grandpa." Autumn looked down at the report and held her pen ready. When she looked up, she suppressed a gasp. She was looking at Justin, but she also wasn't. The arrogant punk was gone, and in his place, a smaller, frightened-looking young man stared back at her.

"Grandpa?" he asked in a small voice. "Is he mad at me?"

Autumn searched his face for any sign that this was

acting, that he was pulling something on her. "What happens when Grandpa gets angry?" she asked him carefully, not taking her eyes off him for a second.

"He hurts people," Justin whispered, his eyes searching the room. "I was supposed to carry out his mission, but I failed. I didn't do what he told me. Winter was supposed to die too, but I didn't do it. Grandpa will be so mad."

Will be? The hair lifted on Autumn's arms at the use of present tense in reference to The Preacher.

"His mission?" Autumn kept her voice soft. "What was his mission? Was that something he came up with?"

Justin's face fell, his eyes hardened, and his jaw became firm. "It's a mission, lady. Good god, you're as stupid as the rest. I said it was a *mission*. Missionaries are *sent*, they are *called*. Missionaries don't just go off on their own randomly."

Autumn nodded, somewhat uneasily. She'd seen the shift happen that Winter had described to her, but still wasn't quite sure she believed it. "Are you saying someone sent Douglas Kilroy to kill people?"

"Not just to kill, but to educate!" Justin slapped the table for emphasis. "He was sent to wake a sleeping people and make them understand!"

Missionaries were sent? Autumn wracked her brain, trying to think back through everything they'd dug up on Justin, on The Preacher, on every last relative in Winter's family. "Who sent him?"

"You don't want to know." Justin was small again and fearful. "You really don't want to know. You think Grandpa was a bad man, but he wasn't, not really, not in comparison. He was an only child, but his father, his father had lots of brothers and sisters. Lots."

"Who sent him on the mission, Justin?"

"Don't call me that!" Justin shifted in his seat as far as the chains would let him. "He hated when anyone called me that."

"Your grandpa isn't here. You're safe."

"No. Not grandpa. Uncle. Uncle is pure evil. He scared Grandpa. Uncle scares everyone. Uncle is a bad man."

"Who is Uncle?" Autumn asked softly, so soft she was barely breathing the word.

"I can't tell you!" Justin wailed. "He'll hurt me if I tell you."

"No one can hurt you, I promise. Tell me who Uncle is. Please."

Justin ducked his head, looking up at her from under his heavy brows. She would have sworn he'd aged ten years in adopting that look alone. "Let me go, and I'll tell you."

Autumn watched his face carefully. Watched it shift from Justin to Jaime and back again several times.

Winter was right.

Her relationship with her little brother wasn't ending. It was only beginning.

Starting now.

The End

Find all of the Winter Black Series books on Amazon.

ACKNOWLEDGMENTS

How does one properly thank everyone involved in taking a dream and making it a reality? Let me try.

In addition to my family, whose unending support provided the foundation for me to find the time and energy to put these thoughts on paper, I want to thank the editors who polished my words and made them shine.

Many thanks to my publisher for risking taking on a newbie and giving me the confidence to become a bona fide author.

More than anyone, I want to thank you, my reader, for clicking on a nobody and sharing your most important asset, your time, with this book. I hope with all my heart I made it worthwhile.

Much love,
Mary

ABOUT THE AUTHOR

Mary Stone lives among the majestic Blue Ridge Mountains of East Tennessee with her two dogs, four cats, a couple of energetic boys, and a very patient husband.

As a young girl, she would go to bed every night, wondering what type of creature might be lurking underneath. It wasn't until she was older that she learned that the creatures she needed to most fear were human.

Today, she creates vivid stories with courageous, strong heroines and dastardly villains. She invites you to enter her world of serial killers, FBI agents but never damsels in distress. Her female characters can handle themselves, going toe-to-toe with any male character, protagonist or antagonist.

Discover more about Mary Stone on her website.
www.authormarystone.com

facebook.com/authormarystone
goodreads.com/AuthorMaryStone
bookbub.com/profile/3378576590
pinterest.com/MaryStoneAuthor
instagram.com/marystone_author

Made in the USA
Columbia, SC
30 November 2022

72426775R00183